David Rice has recreated the sights, sounds, smells and, above all, the emotions of Beijing in the spring of 1989.

—*Jonathan Mirsky, who reported the Tiananmen Square massacre for The Observer*

Shattered Vows
(Michael Joseph/Penguin; William Morrow NY; Blackstaff; Triumph Books; Ligouri Press)

Despite the anguish it portrays, *Shattered Vows* is an immensely heartening and encouraging book.

—*Robert Nowell in The Sunday Times*

Well documented and at the same time an outcry for changing the present disastrous policy.
—*Professor Hans Küng*

The unmistakable force and vividness that only real life can yield... The fruits of this patient listening are pictures we can see, and voices that speak to us.

—*Professor Uta Ranke-Heinemann, University of Essen, author of Nein und Amen*

A call for candor on celibacy.
—*The New York Times*

This courageous exposé... provides powerful testimony. David Rice cannot be commended enough for his brilliant study.

—*Carol J. Lichtenberg in the Library Journal (US)*

I know no study... that compares with this. No one has researched the subject as well as David Rice. No one has listened... with such wisdom and sympathy.

—*Peter deRosa, author of Rebels; Vicars of Christ & others*

His book has the convincing ring of truth... conveys an authentic impression... a very sensitive appraisal.

—*Dr Joyce M Bennett in the*
Church of England Newspaper

This book starkly says the Church is in crisis. Its author is well placed to know.

—*Michael Brown in the Yorkshire Post*

Kirche Ohne Priester

(C. Bertelsmann; Goldmann Verlag: German translation of
Shattered Vows*)*

A book without hate or rancour and an important contribution to the celibacy discussion.

—*Kronen Zeitung*

Rice has established a well-founded scrutiny of the present situation.

—*Braunschweiger Zeitung*

The Pompeii Syndrome / La Sindrome di Pompei

(Mercier Press) (also translation from Newton Compton, Rome)

The Pompeii Syndrome really grabbed me from the first page... it makes you wonder whether we really are in denial about catastrophic threat, because we refuse to believe in the possibility of our own extinction. My test of a good book is always the same - would I loan it to a friend with the proviso that they have to give it back? This definitely meets that criterion.

—*Brenda Power in The Sunday Times*

The Pompeii Syndrome is a genuinely terrifying, totally believable novel, because it could come true tomorrow ... What sets the story apart is the huge amount of research which underpins every paragraph. Rice has spent years studying the situation. He tells us - as the politicians never do - exactly what we can expect if we do not force our governments to

Praise for books by David Rice

I Will Not Serve: The priest who said NO to Hitler
(Red Stag)

Franz Reinisch's refusal to fall in line with an ideology he knew to be morally perverse is as relevant now as it has ever been. David Rice's vivid and sensitive telling of Reinisch's story is both moving and timely and I recommend it highly.

> —*Oscar nominee Lenny Abrahamson, director of Room; Frank; What Richard Did; Garage; and Adam & Paul*

The Dragon's Brood
(HarperCollins)

David Rice's *Dragon's Brood* is a marvellously fresh and immediate evocation ... He has a good journalist's sense of the core of a human character, and a gift for asking questions... His book achieves real depth. The belief that the Chinese care little about individual or human rights... should not survive the pages. Rice's eye is sharp and he has useful things to say about many important topics.

> —*Mark Elvin in the London Review of Books*

Illuminating recorded conversations... with explorations of young people's views on all the issues which have been at the forefront of change. Rice's view of China is not a cheerful one... yet he maintains a justifiable spark of optimism.

> —*Colina Macdougall in The Times Literary Supplement*

David Rice makes worthwhile reading... He accurately conveys the often touching despair of most Chinese surveying the wasteland of their recent past. He cleverly invokes their alternating pride in China's size and cultural heritage and their own sense of inferiority towards richer and freer westerners.

> —*Jasper Becker in The Times (London)*

Where Jung Chang leaves off, David Rice takes over.

—Simon Scott Plummer in The Tablet

This intriguing book opens a wide window on the future which before long we will all have to meet and greet and mingle with... fundamental impression of truthfulness... my respect for an enjoyable, enlightening and important book.

—Tony Parker in The Sunday Times

David Rice has done a commendable job in capturing the spirit of the times.
—John Kohut in the South China Morning Post (Hong Kong)

I trust this book, because of what it says about Chinese faces.... Rice is a keen observer.

—Jonathan Mirsky in The Irish Times

The Dragon's Brood is a singular review of the thoughts and aspirations of a new generation of a people the West has too often misunderstood at its peril.

—Howard Rose in the Sunday Press

Song of Tiananmen Square
(Brandon/Mount Eagle)

Rice has written a gripping and all-too-realistic novel about the Tiananmen Square massacre and the events surrounding it.

—Chris Patten, last Governor of Hong Kong

Utterly fascinating... powerfully affecting... lyricism and immediacy.
—Robert Farren in The Irish Times

change their policies before it is too late. Run, do not walk, to the nearest bookshop and buy a copy. Better still, buy copies for your friends as well.

—*Morgan Llywelyn, author of The Greener Shore;*
Grania; Red Branch & others

A taut thriller... scarily believable. *The Pompeii Syndrome* is fastpaced and explosive... page-turning and thoughtful – a must-read thriller.

—*Cathy Kelly, author of Lessons in*
Heartbreak; Past Secrets & others

Read this book or regret it till your dying day – which could be very soon...

—*Paul Williams, author of Evil Empire;*
The General (book & film), Gangland;
Crime Lords & others

Brilliantly narrated ... this is no ordinary novel, but 'fiction based on fact'... graphically portrays one route to mass destruction and the end of civilization as we know it. The 'Pompeii Syndrome'... may well enter the vocabulary alongside terms such as 'Stockholm Syndrome'. It refers to... denial in the face of impending catastrophe too awful to contemplate.

—*Louis Hughes OP in Spirituality magazine*

The unthinkable becomes obvious. The moment when the obvious turns into reality, it is too late. And yet nothing changes. David Rice is the first one to put into words what many see coming but no one wants to see. Of course not. It would mean that something has to change. Now.

—*Mycle Schneider, international nuclear consultant, advisor to the official UK Committee on Radioactive Waste Management (CoRWM), and former advisor to the Belgian, French and German governments; winner of the 1997 Right Livelihood Award*

An absolutely gripping read.

—*Paul Carson, author of Scalpel;*
Cold Steel; Betrayal & others

The Rathmines Stylebook
(Folens)

We are writing to be understood, and this book will help. Keep what you write simple and short and you can't go wrong.... When in doubt, refer to *The Rathmines Stylebook.*

—*Douglas Gageby Editor, The Irish Times*

Blood Guilt
(Blackstaff Press)

One of the best-timed releases in modern publishing. David Rice had no idea that in the very week of its publication the central question posed by the book would be on the lips of thousands... What becomes of a gunman when his killing days are over?

—*Evening Press*

The great strength of this novel is that it is in no way mawkish and escapes the sentimentality so many people associated with the 'struggle'. The central character is sufficiently authentic to have the reader identify with his personal odyssey. *Blood Guilt* is an insightful, imaginative and well-crafted novel... Highly recommended, especially for those who appreciate the difference between style and pretension

—*Connacht Tribune*

About the author

A NATIVE of Northern Ireland, David Rice has worked as a journalist on three continents. He has also been a Dominican friar. In the 1970s he was an editor and Sigma-Delta-Chi award-winning syndicated columnist in the United States, returning to Ireland in 1980 to head the prestigious Rathmines School of Journalism (later DIT). In 1989 he was invited to Beijing by the Thomson Foundation to train journalists on behalf of *Xin Hua*, the Chinese government news agency, and to work as an editor with China Features. He was in Beijing during the massacre of Tiananmen Square, and later returned to interview secretly 400 of the young people who had survived the massacre. This brought him to the attention of the Chinese security police. It also led to two books, *Dragon's Brood*: *Conversations with Young Chinese* (HarperCollins), and the novel, *Song of Tiananmen Square* (Brandon/Mt Eagle). His books have been published in Britain, Ireland, Germany, Italy and the United States. Rice's No.1 best-selling *Shattered Vows* (Michael Joseph/Penguin) led to the acclaimed Channel 4 documentary, *Priests of Passion*, which he presented. His most recent book, *I Will Not Serve*, tells the true story, in fiction format, of a priest who refused military service under Hitler, as a matter of conscience, and was executed for it. Educated at Abbey CBS and Clongowes, Rice has degrees in both Sociology and German Language & Literature from the National University of Ireland; in Community Development from Southern Illinois University, Carbondale, USA; and in Theology from the Angelicum University, Rome. He now lives in Co Tipperary, has taught Writing Skills at the University of Limerick, and has directed the Killaloe Hedge-School of Writing *(www.killaloe.ie/khs)*.

By the same author

Fiction

Blood Guilt
The Pompeii Syndrome
La Sindrome di Pompei
Song of Tiananmen Square
I Will Not Serve

Non-fiction

Shattered Vows
The Dragon's Brood
The Rathmines Stylebook
Kirche ohne Priester
Yes, You Can Write

In preparation

The Joy of Looking
The Book for the Bully
Look and Grow Mindful
The Little Roads of Ireland
KHS Writing Guides 2-5

CORDUROY
BOY

When did you last see your mother?

DAVID RICE

Author of the best-selling 'I Will Not Serve'

RED STAG
MENTOR

Published in 2018 by:
RED STAG
(a Mentor Books imprint)
Mentor Books Ltd
43 Furze Road
Sandyford Industrial Estate
Dublin 18
Republic of Ireland

Tel: + 353 1 295 2112 / 3
Fax: + 353 1 295 2114
Email: admin@mentorbooks.ie
Website: www.mentorbooks.ie

A CIP catalogue record for this title is available from the British Library.

ISBN 978-1-912514-19-9

Front Cover Design by Anú Design (www.anu-design.ie)

Edited by: Isobel Creed

Visit our website: www.redstag.ie
                        www.mentorbooks.ie

For

Catherine

(aka Kathleen)

My support in all things

The living men that I hate;

The dead man that I loved

— W.B. Yeats

Acknowledgements

MY thanks to the many friends who helped and inspired me in the writing of this book. To the alumni of schools in both Ireland and Britain who shared with me memories of their schooldays, or encouraged me – indeed pushed me – to write, especially George Mawdsley, Dave Courtney, Mike McCarthy, Gerry O'Keeffe, Kevin Hendrick, Victor Davis, Gordon Baker, Roger Marsh, Tom Griffin, Eddie Moxon-Browne, Tom Lauwers, Jim Watkins, John Brophy, Paul Herriott, Dr Brendan Thornton, Mervyn Cull, the late Fr Michael Keane, my brother Dermot, and my brothers-in-law Chris Bruce and Mike Watson. And my thanks too to the women who, though spared the all-male boarding schools, encouraged me to write about them – including Maggie Bresson, Olive Bourke, Mary Glynn, Pippa Newcomb, Marjorie Quarton, Miriam Donohoe, Fiona Clark-Echlin, Julie McAuliffe, the late Rebecca Millane, Hong Kennedy-Bell, my niece Victoria, my sister Noellvie and my late sister Diana. Thanks too to Isobel Creed of The Writers' Consultancy, a gifted editor who takes no prisoners – i.e, who lets nothing by that shouldn't get by (*www.writersconsultancy.ie*); to my late friend Harvey Wasserman MD, psychologist and author, who checked my depiction of the adolescent angst of Jamie; and to Keith Wood, former Lions and Ireland captain, who checked the rugby sequences in the book and was so encouraging. To computer guru Eugene McDonough who, with infinite patience, helped me every step of the way in all computer matters, and created my website, *www.davidrice.ie,* and Facebook page *David Rice author.* To all the members of the Killaloe Writers' Group who, month after month, had to listen to what I wrote (God reward them), and were astonishingly patient and encouraging. And finally to Kathleen (aka Catherine to some of her friends), my partner of twenty-six wonderful years, who always knows from the fanatical glint in my eye that I am going to read her another chapter, and bears it manfully – or rather womanfully, God bless her.

Prologue

RUINS rise everywhere in the West of Ireland. Many are centuries old, their crumbling, tumbling stones bearing witness to the cruelties of a bygone era.

Not all ruins, however, are quite so old.

On the remote edge of Ireland's Burren region, a slender spire soars high above the trees, still pointing the way to heaven. Ivy crawls through the gaping limestone windows below, and crows caw and wheel around the empty bell tower.

What happened here is also part of a bygone era, but not that long gone by.

April 1938

FOR the love o' Gawd, Sammy. Sammy, for Jesus' sake get me a priest. A priest, Sammy, please, *please*. Please, Sammy. For the love o' Jesus don't let me die without a priest....' The screams ended in a retching sound.

The four-year-old boy cringed, unnoticed in the darkness of the alleyway, behind the little red-brick Belfast terrace, listening to the screams of his dying mother. They came from the faintly-lit upstairs window.

A few women in headscarves and overcoats clustered by their back-yard doors, looking up at the window.

'Och, the poor wee thing,' one of them said. 'Sammy should let the padre in if she wants him, papish or not. She'll be gone before the night.'

'Sammy won't do that,' another replied. 'He says Eileen became a Protestant to marry him, an' he'll have her die a Protestant.'

'Somebody should phone the padre, anyways.'

'Norma did a while back. But the man'll not come down here. Not to the Shankill. He wouldn't dare. He'll layve her die.'

The child heard the buzz of the front-door bell, and ran around the end of the terrace to the street. There was a black

Austin Ten at the footpath. A figure in black stood at the front door of the house. The door opened, the yellow rectangle framing his father's gaunt silhouette. The child slunk closer.

'...No papish clergyman comes in this house while she's alive.' His father's voice.

The black figure murmured something.

'I don't give a fuck,' came the answer. 'Not while she's alive. D'ya hear? Now get off afore y'get hurt. It could be dangerous here for your sort.'

The figure turned away, opened the car door and folded itself in. The car purred away, a wisp of smoke spiralling from the exhaust. Cars were rare in that street.

The screaming began again, and the child could hear it from the other side of the house. He ran back to the alley, and into the tiny back yard, where he turned his face to the brick wall and leaned against it, listening.

***

SHE had grown silent up there. Maybe she was sleeping. The child crept in through the back door. The tiny hall was in darkness now. Some light from the street lamp slanted through the oval glass panel of the front door, and picked out his father sitting on the bottom stair. His head was in his hands.

The doorbell buzzed again. The child's father stood up and opened it. The dark figure again.

'She's gone this half hour,' his father said. 'Y'can go up now.'

The figure brushed past him and thumped up the steep stairs.

Silence. Then a roar from upstairs: 'Sammy Jones, get up here. There's something y'hafta see. *Now!*'

His father hesitated.

'*Now!*' roared the voice. There was something so commanding in it that the man slowly mounted the stairs. The child slunk along behind him.

They entered the room. The bare bulb in the ceiling was lit, and the black figure stood by the bed with a sash around its neck. Only the sash wasn't orange – it was purple. 'Over *here!*' it commanded.

His father crossed to the bed, and the child moved unnoticed to a corner of the room.

'What do you see there, Sammy Jones?'

'Me dead wife.'

'What you see there, Sammy Jones, *is the face of a woman whose soul is in Hell.*' The figure lifted off the sash, folded it, and stumped down the stairs.

The front door slammed. The child crept across to where his father was standing. His mother's sunken eyes stared upwards from their sockets, and the cancer had drawn the lips back from the teeth in what seemed like a snarling grimace.

***

THUNK. That's the sound a rope makes when it hangs a man. The sound after the body slithers through the trap and five feet later the rope pulls the neck up short with that jolt that ends all life. *Thunk.* There's no sound quite like it.

Only it's hardly ever heard. Usually it coincides with the last of the death-scream as it's choked, or is drowned out by the crash of the trapdoors halves as they slam into the metal holding jaws.

But what if there's no trapdoor, and the man doesn't scream? Like when a man ties the rope to an attic beam, feeds it down through the hole above the stairs, puts the noose around his own neck, climbs over the banisters and just lets go? Does *he* hear the *thunk*? Or is he dead and deaf the very instant the *thunk* comes?

Or did the little boy hear it? Was he there to hear it?

He never said.

He never said anything.

He never *says* anything.

They just found him sitting on the staircase, canvas schoolbag still on his back, tiny fists clenched on the banisters, and gazing through them at his father's maroon face as it turned gently around and back.

They prised the little fists off the banisters and took the child away.

***

'THE shipyard's going to pay for the funeral,' Reverend Wilson said. 'Mr Soames told me that himself. So that's all right, then.'

'What about the wee boy, Reverend?'

'Aye, that's the question, Mrs Brinks. Seeing as Sammy had no relatives, there's nobody here to take the child. There's only Eileen's people in Enniskillen. There's a sister says she'll take him. They could afford to, I hear. Husband's a solicitor.'

'But they'd be papish, Reverend. The wee boy's a Protestant. We couldn't do that.'

The vicar sighed. 'What else can we do, Mrs Brinks? They're his only relatives.'

'But they'll bring him up *papish*.'

22

'I'll tell you something, Mrs Brinks. If it's a choice between going to the Cottage Orphanage or being brought up 'papish', as you call it, I'd let him be papish. I know that orphanage, Mrs Brinks. It's worse than Rome, believe you me.

'Anyway, the poor child doesn't know he's a Protestant. I don't know if he knows what he is. Or where he came from. Or if he remembers anything. Look at him: he just sits there. Never speaks, and the doctor can get nowhere with him. Maybe prayers will help. And maybe a fresh start at his aunt's.'

June 1943

YOU knew the plane was coming by the sort of rising howl it made – *nyaaaaAAAA* – until it was a sort of a scream – *EEEEE* – and then the sound started going down again – *EEyaaaow* – and it faded and was gone.

Boy oh boy, that one had to be low. There'd be another, maybe two more. They usually came in threes, low over Newry. Jamie looked up longingly.

'Arrah, Ma'am, leave him go,' Sheila the maid said, as she was serving the baked beans on toast. 'Sure I'll keep his warm in the oven.'

'Go on, dear,' Mummy said.

Daddy just nodded vaguely.

Jamie scuttled out down the steps and through the front garden and across the road where he climbed up on the grassy bank. There was the next one all right – a dot getting bigger and bigger. This one was different: it had sort of zig-zag wings coming towards you. Nearly like one of those Stukas in the spotter books.

But this one was blue. And you could see the pilot – glimpse of a pink face. Seeing the pilot was like seeing God. Jamie waved, and the wings wiggled. The pilot had seen Jamie – that was like God seeing you.

EEEyaaaaow. It was gone.

Now there was another dot, getting bigger and bigger. There was a star on one of the wings.

Jamie stared after the dots until he couldn't see them any more. They'd be far past Warrenpoint now. His eyes watered with gazing into the bright evening sky.

He ran back in and upstairs to his two spotter books. Tattered, but he loved them. They had black outlines of each plane – a side view, a view from below, and the view coming towards you. So you could see if the wings were zig-zag.

He sat on the bed. There it was – a *Corsair*. A Vought Sikorsky *Corsair*, the book said. Inverted gull wings, it said. What you did then was, you got the red crayon and put a big red √ on the page. That meant you had spotted the kind of plane shown on that page. There were a lot of √s now – one for the Lysander, and one for the Spitfire Mark IX, and one for the Avro Anson that patrolled lazily every day high over Newry. That Anson was a boring old plane. It never came low, so you never got to see the pilot.

So it was great that the Yank planes flew so low.

'Dangerous young whipper-snappers,' Jamie's Daddy would mutter as he poured a drink at the sideboard. 'Someone should put a stop to it. I'll have to mention it to Colonel Wasserman.'

Of course he never did. He was always saying things like that, but never getting around to it. He said there were dozens of those Yanks over at Cranfield. Wild young fellows, he said.

Something should be done about them. Getting ready to invade Europe, he said.

***

YOU'D often see the Yanks strolling down Hill Street. Some of the Yanks had armbands with *MP* on them. Like the way the Germans in the *Hotspur* had swastika armbands – the ones that were always torturing people and yelling *Donnerwetter und Blitzen.*

Jamie's Daddy had been an MP one time – in some place called Store Mount or Stormont or somewhere. But that had been before Jamie's time. Jamie found it hard to imagine his Daddy swaggering along like these MPs did. And swinging a big brown club, like the Yanks did. The clubs were like something cut from the banisters in Jamie's home.

Sometimes Jamie's Daddy would come home with big quart tins of orange juice or pineapple juice or tomato juice. That Yank Colonel would give them to him. Daddy said it was because he had proposed Colonel Wasserman for the Club. Jamie loved when the juice came, because you couldn't ever get it in the shops. That's because there was a war on.

And Jamie got most of the juice, because Mummy drank tea, and Daddy preferred that stuff from the decanters on the sideboard.

***

MUMMY didn't like Mingy Monaghan. She said he was common. Jamie should mix with Nice Boys. Nice Boys had mothers who played bridge with Mummy. Nice Boys had socks that were always up to their knees. They had garters to keep them up. And shirts and ties.

27

Nice Boys had names like Derek, or Jonathan, or David. They might wear corduroy shorts to school – they'd be beige or fawn – but they'd never wear them on Sundays. On Sundays it was usually a hairy tweed suit, or a blazer and mousy flannel.

Mingy wore corduroys all the time. Even on Sundays. That's because he was common. And his corduroys weren't fawn – they were the colour of shit. That was probably so the shit wouldn't show. And there'd be ink stains on the corduroys. And Mingy'd have boots on, laced up above his ankles. Nice boys wore shoes, not boots. And Mingy's socks would always be sliding down around his ankles, to meet the boots.

Jamie's socks would mostly be half way. Mummy was always telling him to pull them up, but he often forgot to wear garters, so the socks would keep on slipping. So Jamie's socks were half way between the world of the Nice Boys and the world of Common Boys like Mingy.

Jamie preferred the weekday corduroys to the Sunday tweed. Corduroys gave you a feeling of freedom. You didn't have to keep the creases in them, because they wouldn't take creases anyway. Besides, the hairy Sunday tweed was itchy.

Both the Nice Boys and the Common Boys wore their shorts right down to their knees. Too-short shorts were the sure sign of a sissy.

Common Boys said things like *elaskit* and *sumbarine* instead of *elastic* and *submarine*. Things like that. And they held their knives and forks the way you hold a pencil. (Mummy called that *à la crayon*. She liked saying things in French.) Mummy said you could always tell who was common by things like that.

28

And Common Boys (and Girls too) tied ropes to lampposts to make swings. And chalked hopscotch marks on the road, even outside Jamie's house, which made Mummy very cross indeed. And Common Boys called their mothers Mammy instead of Mummy. That was a sure giveaway.

Some of the Nice Boys were Prods and some were Cat-licks. The Prods went to the school with the chocolate-brown blazers, and turned brown themselves in summer.

The Cat-licks turned pink and peeled. Cat-lick boys went to the Abbey Christian Brothers and, when they were older, the *Very* Nice Boys might get sent away to Clongowes, or to Glenstal or Castleknock or Blackrock or Newbridge or Woodcock College. The Prods would go to Portora or Methody or Armagh Royal or Saint Columba's. The Nice Boys' daddies would be doctors or bank managers or solicitors – like Jamie's Daddy – or own a big shop on Hill Street. But not butchers or grocers. Certainly not. Indeed if Daddy wanted to run someone down, he'd say they had 'the soul of a grocer'.

Mingy's daddy drove a lorry. Now *that* was common. The Nice Boys' daddies played golf and drank whiskey at Warrenpoint or Greenore – Cat-licks and Prods all together. And the mummies played Bridge and Canasta and Gossip – whatever Gossip was. And had sherries. Or coffee. Common People never drank coffee. They wouldn't know what it was.

Lots of the mummies had dogs, and they'd be Yorkies or Pecky-Knees or Poodles. *Nice* dogs. Nothing common like greyhounds. Only Common People kept *them*, and Mummy said they actually *raced* them. Same as pigeons. And pigeons were as common as you could get.

MUMMY had two Yorkies, called Judas and Jezabel, and they were mean like teachers. They'd bite you if you came near them. And you couldn't see their eyes, so you never knew if they were looking at you, or planning to bite you.

When Mummy wanted to say somebody was common, she'd sniff and say, 'My dear, they're just very ordinary, you know!' Or, 'My dear, they're *Vin Ordinaire*!'

But the Nice mummies and daddies always seemed to be looking over their shoulder, or maybe looking upwards to Something or Someone, to see if they were doing things right. Jamie had this notion of some kind of shadowy duchess – in his mind he called her Lady Darling – who'd sort of lean down from the clouds every now and then, gaze through her lorgnettes and say graundly in an approving voice, 'I say, jolly good! Precisely how I should hold the fork myself!'

Sheila the maid didn't quite fit common. Yet she wasn't Mummy and Daddy's class. Sheila was sort of outside class altogether. To begin with, she came from far away – somewhere called County Awful or Offly or something (south of the border, somebody said, which sounded like down Mexico way).

She would say *arragh* instead of *och*. Like, 'Arragh, Master Jamie, would y'cop yourself on,' instead of, 'Och, Master Jamie, would y'cop yourself on.'

She had a lovely soft brogue, and was lovely and soft herself too. She was big and soft all over, and you loved to hug her and push your head into her big soft chest, which Jamie often did. Trouble was, she had to wear a stiff starched frilly white apron over her black dress, so it was hard to get at her chest.

The apron went with that funny little white lace thing above her forehead. Maids all had to wear that. Mummy said Sheila was 'agricultural looking', whatever that meant.

Sheila loved Jamie, and was ever so kind to him, and could always find him a wee bite of pastry or something in the kitchen, even though everything was rationed because of the war. She'd even sometimes use her own sweet coupons for a wee bit of barley sugar or a few bull's eyes for Jamie.

***

NOW the mummies and the daddies didn't know that the Nice Boys and the Common Boys hung around together after school. Or maybe they did know, but let it be, provided the Common Boys weren't *too* common.

Because there was a third lot that nobody had anything to do with. *The Animals.* They were the boys whose daddies were Cornerboys. Cornerboys leaned all day against the wall near the Labour Exchange, and did things like get drunk and beat their families. If you passed one of their half-doors in Queen Street or North Street, you'd get a smell. A sort of dark smell. 'Smell of poverty,' Jamie's Mummy would say with a sniff. Whatever poverty was.

Nobody actually *said* they were Animals. It was just a word that Jamie used inside his head. It sort of matched the way people seemed to think, even if they never said the word. Like, there was Dinny McCracken whose father was a drunkard, who came to school in bare feet and no vest in winter and had that smell off him, and wore his daddy's old grey trousers cut to his knees, that ballooned like a skirt, and was twenty minutes late every morning because he had to sell papers at

31

the corner of Hill Street, and held his hand out every morning so Mr McGuchan could give him the twelve slaps with the leather for being late. He must have deserved it or Mr McGuchan wouldn't have slapped him every day.

Only an Animal would have bare feet and that dark smell, and let itself get walloped and hang its head and say nothing. Like a cow would if you beat it.

You didn't talk to Animals. And they had only themselves to blame. That's what Jamie's Mummy said.

The Nice Boys would kick Dinny at lunchtime, because he had no lunch and his mother was dead. And because he was a year older than most, so he must be stupid. And they'd laugh at his skirt-trousers. Sometimes they wanted to pull the trousers off him for the fun of it, but they never did. That was because Dinny had his head shaved, with just a fringe at the front, and pink circles all over his scalp. So you couldn't touch him or punch him or you might get the ringworm.

But you could kick him and throw stones at him, because that wasn't touching. That's another way Dinny was an Animal: it wasn't safe to be close to him.

Sometimes some of the Animals would come along the Dromalane Road where Jamie lived. It would usually be girls that came, and they would be wheeling squeaky prams with no hoods or blankets, and children with wet knickers or no knickers sitting inside the prams, with snots running down from their noses. Most of the girls would have the snots, too. So they got called the Candle Gang, because long snots look a bit like birthday-cake candles. Sometimes the Nice Boys would stop them and push the prams down the hill or up on the ditch. Once a baby fell out. It didn't yell.

The Candle-Gang girls were not nice – they used their nails like claws when you hit them, and used horrible words if you could understand their accent. They had what Mummy called a back-street accent. That was terribly common.

There was a Candle-Gang girl that upset Jamie. She was about 11 and had blond hair nearly to her bottom and was sort of tall and kept her head up. She'd just stand there and stare with blue eyes that made Jamie think of the forget-me-nots in his Mummy's garden, and nobody ever pulled a pram off her.

One day Jamie wanted to shout at the Nice Boys to stop, and wanted to go up to the girl and take her hand and tell her it was all right. But he didn't dare, so instead he spat at her. She gave him a clatter across the face that sent him spinning.

After that he was able to hate her.

***

WHEN Mr Bell came to *Thou-Shalt-Not-Commit-Adultery* in the catechism, he said that could wait till later – ye won't be needing it for a while.

But Jamie put his hand up and said, 'Please Sir, what *is* Adultery?'

'It's what Adults do,' Mr Bell said, and Jamie was satisfied with that. Even his Daddy laughed when he told them at home, and Jamie couldn't make out why, but he was glad to see his Daddy laughing. He didn't laugh all that much.

That was last year. Mr Bell was one of the 'decent' teachers. *Decent* was a special word. Boys knew, without even thinking, who was decent and who wasn't. You just *knew*. Decent meant fair, and that they really cared about you, and didn't really enjoy using the leather strap even if they used it sometimes. Some of the really decent ones didn't use it at all.

Most of the Brothers were decent like that. You felt they really wanted you to learn something, and they cared about you. Brother Hennessy was the Head Brother, and Jamie loved him to visit the class because you could feel he was decent. Holy, sort of.

The teachers who weren't decent were 'mean'. That was a special word too. It didn't mean stingy: it meant sort of nasty. Cruel. Jamie noticed you could tell the decent teachers by the way they were kind to Animals. Animals like Dinny McCracken.

The mean ones were always wading into them with the leather strap. Or making them stand in the corner with everyone sniggering at the holes in their pants. But the decent teachers were gentle to them. Jamie didn't understand why. After all, they were only Animals.

None of it made sense.

Most of the mean ones weren't the Brothers. They were just teachers and were called Mister. Some of the mean ones must have hated boys, even if they were married and had boys of their own at home. Jamie wondered if they were different at home.

When you were let out into the quadrangle where the entrance to the jaxes was, and the two storeys of big glass windows all around you, and 800 boys in behind those windows, you could hear the crack of the leather straps from every side, *crack, crack, crack-crack, crack,* and it was like a

34

fire-fight in *Bataan* down at the picture house. Jamie often wondered how many times those leather straps rose and fell every day. And how much pain there was, if you could add it all up like in arithmetic. A sort of pain factory.

The boys were the same as the teachers – you kind of knew inside you who was decent and who was mean. Boys could be mean in lots of different ways. And you tried to keep away from the ones who were mean, if you could.

Like Willie McGinty, who had two pencils but wouldn't lend one to Jamie, even though ole Murphy was coming down the class and would leather Jamie for forgetting his own pencil.

'I just want to see you suffer,' Willie told Jamie.

Or like Bully Moore who put the stub of a pencil standing up on the seat when Dinny McCracken stood up to answer a question, and it went up into Dinny when he sat down and he was taken screaming out of the class to the hospital with blood pouring through the back of the big cut-down trousers.

About a month later Brother Hennessy came round and told them Dinny wouldn't be coming back. He had blood poisoning, and was in hospital. Brother Hennessy said. But that's not why he wouldn't be coming back: it was because his father had died. Some relative would be coming to take Dinny away.

***

BRANDY Balls was one of the decent fellas. He was common. Brandy Balls was wee'er than Jamie, but he could spit further. Further than anybody. And he could pee higher than anybody else – there was a chalk mark on the back wall to prove it. (Somebody said girls couldn't play that game, but Jamie thought that was ridiculous. Of course they could if they were

35

big enough.) And Brandy Balls could put his fingers in his mouth and whistle so your ears would be hurting. Jamie wished he were like Brandy Balls.

One day Brandy Balls said a new word which deeply impressed Jamie. It rhymed with duck. Mousey McKevitt said it was a Mortal Sin, but Jamie said how could a wee word be a sin? Sins were things you *did*, and there were enough of them to be going on with. The Brothers were always going on about them.

So that afternoon Jamie was dawdling home from school – dawdling because that ole Jennifer was visiting from Enniskillen. Jamie hated her: she was Mummy's godchild, and a sissy. Like most girls.

Jamie was kicking a tin can in front of him when Mummy's friend Mrs McAteer came cycling by. 'And how's my pet?' she said to Jamie. She liked him and always called him pet, which Jamie didn't like.

'Fuck off!' Jamie said, and Mrs McAteer fell off her bike.

Jamie stood watching her struggling to regain her balance, one foot on the ground, bike leaning at a fierce angle.

'You wait – just you wait – till you Mammy hears about this!' Mrs Mac hissed, once she got her breath and her tears under control.

That was when Jamie understood the Power of Language. If it could knock people off bicycles, it could do a lot more. And that power could be Jamie's.

He couldn't wait to try out his new word at home. It was a matter of waiting for the right moment.

That evening during tea ole Jennifer was kicking Jamie under the table. Jamie refused to descend to such below-table level, so he simply said, 'Fuck off, you!'

Time stopped. The tea, pouring from the teapot into Mummy's cup, hung in the air, an amber stream. Daddy's face, fork just coming up to the mouth, froze in a rictus of horror, and turned white. Then sort of purple.

Even Judas and Jezabel both stopped scratching, and waited, legs in the air.

Mummy snuffled and began to cry. Daddy's fork came slowly down and his face came slowly around to Jamie. 'How – how – how *DARE* you, Sir! You little – I'll – I'll – Good God! *Get out of here*! Go upstairs *at once,* Sir!'

So Jamie scurried upstairs and Daddy got up and went to the sideboard. When Daddy called you Sir, he was very cross indeed.

February 1944

POXY Jameson had huge pimples all over his face, with new pimples coming out the side of old spent ones, like those volcanoes in *The Children's Encyclopedia*.

Father Hardy and Daddy drank Jameson sitting each side of the lounge fire whenever Father Hardy came to visit. Mummy would be down in the kitchen with Sheila the maid getting supper ready.

The Jameson in the glasses made Jamie think of the yellow stuff Poxy Jameson was always squeezing out of his pimples. If you added water it would be like the stuff in the glasses. Maybe that's what it was.

Father Hardy was decent. All the priests who came to the house were decent. They were kind and gentle, and would ask Jamie how he was doing at school. Father Hardy would sometimes give him a wee bag of boiled sweets.

But priests were like that. That was what priests were. They were never mean like teachers. And of course they were better class than the Brothers. A priest would never hurt you. They were there to help you save your soul, so they were always kind. Sometimes Father Hardy would take Daddy down to the dining room and shut the door and save his soul, and you could hear them talking quietly for ages, and Daddy would come back up and he wouldn't be so sad.

The priests were there to help you save your soul. Your soul was like a piece of snow-white cardboard shaped like a coffin lid, and when you told a lie it got marks on it. Those marks were venial sins. If you committed a Mortal Sin it turned completely black and if you died when it was like that you went to Hell for all eternity. That was like going down into one of those volcanoes.

It could happen if you ate meat on Friday. So everybody ate fish.

At least, Cat-licks did. There was no point in Prods eating fish, as they were going to Hell anyway.

So you couldn't forget for a minute you were always walking on the edge of one of those volcanoes, and the volcano could erupt like one of Poxy's boils and you could get sucked down into it forever.

That was what dying in the state of mortal sin meant. Every tiny minute of your life you were in danger of losing everything forever. Jamie would lie in bed trying to imagine Hell forever and ever and ever and ever and ever, going on and on and on and never ending. It made him dizzy.

But Heaven must be nearly as bad, going on and on and on forever, like one of those boring ole High Masses that go on and on. And ole choirs that never stop. And clouds of that incense. Like at Benediction. Jamie knew all about High Masses and Benediction, because he was an altar boy.

That's why priests were kind. To save you from Hell. Like Jesus was kind and gentle, in that picture in the front hall with the red lamp in front of it, and such a gentle smile on him. Nearly like a lady. Or in that wee book that showed him in a pink dressing-gown with curly fair-haired boys and girls sitting on his knee and looking up at him.

That's why Jamie didn't believe Mick McGinty, whose older brother was a boarder up at Violet Hill – St Coleman's College. Mick said the priests there had canes and made the boys lie across the bed and walloped their backsides. And one priest had such a temper he beat a boy so many times that the boy had to go to hospital.

That wasn't true. Priests wouldn't do that. Only teachers. Priests were kind and full of love, like Jesus.

There were two kinds of priests. There were the Oblong Fathers in white robes at Trinity Church where Jamie was an altar boy. They had graund accents and were often away giving 'retreats'. Jamie would have liked a retreat – it sounded like some sort of 'treat', but they never offered him any.

Then there were the Circular priests down at the Cathedral. They had sort of common accents and liked money. They wore black skirts.

Father Hardy was one of the ones in white robes, only he put on a black suit when he went out.

Jamie's family always walked to Sunday Mass at the Oblong Fathers. (A better class of people went there than went to the Cathedral, Mummy always said.) They'd always go to eleven o'clock Mass, and they'd nod and say Hello to the people coming back from the ten o'clock Mass. To the Nice People anyway.

***

41

THERE was one Sunday morning they were all walking to Mass (it was the time those Yank soldiers were in town) and Jamie was dawdling a bit behind Mummy and Daddy when he found some kind of balloon on the footpath. It wasn't yet blown up – it was long and grey and sort of slimy and tasted kind of funny when he put it to his mouth. But it blew up nicely, until it was about four feet long, so that finally it looked like one of those airships or zeppelins in the spotter books. Lovely and sort of silvery grey, with a lovely little point at the tip. People coming back from the early Mass stared at it, obviously with admiration.

Then Daddy turned to tell Jamie to hurry up, and when he saw the balloon his jaw dropped in admiration too. No it couldn't have been admiration, because, when Daddy got his breath back and was able to speak, he sort of stammered, 'Oh, dear God in heaven. P-p-put that *down*, Sir! *Now! Put – it – down*, do you hear? *Now!'*

Jamie ran up to show him the balloon, but his father sort of cringed and said, 'Just drop it, will you? *Just let it go. PLEASE!'*

Jamie let it go, and the balloon took off across the street with a roar like some gigantic fart, whirling round and round among the returning Mass-goers. It was magnificent sight, especially seeing people ducking to get out of its way.

For some reason Daddy didn't kiss Jamie goodnight that evening when he was going to bed. Nor the evening after. Not that he seemed cross any more. He just didn't kiss him – that was it. And didn't for some weeks.

***

42

NONE of the Prods were altar boys. Only Cat-licks. And none of the Animals either. They'd be too smelly. Jamie didn't much like being an altar boy, but Mummy said it got you closer to God and could help to save your soul in the long run.

But it could get you to Hell too. Like on a wet winter morning when you had to get up at six thirty to serve seven o'clock Mass, and you'd be on your wee bike going all alone down Queen Street in the rain, and a raindrop would get on your lips and you were wondering if you had swallowed any of the rain because then if you went to Communion you would have broken the fast and that was a mortal sin and you would go to Hell. But you wouldn't dare *not* to go to Communion because Father Hardy might think it was because you were in the state of mortal sin.

If you were serving Benediction you had to use a taper on a huge long stick to light all those big candles way high above the altar and Jamie couldn't get the taper to connect with them, so it took maybe ten minutes to get them all lit. And the coughing down in the church would be telling Jamie to get on with it. Sometimes Mingy Monaghan had to come out and finish the job for him, and Jamie felt mortified.

Sometimes he felt he could do nothing right.

'Tell your Mammy you need glasses,' Father Breen said to Jamie. But Jamie didn't tell her, because the fellas would call you Specky-Four-Eyes if you had glasses, and they would think you were a sissy, and they could take the glasses off you and jump on them.

Jamie couldn't quite understand why Prods couldn't be altarboys. Like Malcolm Bruce and Trevor Watkins – they went

43

to Sunday school in that funny church on Hill Street where the doors were always locked except on Sundays. That's because there was no Jesus in the tabernacle there to visit, so there was no point keeping the doors open.

Prods didn't seem to bother much about Hell or mortal sin. That was probably because they were going to Hell anyway. And they were a bit different about what you had inside your pants. They seemed to think there was more to it than just pissing. Jamie wasn't sure what, but he wondered why you always wanted to keep those things covered.

One Thursday evening in the river field Trevor Watkins pulled Jamie's thing out and made it stand up, but Jamie got upset and ran home. But he didn't tell Mummy because he had felt funny down there and she mightn't like that.

The next day Brother Hennessy came in to talk to them about *Their Bodies*. He must have known about Trevor and Jamie. Jamie felt he kept looking at him when he was talking, and he felt his face getting hot and red.

Brother Hennessy told them their bodies were the temples of the Holy Ghost, and that Jesus covered his face in shame whenever a boy uncovered his body. And if any boy – which, dear boys, may God avert – ever, ever, *ever did anything with his body,* that boy entered a state of mortal sin and merited Hell for all eternity.

The only escape was confession as quickly as possible, before you died in that state and went to Hell.

***

JAMIE tossed all that night and was first in the queue outside Father Breen's confession box on Saturday morning at eleven o'clock. There were three rows of people in the queue, and Jamie was terrified they might hear his shame.

The door closed him into the darkness with a *phut* sound. You stood, because you were too small to kneel. The slide came back with a crash, and Something moved in there.

'*Nominy Patters...*' Father Breen's voice.

'B-bless me, F-father for I have sinned. It's a week since my last confession. I – I ...'

'Yes?'

'I – I...'

'*Yes?*'

'I – I...'

'I can't hear you!'

'I – I did something I shouldn't have done.'

Silence. Then: '*Was it something to do with your body?*'

'Y'yes, Father.'

Silence. Then: 'Was it alone or with someone else?'

'S-s-some-someone else, Father.'

'Another boy?'

'Y-yes, Father.'

Silence. Then: 'How old are you?'

'Nine and three-quarters, Father.'

'O dear God. O dear God in heaven. O my child – *at nine years of age?* Oh, in God's name, child! Tell me, before Almighty God, what did you do?'

Silence.

'*What – did – you – do?*'

Silence.

'I cannot give you absolution, child, if you do not tell me.'

Silence.

'Did you hear what I said, child?'

There was coughing from outside. Either they were getting fed up waiting, or worse still, they could hear everything.

'My child. You must make me a promise. A solemn promise. Promise me, before God, here in the tabernacle, you will never – never – *never* – do – this – thing – again? And that you will avoid that person as an agent of Satan. Promise me, child?'

Silence. Jamie was shaking so much he couldn't promise anything. Or say anything.

The priest waited in silence too. Then he spoke again with a sigh. 'Say six *Our Fathers*, child. I will pray for you. Now go in peace – *if you can.* Do you hear me? *Go,* child.'

Jamie pushed against the door and tumbled out into twenty pairs of eyes fastened on his flaming face. He shambled down the aisle and out the church door. The sunlight hurt his eyes.

Jamie didn't go back to confession for nearly a year. He was too scared. Every Saturday morning he'd pretend to go down to the church, but instead he'd head down along by the canal or wander through Rafferty's fields. Nobody ever copped on.

May 1945

DADDY and Mummy were sitting on either side of the wireless when Jamie came into the lounge. It was early afternoon.

'Well that's it, then,' Daddy was just saying. 'It's over. Well, God be thanked who has brought us to this hour. As Rupert Brooke once said. Different circumstances, of course.'

'What's over?' Jamie asked.

'The War, dear,' Mummy said. 'It's over. We've just heard it on the wireless.'

'Will we get bananas now?'

'Please God we will, dear. But it might take some time.'

Jamie wandered outside, dying to tell somebody that the War was over. But there was nobody there. He wandered down past Hennessy's corner and finally found Mingy Monaghan having a swing from a rope tied to a lamppost. That's because Mingy was common. Mummy had said the Monaghans were *vin ordinaire*, and should never have been encouraged to move to the Dromalane Road.

Mingy climbed off his rope to join Jamie.

'The War's over,' Jamie told him.

'How d'y'know?' Mingy was always like that. Always picking on things you'd say.

'Mummy and Daddy just heard it on the wireless,' Jamie said.

'Them's not your mammy an' daddy, so they're not!' Mingy Monaghan said.

 'Whaddya mean?'

'They're not your real mammy an' daddy.'

'That's not true.'

'It is, so. *Your* mammy an' daddy's dead. You're dopted, so y'are.'

'What's dopted? And my Mummy and Daddy's not dead. They're back in the house listening to the wireless.'

Mingy's nose wrinkled, like it always did when he had something new to tell you. 'Dopted's when your mammy an' daddy's dead, an' other people pretend they're your mammy an' daddy. Like with you. You used to be Jamie Jones, *my* Mammy says – an' you're only called Jamie O'Brien because the O'Briens took y'in.'

Jamie just took off running for home and the tears were running down his face. He could taste the salt on his lips as he hurried up the steps and pushed in the door of the big three-storeyed terrace house with the bay windows. Mummy was just coming down the stairs when Jamie ran in gasping and sobbing and grabbed her around her waist. 'M-m-Mingy Monaghan's been saying bad things,' he sobbed between gasps. 'He says you're not my real Mummy. He says I'm dopted. It's not true, sure it isn't?'

Mummy sat down on the stairs and put her arms around Jamie and pulled him close. She smelled like a mother and Jamie breathed her in.

'Sure it isn't true?' Jamie said again, and pushed Mummy back to look at her. 'Sure it isn't?'

There was something in Mummy's face. Jamie stared at her, then let out a roar of horror and raced up the two flights of stairs to his room, where he banged the door and threw himself onto his bed.

***

'YOU should have told him ages ago, m'dear.' Mr O'Brien was leaning against the sideboard, Waterford tumbler in hand. 'I've said it – how many times?'

'*I* should have told him?' His wife spoke sharply. 'Don't you come into this at all?'

'He's *your* sister's child, m'dear. Not mine. And it was your idea to take him.' Mr O'Brien took a sip from the crystal tumbler. 'Not that I'm sure what a good idea it was. You're hardly cut out for motherhood, with that – that social life of yours. Boy's running wild. And I warned you he'd get his memory back.'

'It hasn't come back, and Dr Flood says it may never. It was that hideous Monaghan boy told him.'

'Did he say – how Sammy died?'

'Nobody could know that here,' Mrs O'Brien said. 'Thank God it was well hushed up at the time. No, the boy just told Jamie he was adopted.'

'But how did the wretched boy find out?'

'I've no idea.'

49

'Someone must have got word from Enniskillen. We never told a soul when we moved here. Unless you did?'

'Henry, that's *most* unfair of you.'

Mr O'Brien turned to the sideboard and took the stopper from the decanter. 'Well, May, at least the job's done for us.' He sighed. 'It's a question of getting the boy used to it now.'

***

JAMIE was dried out from crying. He just lay with his face on the soaked pillow.

Mummy held his hand and talked softly. 'She was three years younger than me, Jamie. And she was so sweet and gentle and beautiful. That's why you're so handsome. And her hair was fair like yours, except it came to her waist when she was a child.

'I want you to remember her as beautiful, Jamie. She was one of the loveliest girls in Fermanagh. And good, Jamie. She was so good and kind to everyone. When she died she must have gone straight to heaven. Always remember she's in heaven, and she's watching over you every minute.

'And she'd want you to go on calling me Mummy. Will you do that, Jamie?'

Jamie's hand tightened in hers.

'That's my boy. And I'll always be a good Mummy to you. You know that, don't you?'

Jamie turned on his back. 'Tell me about my Daddy,' he said. 'My real Daddy. Was he really called Jones?'

'He was indeed. And you could be Jamie Jones now if you wanted to. But maybe it would be silly to change back. And

50

you could call me Aunt May, instead of Mummy, if you'd rather. Do you want to think about it?'

Jamie nodded.

'We didn't really know your Daddy well,' Mummy went on. 'He lived in Belfast, so we hardly got to meet him. But I'm sure he was a nice man, and a good man.

'And he died of sadness. Just died of sadness after your Mummy died. He's with her in heaven now. They're both watching over you. Every minute of every day.'

'Well then, maybe, would you mind if I tried to call you uncle and aunt? Because – because I already have a mummy and daddy, don't I?'

'Of course, darling. From now on, I'll be your Aunt May. That all right?'

Jamie jumped up and gave her a big hug. 'But I'll still be Jamie O'Brien, won't I? I want to stay that.'

June 1947

TREVOR Watkins was a lot of fun to be with. But he could
get you into trouble. And Mummy – Aunt May, rather –
said for Jamie to keep away from him. But she didn't sort of
insist. Actually she hardly ever did much insisting: she didn't
have much time to, with golf and committees and canasta and
bridge and things.

And anyway the two boys walked home together most days –
Trevor from the Prod school that had boys and girls together in
it; Jamie from the Christian Brothers, that had only boys.
Jamie was beginning to think he might like to be in a school
with girls. Even if they were sissies, they might be nice to be
around. They'd be nice to show off in front of – but they could
make a fella feel shy sometimes. Especially when they giggled
together, which they always seemed to be doing.

But Trevor certainly was trouble. He had grown to be the
natural leader of the little gang from the neighbourhood – there
was Noel, Sam, George, Damian, Wesley, Sean, Malcolm, Billy,
and of course Jamie, plus a few lesser hangers-on. About half
were Prods and half were Cat-licks.

Trevor'd come up with ideas like getting Jamie to lie face
downwards on the footpath when old Mrs Heather was

hobbling along leaning on her stick, and a big pool of tomato ketchup on the footpath beside Jamie's neck. And a carving knife sticking out from under his neck, with ketchup on it too. Jamie didn't really want to do it, but Trevor could taunt you into doing anything he wished.

So Jamie lay there, with all the boys behind the hedge watching. And when old Mrs Heather came to Jamie she stopped and peered down. She adjusted her glasses and peered again. Then she took off running without her stick, and up the steps to the nearest house. The boys watched someone answer the door, but then Mrs Heather seemed to fall down.

It was a lot of fun after that, with an ambulance and stretchers and things. It was even more fun when one of the stretcher men slipped in the tomato ketchup, but nobody seemed to ask why the ketchup had been there in the first place.

And then there was the wasp's nest. It was in that loose-stone wall on the side of the road where the fields ran down to the river. So in the evening the boys would wait up the road from it, and when they'd see a courting couple coming along the road, one of the boys would run up to the nest and poke it with a stick and run like hell. Trevor usually got Jamie to do it, because he was the fastest.

By the time the courting couple would reach the nest they would walk straight into a cloud of very cross wasps. The fellas would whoop for joy at the speed at which the courting couple would take off down the road, slapping themselves all over.

It was even better when it was an old couple. You'd never think oul' ones could run that fast. It was such fun they did it lots of times that summer.

***

AND then one day came a boy called Josh – somebody said it was short for Joshua. He had arrived with his family from Lancashire – somewhere in England – and spoke with a funny English accent. The family took the bungalow down by the canal, and word was that his father was a new doctor up at the hospital.

Josh had raven-black hair with a kind of razor-blade gleam to it. When he first joined the group the boys took exception to his ultra-clean knees and well-pressed grey flannel shorts, but they soon overlooked such things after he took on Wesley and bled his nose.

Josh's status rose when it was noted that he could aim a catapult at a cat with deadly accuracy. He could also walk on his hands, and even swim under water down at the river. And he'd talk the hind leg off a donkey.

'Bit of a charmer, I'd say, that young Joshua,' Jamie overheard Aunt May say. 'Handsome, too.'

It turned out too that Josh had a fantastic mother. It was hard to believe that someone so old could still be beautiful. She must have been all of twenty-nine, but she was tall and slender and when she smiled at you you wanted to hug her – as, as a mother, like.

When you called at the door looking for Josh she would sometimes bring you in and give you lemonade and maybe some of those suggestive biscuits. She had a gorgeous gravelly voice that somehow sounded like the biscuits.

Josh's father was one of those big silent types, always busy up at the hospital, or smoking pipes and reading newspapers when he was back at the house. There was a pram with a baby sister in it. Babies are boring ole things, but Jamie's mother seemed to like this one. Indeed Jamie found himself thinking he wouldn't mind having one – a baby sister, that is – if he couldn't have a baby brother, which he would have far preferred.

***

ONE day Jamie came home from school and saw Mrs Credley's little Austin Seven parked at the kerb outside his house – a not unusual sight, indicating the usual tea ceremony within. Mrs Credley was one of Aunt May's Prod friends.

As Jamie came into the lounge, the Gredley was in full flight:

'...saying at the hospital that *of course* they're Jewish. I mean, m'dear, you've just to look at young Joshua's face – '

They stopped dead, teacups at the ready, when Jamie appeared at the door.

'What's Jewish, Aunt May?' Jamie asked.

The Gredley shook her head almost imperceptibly.

'Don't be always asking questions, dear,' Aunt May said. 'And take that schoolbag up off the floor – you know what your uncle will say when he gets home. Better get on up and do your homework. And don't forget your altarboys' meeting tonight.'

The Gredley showed her gold teeth in a wintry smile, murmuring vaguely, 'And how's our little man today?'

***

JAMIE daydreamed as usual over the hated arithmetic, wondering what on earth this Jewish thing was all about. That night after the altarboys meeting he asked Misery McErlane about it.

Misery had a stammer and knew all about everything. 'J-Jewish? That means a Jew. They're – they're not the same as us. An' – an' they k-k-killed Jesus. An' – an' – me daddy sez they started the war, so they did. An' – an' – like I mean, well, like, they're just d-different. That's it – d-different. An' – an' – they're richer'n everyone else, so they are. That's because they t-take everybody else's money.'

Jamie couldn't wait to tell Trevor. He told him when they met after school the next day. Trevor remembered from his Sunday school that Punches the Pilot was one of them.

Trevor's little sister came tripping along behind them and, in view of the seriousness of the occasion, they waited for her to catch up, and permitted her to walk with them. Martha's hazel eyes widened as they told her what they knew.

Tea was deadly slow, and Jamie could hardly wait to get out to the gang. They were all there where they always met, even Martha, on that grassy verge near McAteer's bungalow. All except Josh. There was an exhilarating air of the unknown, of something about to happen, but no one knew what.

'I wonder will he come?' Patsy murmured.

Nobody answered.

Just then he came. They spotted him far away down at Hennessy's corner, walking along with his springy step, then skipping a bit on and off the footpath, then turning a half cartwheel. He was as eager to get to the gang as the others had been. He arrived as usual with a little wave of his hand, a smile, and a thrown-away *Wotcha!* in that funny English way he had.

He must have sensed something then. His mouth opened a little, and he just stood where he was, hands by his side, looking from Trevor to Jamie and back. Nobody said anything, and Jamie noticed that most of the boys were looking at the ground. Patsy was blowing a pink bubble of gum from the side of his mouth, and Wesley was pulling a sticking-plaster on and off his bare knee.

Suddenly Trevor said, 'Hi, Jewface!'

A snigger ran through the group, and Josh's fists tightened down by his sides. He looked at Jamie, but Jamie looked away – he really wanted to smile encouragingly, but he couldn't take sides against Trevor.

Then someone said, 'Fuck off, Jewface!'

Suddenly they were all chanting Jewface, Jewface, *Jewface*, clapping their hands and dancing in a circle around Josh. Like Indians. Josh started to cry, and looked around wildly. He suddenly lowered his head like a little bull and charged. Patsy and he collapsed on the ground in a tangle of writhing limbs. Fists rose and fell. Everyone threw themselves on top of the heap.

It was as if something had got into them all and taken them over. Even gentle Patsy was snarling like an animal. Wesley was roaring, 'Let him have it – punch the Jew bastard.' Jamie didn't want to, but he threw himself into the heap too. He felt he had to. But he didn't actually do any of the punching.

Jamie suddenly felt awful, that they were doing this to someone he liked. That they all liked, really. Suddenly he got a fist in the nose and the blood roared down. Things got confused after that. There was a glimpse of Trevor and Noel holding Josh's arms while somebody brought a knee up between his legs. Then a glimpse of Josh doubled up on the ground, in the centre of a screaming dancing ring. Then coming up for more fight. Then Josh's head locked under someone's arm, and fists zeroing in.

Then Josh breaking through the ring, and tearing off down the road, roaring and crying, with the whole gang whooping after him. Patsy grabbing a stone and throwing it. The stone flying past Josh's ear, and the next thing everyone grabbing stones from the side of the road, running and flinging all at once.

Jamie half-heartedly lobbed a pebble because he didn't want to look bad. When he got a look of contempt from Trevor he threw a bigger one. Someone got Josh a stinging thwack on the buttocks with a hefty piece of rock, and he let out a screech. Then, as in slow motion, Wesley launched a blade-shaped stone that arced gracefully and took Josh right on the crown of the head. Blood appeared like magic and a howl of joy went up. The last anyone saw of Josh was blood pouring down over his neat white collar as he scampered around the bend at Hennessy's corner.

The fellas went home early that night. Nothing seemed much fun after the thrills of the chase. Besides, they found it strangely hard to talk to one another.

***

SOMEONE must have squealed. Probably Martha. Girls are like that. No, maybe not Martha – sure wouldn't Josh have had to tell what happened anyway?

Anyhow, about 10.30 that evening Wesley's father arrived at Jamie's home, and was closeted for about an hour with Uncle and Aunt in the dining room. Jamie sneaked out to the grassy verge but none of the gang was there.

That was ominous, and he crept back home. Uncle Henry was just showing the visitor out, amid mutterings about keeping-the-police-out-of-this-if-at-all-possible-but-I-doubt-if-we-can.

Uncle just looked at Jamie: 'You, Sir. Go up to your room and wait till I come up.'

Next morning Jamie was frog-marched down to the house by the canal, to apologise. Josh, he now knew, was in bed with five stitches in his scalp. Not as bad as it might have been.

Josh's mother opened the door. It was the last time Jamie was to see her, as the family left town within the month, over trouble with someone at the hospital where Josh's father worked. Somebody's Aunty Semitis, whoever she was.

The mother listened in silence to Uncle Henry's harrumphing oration, laced as it was with 'deeply-mortifieds' and 'horrified-that-my-nephew' and 'in-this-town-above-all-places'.

Jamie just hung his head.

When Uncle had done, the mother had a few short things to say, and it was mostly about parents, and about whether they had learnt anything from what had happened in Europe only too lately. That low gravelly voice held a measure of weariness that Jamie could never have imagined.

Then Jamie heard her sigh. She tousled his hair and said something about boys being boys. He looked up from the ground then, and saw her smile wanly, and he suddenly thought there was a terribly old look in her eyes.

Years later he would remember that look, and realise it was two thousand years old.

***

'THE boy's completely out of control, m'dear,' Mr O'Brien was saying, as he refilled his glass.

'Jamie's easily led,' his wife said. 'And it's that hideous Watkins boy that's the cause of all the trouble.'

'Don't we *know* it. We'll have to get Jamie away from him, and that's all about it. He'll have to go away to school.'

'So it's Cock, then?'

'Woodcock College is still the best, m'dear. Strict and severe, but it never did me any harm. Made me what I am, actually. It's what the boy needs right now. And it's still where the best families send their boys. Pretty well the Eton of Ireland, y'know. Mix with the right sort later. Connections, y'know.'

'But could we get him in this September? Isn't it a bit late in the year, now?'

'Probably manage it. I'll write to the Provost – I'll remind him I'm an Old Boy m'self. An Old Woodcock. That should do it.'

September 1947

YOU could hardly hear the hissing of the engine as the whooping crowd of boys in bright red blazers swarmed off the train at Ennis and straight through the station to the gravelled park outside, where a couple of ramshackle blue buses waited. They clustered, elbowing and shoving, around a bus door, where stood a stubbly red-faced man with a tweed cap.

'Half-a-crown each,' the man roared. 'An' none o'yiz gets on till ye pay. Had enough of that last time.'

Jamie was the very last to board. Stubbles took the proffered ten-shilling note, fumbled in his coat pocket, and said: 'Look, I'll give y'yer change when we get there. Haven't time now.'

Jamie had to be pushed inside almost on top of the others before the driver could close the door. He could hardly turn around, but at least he had the view through the front window.

'Never trust a peasant,' somebody said, somewhere behind Jamie. 'They're all peasants here you know.' The voice had a sort of hoity-toity ring to it, such as Jamie had never heard before. He tried to turn to see who was talking, but he couldn't move with the crush.

The bus lurched off through the town, and soon was spinning between fields lined with stone walls.

'Peasant country,' the voice said again. 'People here haven't an arse in their breeches.'

Jamie could see the driver's neck reddening, but the man said nothing.

'But wait till we get to the Burren, you new lot,' the voice said. 'They don't even *have* breeches there. It's so poor it's like the moon. Acres an' acres of rock – nothing else. Nobody can live there – 'cept us, of course, at Cock. Gentlemen exiled in the wilderness. An' there's caves the size of cathedrals down underneath the Burren, with rivers running through them. An' there's swallow holes going down into the caves an' you could slide into one if you ever try running away from Cock. Some fellows ran away an' were just swallowed up an' never seen again.'

The bus slowed across a bridge and through the narrow main street of some small town. Someone said Corofin. It swung right, and there were more of those tiny fields and loose stone walls.

Then suddenly no more fields. Just acres of what looked like flat grey concrete going on and on to the horizon, where it seemed to merge into the grey September evening sky. And boulders the size of buses lying here and there, as though only just hurled there by some giant Trevor after stoning someone Jewish. Jamie shivered, as much from the bleakness of that memory as at the bleakness of the scene.

Now there were hazel bushes on either side of the road, then there were trees, more and more of them that became gradually bigger, finally forming a green tunnel into which the bus plunged.

Now here a crossroads and, with a grinding of ancient gears, the bus turned right under a massive stone archway, and lurched up a gravelled avenue that wound through the trees for what seemed to be miles.

The trees fell away to reveal sudden acres and acres of vivid green, graced with the white H's of goalposts, and clusters of red blazers. At the far end a slender spire rose above a clock tower, on either side of which ranged grey limestone buildings. In the windows lights were beginning to glitter.

As the bus door opened and the boys and bags spilled out onto the gravel, the clock tower boomed the *dong-ding-ding-dong* of the quarter hour.

'Welcome to Woodcock College,' the hoity-toity voice said. 'Preferably shortened to *Cock* College. You are now in the caring hands of the Fathers of Heavenly Compassion. Come into my parlour said the spider to the fly.'

Jamie turned to look. The voice belonged to a fellow about the same size as Jamie, but considerably plumper, with a face that to Jamie looked sort of spoiled.

Jamie waited for his change until all the boys were off the bus and gone through the yawning gothic doorway. The man slammed the door and walked around to the driver's side, ignoring Jamie.

'My change, please Sir.'

'You can fuck off, ya little cunt. I heard what yiz said. Well now ye've met your first peasant.' The man climbed up, slammed the door, and the bus scrunched away across the

65

gravel, leaving Jamie standing alone in front of Woodcock College. And half his money gone.

***

EVERYTHING was a shock at Cock. It seemed a foreign country. The smells, more than anything else. The dormitory smelled of death. Well, like a coffin, anyway. Jamie had once smelt a coffin in front of the altar in Trinity Church, and the dormitory cubicles had the same varnishy smell as that coffin. It gave him the shivers. And the boot-room, where you put on the football boots to go out to rugby, stank of mud, feet and ancient leather.

And the priests had a hard cruel smell, not like Aunt May's soft smell. They smelled of damp black cloth and sort of sharp under the arms. Then there was the ancient sour smell of the blue-slate urinals, and the permanent stale odour in the jaxes. And the damp inky smell of the squares of torn newspaper in lieu of toilet paper. (Jamie wondered did the ink stain your bum, but he could never manage to see if it did. And he also wondered how many people they employed to tear up the newspapers, or where they could ever get so many newspapers. He could imagine a big hall full of people tearing up newspapers all day.)

And the male odour of a rugby scrum, comprising farts, sweat, and stale breath, laced with the occasional tincture of dried urine.

The sounds were different, too. The swish of a priest's black robe as he swung off the corridor into the classroom. Whip, whip, whip went the robe in time with the strides.

And the bells – oh, the clamour and the clangour of the bells. There were bells always and everywhere: there was the grinding of the electric bell that woke you gasping in the morning; and the brass handbell to get the boys out of the dormitory; the clang of the iron bell in the chapel corridor as you lined up in total silence to walk into morning Mass; the brass handbell at breakfast to make you stand for grace and the same bell again for grace after meals; the handbell after breakfast, at shitfast, to get you out of the jaxes so Revvo Fitz could close and lock them; another handbell (or sometimes a whistle) to call you in from walking the track in the morning; more electric bells in the corridors to start class and end class; and the iron bell again for evening devotions.

And, high above all, the booming brazen bells in the clock tower that tolled every quarter hour of day and night. At least, Jamie thought, they were counting away the hours till you could get home for Christmas. Indeed all the fellows had calendars stuck to the underside of their desk lids in the study hall and they'd mark off every day as it passed, inching freedom that bit closer.

And the fellows sounded different too. To Jamie's northern ears they had what he would have called brogues, but some had awfully graund ones with sort of long languid vowels. They were the fellows from south Dublin, somebody said.

The fellows had different words for things, too. If you farted you were 'offside'. Doing your homework in the study hall was called 'doing your ekers'. If you were hungry – which was all the time – and another fellow in the hamper room had a cake, you'd beg with the words, 'Give us a scrounge.' The answer, however, might be quite conventional: 'Fuck off!'

The fellows were divided into *Juniors, Intermediates* and *Seniors*, groups that were strictly forbidden to talk to each other, but nobody used that terminology. Instead everyone called them *Bottom Cocks, Middle Cocks* and *Top Cocks*.

If a fellow bested another fellow in some way, he'd jerk two fingers up in the air and say, 'Get the razz!' If a fellow cracked a joke that wasn't that funny, the other fellows would pretend to tickle their armpits while saying, 'Ciuch, Ciuch!'

***

FREE days were called 'Jollidays'. On a Jolliday you got an extra half hour in bed; a sausage at breakfast; a High Mass with litanies at eleven; and the usual rugby in the afternoon. The litanies at Mass would go on and on forever, with utterances like – *Propitius Esto*, to which the whole chapel had to reply, *Libera nos Domine.* Actually some of the fellows would reply with their own version, 'Never on a Sunny Day.'

And then there was that cathedral of a dining hall, resounding to 350 of those brogues now bellowing, with all their owners, seated 18 to a table, vying to be heard between echoing bare stone walls and vaulted roof.

Then the brutal bang of bare backsides being battered with that enormous specially-designed leather paddle. That was the most fearful sound of all. It came only at night, after everyone was gone to bed – everyone but those who were lined up outside Smegmas's room or Revvo Fitz's room for their turn to be bared and battered. The fellows said the paddle collided with the flesh at eighty miles an hour. Each bang was louder than the crack of a gun and, as each bang came, a frisson of fear would waft down the silent dormitory. Sometimes there'd be a scream from Smegs's room, maybe after about the eleventh bang. That's when the blood would be on the paddle.

Everything looked different, too. There were simply no women. None at all. You never, ever, saw one. Well, there were rumours that that the infirmary contained a good-looking nurse that the fellows called the Gorgon, but you'd have to be very sick before you'd even see her.

Only males served in the dining hall. They were kind of sad, some quite old, and they wore brown shop coats with gravy stains on them. They were called skivvies. When you wanted another jug of water you snapped your fingers and shouted, 'Hey, Skivvy.'

There were so many things Jamie had never seen before. Like the mattress hanging from a dorm window when some fellow had pissed in the bed. That served two functions, a fellow called Cairns explained to Jamie: firstly, it dried the mattress in the sweet-smelling fresh air and, secondly, it humiliated the pisser so he'd learn not to do it again. Apart from the humiliation of being walloped for bed-wetting. It was all very effective.

Except it didn't seem to work with Pisser Bates. Pisser was holy and always praying in the chapel, but it didn't seem to stop him from wetting the bed. Neither did the walloping. Pisser always walked alone and never talked to anyone. That was because he was holy. Or maybe it was just that nobody talked to him because they said he smelled of piss.

Nail biting was effectively dealt with too. Revvo Fitz, the assistant dean, had a list of nail biters, and these were lined up every Saturday morning for inspection. If the nails had not grown perceptibly, those bitten hands would receive four wallops (called 'handers' at Cock) for each bitten finger nail. It worked.

You hardly ever saw the priests outside of class time, except you might see them heading off with their golf clubs to play at Lahinch. They lived across in the Manor, where the Provost had his offices, and weren't supposed to have anything to do with the boys outside of class. Except for Smegs and Revvo Fitz, and Shittles the spiritual director and one or two others who could talk to the boys.

The 'revvos' weren't really priests – they were the ones that were putting in time until they would be ordained.

The revvos were called *Sir*, and the priests were called *Father*, except when they taught in the classroom. Then you called them *Sir* even if they were priests. It was all a bit confusing.

The jaxes looked different from anything Jamie had ever seen. There were no seats – just the bowl and the holes in the porcelain where the seats had been removed. Somebody said the walls of the cubicles were whitewashed once a year, but it didn't look like it. Fellows had used fingers to write things in shit, like 'Murray loves boys' – whatever that could mean. One of the cubicles had the print of a hand, perfectly outlined in shit. Jamie tried to imagine the trouble some fellow had gone to to achieve that. It was extremely well done. That hand must have taken some scrubbing afterwards.

You only got ten minutes after breakfast to use the jaxes. After that Revvo Fitz rang his bell, to get everybody out, and then the jaxes were locked. So you had to hurry. That's why it was called *shitfast*.

The fellows looked different from at home, too. You dressed differently here. At home corduroys were always fawn or beige, except for the shit brown of the Common Boys, but here the uniform was grey corduroy shorts that were stiff as corrugated iron, along with a bright red blazer. That was for the Bottom Cocks. The Middle and Top Cocks wore long grey cords, along with the same red blazer. Grey must have been higher-class corduroy, was all that Jamie could think. More suitable to Cock College. Certainly Jamie had never seen grey corduroys before.

That first breakfast in the dining hall was a bit of a shock. You were 18 to a table, and the nine fellows at Jamie's end had finished their porridge, while the skivvies were pouring out scalding tea from those enormous two-handled teapots. A skivvy came across with three plates of rashers and eggs, put one in front of Bentley-ffrench across the table, and ones in front of two other fellows. (Bentley-ffrench was that fattie with the hoity-toity accent, Jamie had learnt, and was proud of the two small *f*'s in ffrench, but the fellows called him just Bentley.) Jamie licked his lips with anticipation, as Bentley tucked in. But no more plates came.

'What about us?' Jamie said. 'Aren't we getting any?'

Bentley looked up with his mouth full. 'Did your oul fella pay for it?' he asked, spluttering out a morsel of egg.

'Whaddiya mean?'

71

'Did your oul fella pay for extras?'

The fellow called Cairns said gently: 'Extras are – well extra. Your people'd have to pay for you to get them. Maybe you could ask them to. You'd be getting rashers and eggs three times a week. An' a glass of milk at night. Things like that.'

'Bet his oul fella couldn't afford it, Cairns.' Bentley snorted, and some of the others sniggered. But Cairns didn't snigger.

Jamie had the feeling that Cairns was 'decent'. Like some of the decent fellows back home, whom Jamie was already missing. Cairns was a bit taller than Jamie, and was quiet, but nobody ever messed with him. He had dark reddish curly hair and a cluster of freckles on either side of his nose, and a face you could trust. He had a sort of jaunty way of carrying himself – not arrogant, just cheerful, like. Confident, maybe.

Dempsey and McArdle seemed decent enough too. At least they were friendly and would talk to Jamie. Most of the others went around in their own little groups and you couldn't break in. They were the ones who had already been at Cock for a year or two.

The fellows who belonged to no group at all were known as the 'Oddfellows'. They went around alone. Like Pisser Bates.

***

FELLOWS seemed to behave in a different way at Cock, different from anything Jamie had ever encountered. Like again at lunch that first day in the dining hall, when there was not enough water in the jug for all nine at that end of the table. Dempsey and McArdle got none, and neither did Jamie.

When the refilled jug was slapped down the same fellows grabbed it again.

'Hey, what about us?' Jamie protested.

'Fuck you!' Bentley said.

So Jamie reached over and tipped the full tumbler into Bentley's crotch.

That was another shock – no one ever used first names. You were Bentley and Dempsey and McArdle. So Jamie became just plain O'Brien. The only exception was if you had a nickname. Like Bates had. They always called him Pisser: never Bates.

Bentley's cronies jumped Jamie outside the dining hall. He fought the way he knew – claws into faces, teeth into arms, knee up into crotches. He had Bentley's head in an arm lock and was hammering it with his fist when they were dragged apart.

'Go up to my room and wait for me there!' A massive priest, with enormous eyebrows and a belly pushing out his cassock, towered over Jamie. He strode away, shiny boots creaking.

'You're for it now,' Bentley smirked through the blood on his face. Smegs'll fuckin' kill ya.'

So this was the Smegma they all talked about – Smegs for short. Jamie had to ask the way to his room. It was at the top of the stairs outside the Bottom-Cock dormitory.

You wait and wait and then you hear the creaking boots coming up the stairs. Jingle of keys, Smegs swishes past and the door slams.

Door opens and Smegs's holding something like a paddle. Only it's shiny and swishy. And it's enormous.

'Right hand!' Smegs says. This isn't like the Brothers' straps. It's what an electric shock must be like. The pain is so awful that you almost lose count of the paddle slamming down. ...Five six, seven, eight, nine. You feel you're going to faint.

'Left hand!' It starts all over again. ...Five, six, seven, eight, nine.

As you stumble down the stairs your hands seem swollen half as much again. Imagine, priests actually sat down to design that thing, Jamie found himself thinking, so that it would create as much pain as possible. Same as torturers designing their instruments. And that Smegs putting all his energy into making somebody suffer. Same as a torturer. And him a priest.

'That's what he does all day,' Dempsey told Jamie as he nursed his swollen hands. 'Just sits in that room all during class time, and the fellows get sent up to him with notes for four or six or ten biffs – by the way, they call them 'handers' here. It's his life. That and walloping the arse off fellows at night. They call that 'buttocking', by the way. Oh, an' he trains the Bottom-Cock team too. To get some variety into his life.'

'You'll have to finish the fight in the gym tonight,' the fellows told Jamie over supper. 'You wait and see.'

'An' I'll fuckin' kill ya,' Bentley added.

'O'Brien! Bentley!' Smegs was standing outside the dining hall as they came out from supper. 'Down to the gym. Gloves on.'

Jamie had never put on gloves before and his hands were shaking. They were still swollen. Somebody tied the laces for him.

Later he could recall the taste of the blood as it trickled into his mouth. He came away from that fight with a bloodied nose.

74

But that was nothing to the black eye that Bentley sported for the next few days. Jamie hadn't a clue how to box, but then neither had Bentley, and Jamie's latent but innate ferocity eventually gave him the edge.

***

THE fellows were all crammed onto the benches in the Bottom-Cock recreation room, to hear Smegs give the first *oratiuncula* of the term. That's what his weekly spiff to the fellows was called – that was the Latin for 'a brief utterance'. He sat on a huge leather armchair that four fellows had to carry down from his room every time. The chair was put on a dais, so as Smegs could look down at the fellows.

First on the agenda was bed making. Taking up his black leather prayerbook, he wrapped his large handkerchief around it to demonstrate how to put on a sheet.

'I bet it's full of snots,' Bentley whispered to no-one in particular.

Next topic was the school motto – *Conquer for Christ: Be Strong.*

'You are born to rule,' Smegs said, 'and never forget that as long as you live. The politicians who have been sitting for the last twenty-five or more years in that so-called parliament, which they choose to call their *Dail'* – a sniff – 'labour under the illusion that they run this country. But an illusion it is, because this land is really and truly run from the Law Library, by its barristers and its judges; from our boardrooms and from the employers' conferences and the chambers of commerce, by our leaders of industry. And from the Medical Council, by its consultants. And from our financial institutions, by our eminent bankers. These are the people who really run this country, guided of course as always by their bishops in Maynooth.

'And where do all these men come from?

'As in France, they come from the *Grandes Écoles* – our great schools – like Blackrock, Clongowes, Glenstal, Castleknock, Newbridge – but above all, our own illustrious Woodcock College. It is here in Woodcock that the elite of the future Ireland are formed. Those who shall rule. And those who do not rule here in Ireland will always find a place in Britain's officer corps.'

Smegs brought his huge fingers together. 'But, before you can rule, you must *be* ruled. And that is my function here. And rule I shall. I shall rule you with a rod of iron' – a flicker of a smirk – 'or rather, a rod of leather.

'And that leather will rise and fall without mercy. There will be no room for weaklings among us. No place for sissies. Such I shall treat as dogs. Remember what James Joyce wrote about Clongowes:

> It can't be helped, it must be done,
> So down with your breeches and out with your bum.

Well that will be fulfilled here at Woodcock, too, but to the power of ten.

'And I shall have the validation of Scripture for my rule, for it says in the Book of Proverbs, 23, 13: *Withhold not correction from the child: for if thou beatest him with the rod, he shall not die.* And the next verse says more again: *Thou shalt beat him with the rod, and shalt deliver his soul from Hell.* So I have my

76

mandate from Holy Scripture itself. And that mandate I shall fulfil, to the letter of the law, with every single one of you here. None of you can hide from me. None of you. Do – not – even – try.

'And do not think you can whine in your letters home. Remember that your parents or guardians all signed a form accepting the discipline of this institution for their charges, and undertaking to uphold it in all circumstances. They recognize what is right and good for you.

'Besides which, we read your letters home anyhow.'

Smegs paused, and gazed down at the silent boys. 'Some of you of course will hate me for the discipline I enforce. Some of you already do hate me, and I know that full well. You cannot hide it from me.

'Well, to such I speak the words of a great Caesar, *Odiunt, dummodo timeant.*' He gazed down. 'You there. Translate!'

'Er, Father. Uh, "Let – let them hate – uh – provided that they fear."'

'Right, boy. Let them hate, indeed. And remember – let all of you remember – there is no escaping me. No escape. Ever.'

***

SMEGS was wrong. There was one escape, and that was the rugby. When you got out on that field, the world was yours to make of it what you wanted.

At first Jamie was put in the forwards, third row on the outside – 'breakaway' as it was then called. But soon his speed and acceleration were noted, and he was soon moved into the back line – outhalf, or second centre sometimes, but mostly out on the wing.

And it was on the wing you could excel: when the ball came out along the back line and was finally in your hands, you just went for that line up there, threading your way through all those inept attempts to tackle. And when you slammed that ball down over the line it was as close to heaven as you could ever come. No, there was one thing better – when you were so far ahead that you could run right behind the posts and touch the ball down there.

Jamie wasn't so keen, however, on having to lie down and hold the ball for the fellow to take the convert in windy weather. He sometimes remembered that Rowel Friers cartoon in *Dublin Opinion*, where the ball remains in the headless man's hands, while the head sails merrily between the posts.

At first Jamie couldn't quite grasp why it was the backs rather than the forwards who did the scoring. You'd think that the forwards, being up front, would have that function. It was Cairns who explained that the forwards were like a sort of heavy cavalry whose job was to break through the enemy lines and let the troops through to score.

With Jamie's bad eyesight, and not being able to wear his glasses on the field, taking or giving a pass could be a problem. Sometimes there were knock-ons and forward passes and fellows shouting Oh-for-Christ's-sake-O'Brien, but these were mostly forgiven for Jamie's speed and manoeuvrability and the trys he made when he did manage to hold on to the ball.

And tackling could be fun, too, when you got over the fear of it and learned to get it right. With the bad eyesight you just went for the colour of the jersey, of course. You went in from the side and took the fellow just below the waist and simply slid downwards, tightening your arms as you went, and if you did it right you pulled his knees together so he had to go over, and no one got hurt, but the fellow's face went right into the mud. So did yours, of course, but it was worth it.

And Jamie felt ten feet tall the day Revvo Hanley the ref said, 'Your tackling is absolutely magnificent, O'Brien. So we'll forgive you that forward pass. Keep it up, boy.'

Within six weeks Jamie had been moved into First Division, which meant he might soon get on to the Bottom Cock team to play Glenstal or Rockwell. The downside of that, of course, was that First Division had Smegs as trainer, so you couldn't get away from him even on the pitch.

Still, Smegs mostly let Jamie be, as his bursts of speed were invaluable. And when he twice got through to score in the game against Glenstal, Jamie felt that maybe he was safer than most of the fellows in Bottom Cock.

***

HE wasn't that safe at all, however. As certain events in November revealed.

The trouble began with *shitfast* – that ten-minute period after breakfast when the jaxes were open. (There seemed to be some fear of what fellows might be up to if the jaxes were left open all the time, but Jamie couldn't imagine what that might be. Smoking, probably.)

'All right, all out,' Revvo Fitz would shout while clanging his bell, after the ten minutes were up. 'Come on, you, in there! Move it!' And he'd hammer on the still-closed cubicles.

So you literally had to shit fast. It was all right for fellows who could do their business quickly, but not everyone could.

Some would come tumbling out still trying to button up their shorts. Jamie was one of those. Always had been a slow one. And he couldn't change now. And if he couldn't go in the morning he couldn't seem to manage it at all.

So one day he stopped going.

He'd had a bright idea – he'd hold it in all day, and at least try to go at night time. There were jaxes upstairs above Jamie's dormitory. To get to them you had to go through that open dorm with rows of beds where the youngest fellows slept. He'd sneak up there after lights out and use the jaxes there.

It worked, sort of, for about a week. Then one night as he was sneaking down between the rows of beds, in pyjamas and bare feet, somebody gave a whoop and threw a pillow at him. It hit him in the chest and he held it. Like you'd hold the ball when it was passed to you on the wing. Instant reflex.

The door at the far end opened and a flashlamp dazzled Jamie.

Smegs's voice: 'O'Brien. Go to my room and wait for me there.'

The little fellows in the beds shivered as the eighteen bangs resounded – nine on each hand. And O'Brien went back down to bed without ever getting to the jax. His hand couldn't have held the squares of newspaper anyhow.

So the shitting had to stop. There was one last try, when Jamie used the charlie under the bed. But that was reported by the dorm janitor, and Jamie got twelve for using it. It's only for emergencies, Jamie was told.

So the shitting had to stop. And it can. Shitting can actually stop. There were nights when you squeezed yourself tight to

80

hold it in, and the pain could be something awful. Utterly agonizing. And you'd get dizzy. But finally your bowels realised they were bested, gave in and simply stopped trying.

And the same again the next night, and the night after.

And the week after that. Where the shit went, Jamie couldn't fathom. Into the bloodstream, maybe. But somehow or other you didn't need to shit any more.

It helped, of course, to stop eating. A spoonful of porridge in the morning, and pretend to eat dinner. No one seemed to notice.

It was worse when the headaches began. There were no stomach aches – it was just sort of dead down there. A bit like concrete. But the headaches were hell. As if your skull was cracking or bursting open. Maybe that's where the shit went. Into your brain. And you'd be sent out from class for six because you had a headache and couldn't concentrate.

You couldn't play rugby any more. You tried but you could hardly run. You'd be half bent over most of the time. But you still tried. The fellows didn't know what to make of you.

Then one day a ball came out along the line and when Jamie caught it he doubled up and just lay curled up on the ground.

There was little to remember after that. The infirmary; then an ambulance; then some hospital in Ennis. And Jamie with hallucinations and screaming about aeroplanes coming to take him away, and holding on to the bars of the bed so the aeroplanes couldn't get him; and people pushing pumps up into him; and some doctor looking grave and shaking his head and demanding to be shown some stool or chair or something.

When it was all over Jamie heard them say he could have died. *Should* have died. A miracle, they said. They sent him home after he was let out of hospital. It was only two weeks to Christmas anyhow.

January 1948

WHEN Jamie returned five weeks late to Cock after the Christmas break, there was no talk of what had happened. Perhaps the fellows didn't really know. Or maybe they just pussyfooted around it.

But there must have been enquiries and things that nobody knew about. Because now the jaxes stayed open after breakfast. For half an hour, that is. After that they still locked them.

It was the winter of the Big Snow. There were tales of Wicklow people marooned and hungry in the mountains. The snow on the rugby pitches was deep and hard, and in the windless air the snow stayed on the perimeter trees that surrounded the acres of playing fields, making the leafless branches look as if they were hawthorn in blossom.

'Midwinter spring,' Cairns said. 'T.S. Eliot,' he said. Whoever that was. Cairns could come up with things no one else knew, but never really flaunted it.

And beyond the trees, when you looked from the dorm windows, you could see the Burren all white and gleaming, instead of the awful dreary grey it usually was. Jamie wondered did the snow make its way down through those swallow holes and fill up those terrible cathedrals under the Burren.

It was a time of chilblains, and newspapers between the blankets to keep the cold out of the beds, and your breath coming like smoke. The chilblains were on your toes and your fingers. The toes were bad because you couldn't get at them through the shoes to scratch them; but the fingers were worse because when the leather paddle hit the chilblains you wanted to scream.

There was no rugby, because of the snow, so maybe it was just as well the three-day retreat was starting.

***

THE aroma of quenched wax candles mingled with the remnants of the incense from Benediction. In later years that aroma would always bring back to Jamie what was about to happen now.

The boys sat in Cock chapel, transfixed. That visiting priest could transfix you and he knew it. He had started by saying how the annual retreat was one of the few real chances of saving your soul, but that it meant absolute silence – total and utter silence for the next three days.

'There will be silence,' he said, 'beginning five seconds from now. Five. Four. Three. Two. One.' He raised his hands, brought them together with a clap. 'Your retreat is now on,' he said.

The boys sat as if they were stones.

Over the next two days the priest took them in spirit to see their own graves, had them stand and stare down at what was inside the coffin – 'that Thing that was once you, rotting in its hideous stench, that now has no eyes to stare back; that has no arms that it could raise aloft in supplication. It would be useless even if it could – the time of supplication and mercy is over. Look with horror now on that thing *that you will someday become.*'

Then the priest started going on about friendship, but Jamie didn't know what he was on about. Friendship, the priest said, was a hopeless thing. 'Your souls are spheres revolving in different orbits from one another, my dear boys. They can never truly meet. Set no store by friendship, as it can bring you only grief.'

He told them how their faith permitted no questions whatsoever. 'To question anything you are told, even for a single instant, is to harbour doubt. And that is a mortal sin against your faith. And for that you merit Hell for all eternity.'

A holy nun once had a vision, he said, where she saw a four-year-old child burning in Hell. 'God had blessed that child with precocious intelligence, and the child had used its free will to harbour one single doubt. One single, tiny doubt, dear boys. And that child died, and went to Hell for all eternity. For – that – one – doubt.'

It was a silent school all those three days. The only sounds in the refectory were cutlery clinking and mouths munching and masticating. Plus the occasional moan of Bentley's farts. The only sounds in the corridors were the routine clangour of bells and the crack of leather on flesh as Smegs walloped fellows who had been caught breaking the silence or reading non-religious books.

The fellows walked the corridors with heads down, avoiding each other's eyes, or sat in corners reading holy books. Bentley of course was reading *Biggles Flies West*, but he had wrapped it in the dust jacket of a book called *The Life of Saint Louis Marie de Montfort.*

On the second day all three lectures were about *impure thoughts*. 'Foul and filthy images of females can come to you in the stillness of the night. They are the secret gift of Satan, boys.' You could almost hear the priest swallowing his saliva. 'And the stirrings of your body that follow such fiendish images are Satan's silent caresses.

'And never forget that any impure thought whatsoever is itself a mortal sin. There are three conditions for a mortal sin. Firstly, grave matter. And a foul thought is always grave. Secondly, full knowledge of the sinfulness. You have that full knowledge now, as I have just given you that knowledge. And thirdly, full consent of the will. That is the only thing that might save you from Hell – that the thought came unbidden, and that you banished it. Or that at least you did not fully consent to it. 'If you did consent, you are in the state of mortal sin and you merit Hell. And if you die in that state, without having confessed your sin, to Hell you will most certainly go.'

***

IT was on the third day that the Thing happened. It was the final sermon, and a frisson of anticipatory joy was rustling through the crowded benches. Father D'Arcy-Matthews stood there, tall and narrow and black, and told the boys how other people, especially people you loved, could bring you to damnation.

'A Belfast priest told me, only the other day, about a sick call he had some years ago, which he will never forget until his dying day. A good Catholic girl had given up her religion to marry a Protestant. *A Protestant.* The girl became an Apostate, dear boys – someone who, for a brief worldly lust, had turned her back on God.

'But after a very few years of godless lust, this young woman fell gravely ill. She knew the tomb was yawning for her, and that Hell awaited her beyond the grave.

'And so she decided to repent.

'But repentance was not to be hers. She asked that a priest be sent for, but her husband refused her. For three long months she begged him. No, he said. And No again. And again No. You became a Protestant to marry me, he told her, and a Protestant you will die.

'Someone even sent for the priest, and he came, but the husband turned him away from the door. Two or three times, that happened, I was told.

'That girl begged and wept and screamed for her husband to save her from Hell by letting in the priest. Until she could scream no more.

'Now she could only gurgle at him, trying to utter "priest" through the death rattle in her throat. But that Protestant husband, like many Protestants, alas, was a hard man.

'However finally he did allow in the priest. Except that he waited till the woman was dead. And do you know what that priest told me? He told me that when he stood by that deathbed, and looked down at the face on that pillow, *he knew he was looking at the face of a woman whose soul was in Hell.'*

THE boys were all gone to the dormitories, but Jamie sat on in the chapel. His mouth was open and he stared at the place where the priest had stood. But he saw nothing there.

What he saw was a face on a pillow. A face that was almost a skull, with cheekbones pushing the yellow parchment skin, and glassy sunken eyes locked on some sight that no one else could see. And teeth bared like fangs. And a black figure with a purple sash saying Sammy Jones what you see is the face of a woman whose...

Jamie closed his eyes, so as not to see that – Thing.

And it went away.

But now he saw that same face close to his, but different now, with laughter and pink cheeks, and eyes bright with joy.

And the teeth now not fangs but white and beautiful and the lips red. And Jamie being jounced up and down and that beautiful face singing –

> Bumpety bump, bumpety bump,
> Here comes the galloping major.
> Bumpety bump, bumpety bump,
> As proud as an Indian rajah.
> All the girls declare
> That I'm a gay old stager.
> Heigh ho, clear the way!
> Here comes the galloping major!

And Jamie giggling and chuckling as if he was going to have hiccoughs.

There was a tiny red-brick walled yard, and a hall with brown lino, and a front door with an oval window in it. And

88

frosted glass so you couldn't rightly see through it. In the daytime you could glimpse the milkman's white coat through it, but only just the shape. *Like the black shape that night.*

And there was a sort of flat glass thing with ridges on it and his mother was rubbing clothes on it in the sink. Lots of suds, and Jamie was grabbing some of the suds and blowing them around the scullery. And his mother was singing, 'I'll tell my ma when I go home, the boys won't leave the girls alone...' She was always singing. And her voice would make you feel happy and safe.

His *mother*? Oh yes, he could see her now. She was so pretty. And so smiling. And her hair smelled of – of heaven.

It was like the curtains opening in the picture house. A new place – new scenes one after another. No. No, not new. Ones that were there before. Sometime.

There was a man there too, in blue dungarees, and he had his arms around Mammy – yes that's what she was called – Mammy – and he was running his hands up and down her back, very far down, and he was putting his lips on her lips and she would pull back to laugh and Jamie wanted to be lifted up and Daddy said wait a minute Jamie we'll lift you up in a wee while.

And Jamie sitting in a go-car and people on the street saying, 'Och, sure God love him. Isn't he the spitting image of his Daddy?'

And Jamie standing with Mammy and Daddy between shiny benches in a little wooden hall, and them singing with their best voices and everybody else singing together, *A Mighty Fortress is our God*, and a Reverend up there conducting, and everyone's face shining with love and happiness and the organ going as if it was heaven itself.

And Mammy telling him she was going off to get a new baby sister for him, or maybe a baby brother – she wasn't sure what they had on offer right now. But coming back without one. Shop was closed, she said. For renovations. For what? Something like that anyway.

And Mammy away again. But still not coming back with a baby brother. And her hands a sort of creamy yellow when she caressed Jamie. Like she was Chinese. Weren't they yellow in that Aladdin book?

And then Mammy and Daddy shouting. They never did that before. And Daddy going out and slamming the front door behind him. And Mammy curled up on the sofa and gasping and sobbing. But mammies don't cry, do they? Jamie crept up and put his arms around her and yes she was crying and she hugged him and hugged him until he was all wet from her tears.

And then that silence upstairs when Mammy went up there and never came back down and they wouldn't let Jamie up except maybe once and then he screamed because she was so yellow and he thought it wasn't his mother.

Now he knew the yellow was because his mother was going to Hell.

Keys rattled and the sacristan Brother came up the aisle. Jamie liked him, even though he was only a Brother.

'Enough of the prayers, now, young man,' the Brother said gently. 'Time for bed.'

90

Jamie ran out and down the long corridor, now only dimly lit. He didn't see it, nor the gothic glass doors that swung back with a creak when he pushed through, nor the other long corridor nor the dark, wooden stairs worn by decades of boots that led to the dormitory. All he saw was a white pillow with a yellow face on it. And the fangs.

'You're late.' Smegs stepped out of the shadows. 'Go to my room and wait for me there.'

The pain of the leathering was as awful as ever. Worse, because of the chilblains.

***

'O'BRIEN!' yells Father Hedigan, the teacher. 'Write yourself a note for six! I'll have none of this daydreaming.'

From the next desk Bentley gives him a contemptuous kick on the shin and Jamie stops thinking about Hell for a moment. He climbs out of his desk, and goes up to the teacher's rostrum.

The punishment book looks like a book of raffle tickets. Under *Poena Sumenda* you write the figure '6'; under *Quam ob Causam* you write, 'Not paying attention'. Then you tear along the perforated line, hand the ticket to the priest to sign, and leave the room, closing the door gently.

You go through the motions automatically, as you've had lots of practice lately. It's a daily routine. Besides, your mind's only half there.

You walk slowly along the corridor. Muffled classroom sounds come from behind each door as you pass – old Murph yelling at someone in second-year maths; a Greek class reciting in unison *...kai ho logos en pros ton theon*; Hedigan in

91

Latin class orating, *Delenda est Carthago.* Turn the corner, down another corridor and up the stairs to Smegs's room. Tap on the door. Silence. Tap again. A swishing of robe from inside and the door opens. Pong of armpit and cigarette. You hand the note over silently. Smegs reads it, goes to a cupboard and comes back to the door with the paddle. You get a whiff of the dull leather of it. You hold your left hand out, and then, when he's finished with that, you hold out your right hand. You don't have to be told any more what to do.

On the way back you squeeze your hands in your armpits to ease the pain. But you're pretty used to it now. Besides, you have to be thinking about Hell. Well, about the sins that will bring you there.

***

IT all started with Mammy being in Hell. For a long time you couldn't think of it – all you could think of was the evil yellow face on the pillow. And the fangs. It's a terrible thing to have a mother in Hell. For all eternity. Every time you thought of it you wanted to vomit. Sometimes you did.

You wanted to talk to a priest about it but there was no one to go to. The priests who taught you swished away as soon as class was over: they weren't supposed to have anything to do with the boys outside of class. And you couldn't go to Smegs. His job was inflicting pain.

That only left Shittles. Shittles was supposed to be the spiritual director, and was the only priest the 340 boys could go to. But he walked like a girl and you couldn't take him seriously. Nobody ever went to him, except a few of the sissies. He seemed to like sissies, especially the nice-looking ones.

But you could go to confession – two of the priests heard confessions every night between eight and nine. So you asked Father Moran in confession if people could ever come out of Hell, and he said no. Never. So then was it any good praying for them? He said no.

So that was that. You were stuck with a mother in Hell. Even though she had once smiled and laughed and danced you on her knee, she was in Hell now. For all eternity. In the end you had to try and stop thinking about it because you couldn't go on vomiting. But it was so hard not to think of it.

Then awful things started to happen. It all began slowly, but in the end you began to believe she was possessing you from Hell. First, filthy *filthy* thoughts started coming into your mind when you were asleep, like pulling the knickers off Ann Morgan in the tennis club at home, and when you awakened you were covered in fish soup. At least that's what it smelled like, so you stopped taking the fish soup on Fridays. But the filthy thoughts kept coming and the soup kept squirting out, so you stopped taking any soup at all, even though you were hungry.

Then one day your body started acting as if you really were possessed. Your willy started standing up between your legs and you couldn't stop it. And it wouldn't lie down. Sometimes the skin would pull back and it was so sore you could hardly walk. And when you togged out for rugby the willy would start bulging inside the white shorts so everybody could see it, and you tried to keep sort of bending over so it wouldn't be noticed, but some of the fellows would snigger. And when the ball came out along the line to you and you had to run with it – you were nearly glad to be tackled.

And then hair started growing in dreadful places where you'd never expect it. Was Mammy possessing you to turn you into an animal, some sort of hairy monkey?

Then the Thoughts started coming, not just while you were asleep, but while you were awake. *The Filthy Thoughts.* They were the worst, because the priests had said even a single impure thought was a mortal sin and would take you to Hell for all eternity. It was always 'grave matter', they said. And of course you had full knowledge of how wrong it was. So the only thing could save you from Hell was if you didn't consent to it.

So a thought would come – maybe about Ann Morgan's wee white tennis skirt coming up when she hit the serve. The knickers that showed. You immediately turned your thoughts to something else, like maybe would there ever be a parcel from home.

But did you turn your thoughts away fast enough? Even an instant of dallying meant consent. And that was a mortal sin. Hell for all eternity. So think now. Did you dally? *Did you consent?* Stop everything else and think this out. Was there the teeniest, weeniest hesitation, the teeeniest consent? If so... there's no teeny-weeny Hell. It's for all eternity.

You'll have to go to confession again tonight. You've been every night this week. You can hear the priest sigh as he recognises the same voice. Oh, him again!

'Look, I *told* you. Stop thinking about sin. Just turn your thoughts to something else. I'm giving you permission not to examine your conscience. Don't – examine – your – conscience: do you hear me, boy?'

But then you wonder did the priest hear you right. Or did he understand it right? So maybe he gave the wrong advice. So you could still die in mortal sin.

Anyhow here's another thought coming. About Ann Morgan peeing. And what's there between her legs. Now that is gravely sinful. Did you consent? Think. Just think for a minute. Think it through. No, no, maybe not. No you didn't consent this time. You got by. But here's another thought coming – keep it away, *keep it away* – about Ann's mother this time. Oh no. No, not her mother. No. Oh yes. Those big breasts – do they have purple tips? Now that's filthy. That has to be a mortal...

CRACK across the head. Father Tracy standing over you. It must be maths class now. 'Did you even *hear* my question, O'Brien? No, you didn't. Write yourself out a note for twelve, O'Brien. I've had enough of this mooning.'

***

'ANY boy who doesn't like rugby must have a mental kink.' Smegs was giving the *oratiuncula* – his weekly utterance to the Bottom Cocks.

The boys sat crammed together on the benches, listening in silence to the words from the massive leather armchair. Utterance from the throne, Jamie thought.

'There are boys down there among you who, unfortunately, are of that sort, and we all know who they are. It is up to you to force them to change, whether on the field by tackling them into the mud so they *get* to like it, or off the field by showing your utter contempt for them. Hammer into them our motto – *Conquer for Christ – Be Strong.*

'As for my contribution, let me say this – I know every single one of those boys – so-called boys – and to each one of them I say – if I see any one of you standing or walking even for an instant during a rugby session, you will come up to my room afterwards. And you know what that entails. *You hear that, Bates?*

'There is no place here for weaklings – remember that. And I will not tolerate their pernicious influence among us.' Smegs slammed his ledger shut and swished from the room, trailing clouds of armpit.

Jamie had only half listened as he had stuff to tell in confession later, and he was trying to work out how he would explain it to the priest.

Anyhow Smegs's words didn't much matter because at least Jamie was still pretty good at rugby. If only he could wear his glasses so as he could see better. Then he mightn't fumble some of those catches. Or give that forward pass like yesterday. But one ball in the face and the broken glass would be into your eye. And you could hardly tackle if you were wearing glasses. Didn't some film stars have lenses put right on their eyes? Jamie would have loved lenses like that – there'd be no more fumbled catches if he had those.

Still Jamie was as fast as ever when he got the ball. And on the wing you could wait till the ball came out to you. And there was still that fabulous thrill when you got a try. You could forget Hell for a moment or two. And Jamie was getting better at throwing in the ball after it went into touch, which the wing did in those days rather than the hooker. You cradled the oval 'pill' in hand and forearm and sent it right between the two waiting lines. If you handled it right you could get it into the right pair of hands. Some of the wings were starting to call out codes, but Jamie hadn't got to that yet.

And at least on the rugby field the fellows were too busy to shun Jamie's mournful mortal-sin face. And sometimes, sometimes, if he really got involved, or managed a try, he could forget his sins for a few blessed moments. The sins waited, of course, for the moment he slowed down again. But maybe with that match coming up against Rockwell he'd get his mind off the sins for a while.

***

IT was in the week before the match against Rockwell that Jamie got knocked out when tackling Bentley. He must have gone in wrong, because Bentley's knee went right into the side of Jamie's jaw. He woke up on the sideline with a ring of faces looking down at him. One of the faces belonged to Smegs.

They told Jamie he had been out for twenty minutes. When they helped him up his back hurt a bit, and he winced.

'It's a man's game, O'Brien,' Smegs said.

And they just got on with the match, and Jamie scored twice, in spite of a dreadfully painful back and a jaw that was swelling by the minute. He'd be a cert for the team against Rockwell now – if the jaw and the back stay put.

As they walked in off the pitch, the sins came back to roost, and Hell yawned for Jamie. No wonder the fellows backed off Jamie O'Brien once he was off the pitch.

***

JAMIE tosses that night in the dormitory, listening to the snores and snuffles and belches from the other cubicles. His swollen jaw throbs and his back hurts, but the tossing is more to do with a thought that has poisoned his mind as he climbed into his pyjamas. Do girl's pyjamas have an opening like that, or not? And what is it like inside there anyway? How different are they? No, no. It's a sin to think that. Stop it. Don't let it take hold. Oh Jesus help me. Did I cause the thought deliberately? I gave in to it. I know I did. Did I? Oh Jesus help me. Wait till I think, now...

The curtain rustles and Smegs comes in to the cubicle. Jamie can just discern the white shirt in the darkness. The man seems huge in the tiny cubicle. There's a slight whiff of decanter, like off Jamie's uncle.

'I'm going to massage your back,' Smegs says. Very quietly, so as not to wake anyone. 'Take off your pyjamas.'

Jamie sits up and takes off his top.

'Everything,' Smegs said.

Jamie pushes back the blankets and raises himself up to take off the pyjama bottoms.

'Now turn over and lie on your stomach.'

As Smegs approaches the bed the decanter smell is stronger, enriched now with armpit and cigarette. Jamie can hear the man breathe.

The hands are warm and firm as they touch Jamie's back. Jamie winces as a thumb presses.

'That where it hurts?' Smegs asks.

'Yes. Just around there.'

Expertly the hands move up and down the small of the back, kneading, pressing, caressing. Hands that have caused so much pain, now comforting. Easing. It feels good. Jamie sighs and relaxes. Maybe that sin can wait.

Knuckles are moving up and down the backbone, almost playing it like an instrument. Tension drops away. The man has a gift.

Now flat hands slide gently but firmly across the small of the back. Sideways, upwards, downwards, now in a circular motion. Those hands know what to do and where to go. Jamie hasn't felt this relaxed in ages. Yes, maybe the sin can wait a little.

Now the hands slide downwards, across the buttocks. Kneading. Caressing. The hands stay there, now no longer caressing. Just resting. Then caressing again. Then resting.

They're staying longer than they need. And, hold on – why there anyway? Nothing got hurt there. Smegs is breathing short shallow breaths, and Jamie's heart begins to thump, almost in time with Smegs's breathing. Now a hand moves to an inside thigh.

'Please, no,' Jamie whispers.

The hand moves upon the thigh…

'No, Father. Please. *Please.*'

The hand slithers underneath Jamie and gently cups his genitals.

'Oh no, please. No, please. Please – *I'm going to scream.*'

The hand is gone. Smegs is gone. Only a twitching of the cubicle curtain and that miasma of armpit and cigarette and decanter suggests he was ever there.

The dormitory has never been so silent. Not a snuffle out there. As if everyone has been turned to stone.

THE team to play Rockwell was up on the green baize board when the fellows came back from morning class. Jamie's name was not on it. And when the lists went up after lunch for that day's rugby, Jamie was back down in Second Division. And that's where he remained.

But Jamie hardly noticed. He had been involved in grave sin with a priest. He must have led Smegs on. Jamie was the guilty one. Smegs must be totally shocked that Jamie could lead him to such a thing. But it was something Jamie could never confess. No one would ever believe him. No one could possibly believe that a priest could – that a priest could... Maybe Jamie just dreamt it? He had such a filthy mind, yes, maybe he just dreamt it. Or maybe made the dream come true?

Whatever it was that had happened, this much was certain: Hell gaped for the living thing that was Jamie O'Brien.

May 1948

JAMIE O'Brien stood on the edge of Bottom Cock cricket pitch looking out across to the rugby fields which were now already meadows. His team was fielding but no ball had yet come his way. It was the second week of the summer term, and the breeze patterned the high grass on the nearby rugby pitches. It was hard now to imagine the silvery mud of last term and your face going down into it after a tackle. Even the smell of the mud seemed a distant memory.

The three cricket pitches were alive with white-flanneled figures. The quiet *tock* of a ball reached him from the Top Cock pitch, long after he saw the bat connect with it. Beyond the playing fields the encircling beech woods shimmered in the frail green of early summer.

Fielding left plenty of time to look around. However the scene did little for Jamie. He was not yet of an age to perceive scenic beauty, and besides, he was depressed as hell. As Hell.

Things hadn't been good at home during the holidays. Uncle Henry hardly spoke at meals at all now, and did a lot of staring out the window or going to the decanter on the sideboard. And Aunt May was scuttling around from her committee meetings to her golf, to her bridge. Or her canasta.

Only Sheila the maid had been the same as ever. 'Arragh, sure aren't you thin as an ole rake, Master Jamie,' she said when he came into the house. 'I'm going to have to fatten you up, so I am, while you're here amongst us.'

And Sheila had done her best. There was bacon and cabbage, and egg champ, and puddings galore – everything that could build up Jamie's growing body.

But Sheila couldn't do much for his mind or his soul – his soul that was in a state of mortal sin for having led astray one of God's priests – and his mind that had lurched from one spasm of guilt to the next. It lurched still more, now that he was back at school, where it had all happened.

'Did your daddy hang himself?'

'What?' Jamie turned around to find Bentley, Fitzmaurice and Hutchinson grinning at him. Their team was batting, so they were free to wander around.

'Your daddy hung himself. Years ago in Belfast.'

'That's not true!'

'It's true all right. McGinty found out in Belfast during the hols. He heard all about what happened.'

'It's not true, Bentley! It's not true!'

The three boys swaggered away. Then they turned and chanted in unison,

'
Hang 'em high,
Hang 'em high,
Happy happy hangman,
Happy happy hangman,
Hang 'em high.
Hang 'em high.'

Amid hearty guffaws the boys headed off. They looked angelic in their white flannels.

'O'Brien, for Jesus sake,' Morrissey his captain was yelling at him. 'The ball, you fuckin' eejit!'

The ball was rolling merrily past him towards the boundary. Jamie ran after it, grabbed it and hurled it towards the wicket. The batsman had already loped home.

'Cut out the day-dreaming, O'Brien!' Morrissey yelled. 'This is fucking cricket.'

***

'YOUR father died of grief.' All during study that evening Jamie found his aunt's words running through his mind. He died of grief. He died of grief. Your father died of grief.

There was no way he would get his eckers done. There was no way he could concentrate. That meant he'd be sent out for six tomorrow for not having his algebra done, and probably eight from Hedigan for not knowing his Latin third declension. *Rex, rex, regem, regis...* What comes next? It just won't come. Your father died of grief.

Bentley turned around in his desk, put his hand to his throat and squeezed. He made his tongue bulge out. Some of the other fellows were looking around and grinning.

Revvo Thorne, the study-hall prefect, sensed something and moved down the hall towards them. He stopped a little way behind Bentley, and stood silent and unmoving. Bentley let off a long, silent fart and Thorne moved away. Bentley had the foulest farts in Christendom.

Your father died of grief. Jamie recalled the vision he had concocted for himself of his father dying of grief, after his aunt had told him. He saw a tall, beautiful man gazing down at a grave, broad-brimmed hat in hand, and weeping. Like something from *Gone with the Wind*. And then that same man laid out on a bed, peaceful at last after his long grieving.

The thought of a purple face and bulging tongue and neck narrowed into an hourglass was unthinkable. Purple face? Where had that notion come from? Bentley had said nothing about a purple face.

The coffin smell of the dormitory hung heavy in the air that night as the boys trooped in. Jamie stopped when he reached his cubicle. The curtain was pulled back, and from the crossbeam dangled a neat hangman's noose.

***

JAMIE was right about the next day's classes. Father Tracy sent him out for six handers for the algebra. Then six more for not paying attention.

When Jamie got back and sat down, nursing his flaming hands, Bentley and all the fellows pulled white strings from their pockets. Each string ended in a tiny noose. They held them out towards Jamie, swinging them like pendulums. Bentley went one better, as leader of the mob – he had a bit of clothesline tied in a noose, which he moved up and down as if he were dispensing incense at Benediction.

'What's going on here?' old Tracy asked. 'What the dickens is this? Put all those things away. What the dickens are you up to? Put them away, I said.'

Class resumed, but Jamie found it even harder to pay attention.

Hedigan's Latin class was the last before lunch. Jamie had started to tremble, and when Hedigan asked him to conjugate, he stammered and stopped. There was this long silence, while Hedigan wrote out a note for eight handers. Hedigan's little chin quivered as it usually did when he was sending someone out to be walloped. The fellows were smiling up at Jamie.

By the time Jamie got back his hands were numb. As he came into class he saw that the nooses were out again, and Bentley was swinging his piece of rope. Something snapped inside Jamie, and the next thing was he was across the desk on top of Bentley and putting a fist right into his left eye, and then he had Bentley's rope around the fellow's neck and was tightening it so that Bentley's tongue really did bulge. And it was all happening in a sort of red mist.

At some point Jamie was aware of people pulling him away and of Hedigan squawking like a hen, of Smegs looming through the red mist.

A thunderclap across the face, from the flat of Smegs's hand, accompanied by lightning flashes inside his head, brought Jamie to his senses.

'Tonight, outside my room,' Smegs said. 'In your pyjamas.'

Pyjamas were for taking off. This meant the dreaded buttocking.

Bentley was weeping and snuffling and trying to get his breath, while a few of his cronies tried to comfort him.

***

A FULL moon gazes down from a clear night sky as Jamie runs across the Top Cock cricket crease towards the line of forbidden trees. It is spooky under the trees. He runs under

105

leaves that shine bluish where the moonlight penetrates. His feet crunch on ivy leaves and he can hear his own breath as he runs.

Something screeches high above, and a tiny creature scuttles away through the ivy. Running away can be scary. Jamie keeps going in a straight line.

The trees end and Jamie stands gazing at a flat, concrete-like surface, full of cracks and scattered with boulders which cast sinister shadows. It's like a dream where the moon itself has come down and Jamie is standing on its surface, but that can't be, as the moon is still up there gazing down on him.

The flat stone just goes on and on, and in the far distance is that low hill you could see across the trees from the top windows of Cock.

Jamie starts off at a run across the flat surface. But it's far from flat, and his right foot goes down into a crack and he pitches forward hitting his head off the rock. There are sparks inside his head and the blood coming from his forehead is black in the moonlight when he wipes it off. Some of it runs into his eyes, and he can taste it in his mouth as well.

The leg caught in the crack is in agony, but it's not broken: at least it holds him up when he stands.

Jamie runs more carefully now, but his left foot goes into another crack and scrapes his shin, so he slows to a walk, and picks his way around the dark cracks that run everywhere.

The place is like a school playground from millions of years back, where boy giants must have played, and the stones they rolled and threw at each other are still lying there. And the pavement is all cracked like a playground would be if it was old, but some of the cracks are so big you could fall right in.

Some of them look deep too. Jamie remembers Bentley talking about the caves like cathedrals down there, with rivers running through them. What if a crack went down into one of those caves? And Bentley said the rivers rush terribly fast, and they enter the Atlantic under the surface far out from the shore. So you'd never be seen again if you fell in.

But you'd be drowned anyway, and even before that you'd be killed by the fall from the roof of the cave down there. It would be like falling from the roof of Cock chapel down onto the benches, only there'd be rushing water there instead of benches. And even if you weren't killed you'd freeze to death in that underground water.

You shiver at the thought of being underground, and no moon to shine. And no light ever. But you'd be dead, so there'd be no light for you anyway. Anywhere.

You wipe more blood out of your eyes as you limp along. Your left shin is starting to swell. Your sock feels squelchy with the blood that's seeping in. And your shoes are starting to slip on the stone: they're only light house shoes, and the blood makes the leather slippery.

The rocks are getting bigger now. Maybe it's just the moonlight. No, some of them are the height of buses stood on end, and some of them are standing on tiny bases as if they could topple over any minute. And there's one lying on its side, so it has already toppled.

Some of the rocks look like giants standing on tiny feet, gazing darkly down at you in the moonlight. And the rocks making shadows on the ground so dark you don't know what's waiting for you in the shadow. Maybe some animal or maybe a chute down to one of those underground cathedrals.

And now the rocks are closing in and getting taller and taller and it's darker with so much shadow, although the moonlight is seeping in between the rocks. Now there are two giant rocks closing off where you want to go, and there's only a tiny space between them to push yourself through.

When you try to push through, a rock moves and you scream. So you stop and you're trembling. The rock moves again, just a tiny bit, back to where it was. But it makes no sound. Now your shorts are wet and so is your leg with the fright. And you stand between the rocks afraid to move.

Then your heaving chest touches the rock again, and it moves again and you know it could crush you so you push through the gap and you fall flat on your face, banging your left cheek this time and the knuckles of your left hand.

But it's no place to be lying if that rock could topple down on you. At least it's bright moonlight here, so you get up and hobble on. The ground is sloping upwards now, and there are not so many boulders and it's not smooth stone any more but small loose stones and it's hard to clamber up.

You keep on going and it must be hours now since you started. The loose stones are suddenly gone and the rock is smooth again under your feet. It starts to rise in sort of ledges and you sit down on one of the ledges. They're like steps leading up to something.

The blood is dry now on your skull, and your left shin is throbbing, and each throb comes a little bit after the throb in your skull. And your heartbeat is ahead of them both.

You look back to where you came from. Everything down there looks grey and smooth in the moonlight, and that dark line near the horizon must be the trees of Cock. Yes, because there's the spire beyond the trees, glinting in the moonlight.

***

WHEN Jamie awakens the moon is just sitting on top of a rock and it's a brown colour. There's the black outline of some creature perched on the rock in front of the moon. It doesn't move, but Jamie knows it's watching him. Then it's gone without a sound and there is the momentary glimpse of a bushy tail.

The plain below is dark, but there are lights moving far away down there near the trees. They must be searching for him. Jamie stands up and his back and shoulders scream with the cramps. He heads off up the hill away from the flickering lights.

Then the rock floor starts sloping downwards and Jamie can't see the lights any more when he looks back. The moon is gone now and it's pitch dark except for a few stars. Suddenly Jamie is scared.

You can't see the stones any more – you can only feel them. But you have to keep going to get away from those lights that you can't see any more. You keep falling all the time now in the darkness, and both elbows are bleeding now and so are both your knees. You are sore all over now, with the head and the knees and the shin and the cramps in your shoulders and your back.

Suddenly you're slipping downwards and you can't stop yourself and there's wet mud under your feet and the mud is nearly vertical now and you're falling and then you stop with a jolt. You're lying on your back and on some kind of slope and it's wet and muddy. You look up and you can only see a few stars and everything else is black so you must be at the bottom of something.

No, not right at the bottom because you can hear rushing water far below and the water has a hollow echo to it. Like it's down in one of those underground cathedrals. You gently move your left hand down the slope where you are lying and your hand comes to the edge of the mud *and there's nothing there.* That's where the sound of the water is coming from.

You shift your body to move up from where there's nothing and instead you feel yourself sliding down towards the edge. So you stop moving at all.

You stay that way for hours and hours and hours and all you can do is breathe very gently. You can't even cry because the shaking makes you slide nearer to the edge. The water down there roars as if it's hungry for you.

It must be getting brighter, for now you can just see the jagged rim of the rocks up there against the sky. They are all around you, as if you're at the bottom of a giant funnel.

'Not a sign,' a voice says. It's quite near. Someone replies, but it's fainter. Then both voices fade.

'I'm here!' you yell. 'I'm here! I'm here! Down here!'

No reply.

'Help! Please help! I'm down a hole! Help! Please don't go!'

A faint light sweeps the rim of rock high above. Then it's gone again.

'I'm down here,' you yell. The vibration makes you slide a little, and the edge is at your shoulder. You stay quiet. There are no more lights.

And then suddenly a light is shining down into your eyes.

'Martin, he's here!' Father Flynn's voice. 'Oh my God, boy, don't move an inch. Just – just hold on there. *Just – don't – move!* D'y'hear?'

A conference up there. 'But we haven't *got* a rope,' a voice says.

'Well, *get* one!' Flynn again. Sharp. 'No. Get *two*, d'y'hear?'

More conference up there. 'Anything broken, boy?' Flynn calls down.

'I don't know,' you whisper. 'I don't think so.'

'Speak up, boy! We can't hear you!'

'Nothing broken,' you shout, and you slide a tiny bit more. You want to scream but you daren't.

More talk up there. Flynn: 'We're switching off the lamps now, boy. Save batteries. This will take time – we've sent for ropes. Just stay still down there.'

The wait seems like hours. Maybe it's not, but the sky is bright by the time the rope arrives.

And then Father Flynn is beside you, and lifting you slightly to get a loop of rope under your arms. He gets another loop under your crotch. And now you're being hoisted up the slimy mud slope and suddenly you're over the rocky edge. Father O'Hare and three revvos are there and they look strange in white shirts and black pants instead of their robes. A couple of the skivvies are there too, hauling on another rope to bring up Father Flynn. There's no sign of Smegs.

Everyone stares at you, and you stand there ashamed of your piss-soaked shorts and legs slimy with mud, and aching all over.

Father Flynn comes over the edge, lifts off the rope, and looks at you. 'You're in big trouble, boy!' he says. 'Very big trouble!'

***

IT'S evening and the little infirmary ward is quiet. The other five beds are empty. The clock says 9.25.

Gorgon the matron comes in with a cup of tea and two of those suggestive biscuits on the saucer. She's the one soft thing in the whole of Cock. She might even have been almost pretty before she hit thirty.

'I'm afraid it's back to the big bad world tomorrow, Jamie.' Her voice sounds like the suggestive biscuits. Gravelly, sort of. Like Josh's mother, before – before what happened. 'You've come on grand these last few days. You'll be well able for them all, now, won't you?'

After they had brought Jamie in, that awful morning, once Gorgon had made sure no bones were actually broken, she had run a bath with clouds of steam, deep enough for Jamie to drown in.

'Just you soak away there, now,' she had told him, 'and we'll attend to those cuts and bruises when you're clean as a whistle.' She left him fresh pyjamas, and whipped away his filthy shorts and things, so quickly that Jamie hadn't had time to be embarrassed.

Those were a wonderful few days, all alone in the little infirmary, with a bit of mothering from the Gorgon from time to time. But tomorrow, it's going to be over. All things come to an end, the way the priests keep saying in those sermons.

The phone rings with a strident tone that brings the outside world harshly into Jamie's little haven. The matron goes out to the corridor to answer it.

Her voice seems to be raised, and Jamie tries to listen, but can't make out what she is saying. There seems to be some sort of argument. She comes back in and the way she looks at Jamie frightens him.

'Father Smith wants you across in his room, Jamie. Better get your clothes on. They're in the locker there – all nice and clean now.' She hesitates. 'Just your shirt and pants will do. And those slippers.'

As Jamie leaves, the Gorgon squeezes his arm encouragingly, but she doesn't seem able to say anything, and she doesn't look him in the eye.

***

'ENTER.'

You push in the door and Smegs is behind his big desk. There's a smell of leather armchair, armpit and ashtray.

'Go across to the chair and take off your clothes.'

Your fingers tremble as you undo the buttons and let go your grey shorts. They slip easily down to your ankles. You slide the little white underpants down and step out of them. At least they're clean – no time to get skid marks.

113

The flaps of your grey shirt still hide most of what matters. You stand there, one hand holding the other to keep from trembling. Your breath's getting a bit quick.

'I said, *take off your clothes.*' Voice from the desk. '*Everything.* Didn't you hear?'

Your hands are really shaking now, as you try to get the shirt off over your head, and then the string vest. You turn away to face the wall – there's a fireplace there, with an electric fire in front of it, one of its two bars glowing dull red. You bend down to pull off the slippers.

'Stay exactly as you were.'

You stand up, and manoeuvre the slippers off while hopping on one foot. Then you remember that it's a mortal sin to be naked in front of somebody. So you put your right hand in front of your willy – it's not even twitching, you're that scared.

'Hands by your side,' Smegs says.

He's working away with a fountain pen at his desk. But he can't be correcting ekers, because he doesn't teach any classes. He just keeps working away with that pen, looking up from time to time. His jowls look soft and puffy. The whiff of armpit is strong now.

Smegs stands up and he's huge in the room. He crosses to a cupboard, and its door creaks as he opens it. He reaches in and takes out a thing like as big as a canoe paddle, only it's flexible and he swishes it up and down and it creaks as he swishes it.

'Get over the arm of the chair.'

You can smell the leather chair as you bend over it. Your hands reach out to hold the other arm. You wait, and you wait

114

some more. The paddle creaks as it's tested in the room behind you. Would you feel like this, waiting to be hung? Waiting for the bang. Maybe you'd smell the rope around your neck. Did my Daddy smell the rope, before – before...?

When it comes, it's the deafening crack of a shotgun, but the crack comes not so much through your ears as up through your body to your throat, and your whole insides lurch up into your gulping throat with the agony and you go 'aaaagh'. Nothing in the world exists but this searing, numbing flame within your flesh. You jerk upwards, hands clutching for your buttocks, throat trying to swallow, and your head swims like you're going to faint.

'Get back down over the chair.'

When you have the worst agony in the world, how can it get worse? Smegs knows how. By the end of the next eleven bangs, you are lying across the chair just shaking all over, gasping for breath, tears tumbling from your eyes and snots tumbling from your nose, and when Smegs says 'Get up!' you can't.

'*Get up!*' Smegs says again.

You try, but your knees give way under you. You crouch there on the floor, leaning against the leather side of the armchair, sucking for breath.

Smegs goes to the door and throws it open. He roars up the dormitory: 'Morrissey! Flanagan! Get O'Brien's dressing-gown and bring it here.'

Flanagan lifts you and holds you there while Morrissey gets the dressing-gown on to one arm. Then Flanagan shifts his hold so the gown can go on to the other arm. They tie the cord roughly.

'Take him back to the infirmary.'

As the two boys manoeuvre you through the door, almost doubled up and your feet hardly touching the ground, Smegs speaks:

'Don't you ever, ever, *ever*, attempt to run away again. Do you hear me, O'Brien?'

June 1948

THAT summer was a time of angst, hatred, sin, tennis and swimming. Sort of in that order. The angst began when Jamie arrived home to discover that Aunt May's Morris Eight had been sold. They still had Uncle's big Rover, but he wasn't driving it any more. Instead, Aunt May drove him to work each morning. Or sometimes he'd walk.

'He hasn't got a licence at the moment, dear,' Aunt May told Jamie. 'It's some technical nonsense, and it should be cleared up in no time.'

But it wasn't. It stayed that way all summer. And it wasn't just that: that was a sort of miasma of anxiety throughout house, which Jamie couldn't but breathe in. It showed in Aunt May's face which could tighten up when she was pruning the roses in the garden and thought Jamie wasn't looking. Indeed she was starting to look a wee bit older.

Only Sheila, bustling around the house, dusting and cleaning and fussing over Master Jamie, was her old self. Or was she? 'I've made y'a very special apple dumpling, Lovey. Cloves an' all,' she might say. 'We have to build you up, now – sure you'll be takin' over here some day, won't you now?'

Now why would she say that?

And then there was the silence at mealtimes. It wasn't a hostile silence: it was just that Uncle Henry hardly said anything, and stared a lot out of the dining-room window. And the look that Aunt May would give him wouldn't be angry but sort of sad. Sometimes even loving.

***

IT was a time of hatred, too. Jamie's hatred. But in a way the hatred helped to cope with the sin. It worked a bit like this: Jamie would be wrestling with his latest impure thought: there had been shots of Maureen Connolly – Little Mo – on the Pathé News down at the picture house – she had been winning all sorts of tennis in America and was exactly the same age as Jamie – but had Jamie taken pleasure in that momentary glimpse of the knickers under the tiny white skirt as she went up for the serve? Had he given in to it? Had he dallied the tiniest bit? Think, now. Concentrate. Just concentrate. Then suddenly Jamie would remember Smegma, and a sort of redness would erupt inside him, starting in the solar plexus and lurching upward into his brain, until there was almost a red mist in front of his eyes. The hatred was so incandescent that it burned everything else out of Jamie's mind – even those thoughts of Little Mo and the sins she occasioned.

But of course it didn't drive out the sins themselves, which were still there like the smoking hot rocks after a forest fire has died down.

Yet the hatred did help. It brought a brief relief whenever it came. And at times Jamie felt himself almost enjoying it.

Then there was the tennis. The club was OK for the first couple of weeks, until it too became an Occasion of Sin. That happened when Ann Morgan came back from her holidays in Portrush.

Those first weeks had been enjoyable: Jamie could well hold his own at tennis and was respected for that. Although he had developed an acute shyness that could sometimes leave him nearly speechless, there was nearly always someone to ask him to join a foursome. And once you're out on the court, shyness doesn't matter.

Then one day, just as he was tossing up the ball to serve, a pair of hands came from behind him and covered his eyes. 'Hiya getting' on, wee man?' said a familiar voice.

Jamie turned. 'Ann? Uh, hello.'

'What are y'blushing for? Red as a beetroot, our Jamie.'

Jamie couldn't think what to say.

'I'll take y'on when this set's over. Just you and me.'

'All right, Ann.'

Jamie and Ann were fairly evenly matched, and they managed some good sets that week. But it could never have lasted, and all because Ann seemed the image of Little Mo. Oh Jesus, the wee white skirt. And what was under it when she went up for the serve. Jamie didn't know where to look.

He'd have to leave the club. It had become an Occasion of Sin. Better give up tennis than give up your soul. There was no way out. So Jamie stopped going to tennis.

***

WELL, at least there was the swimming left. So now here was Jamie on his bike, regularly cycling the six miles to Warrenpoint to the open-air seawater swimming pool on the promenade. It was only thruppence to get into 'the Baths', as

119

they were called, so Jamie could just afford it three times a week. Jamie's swimming wasn't as good as his tennis, but he could do an adequate breast stroke and side stroke which, if hardly elegant, could take him up and down the pool.

There was only one problem, though. When Jamie had learned to swim all those years ago (four, to be exact), there had been two separate swimming pools, one for men and one for women. But in the past year some lunatic had decided to join them into one big pool, so that men and women were now in there together.

In the end it became worse than the tennis club. If Jamie didn't know where to look when on the tennis court, there was literally nowhere to look when at the swimming pool. And here it wasn't just short skirts and a brief glimpse of knickers. Here the knickers were right in your face, everywhere you turned. Next to nothing, they were. Bikinis, people were calling them. Occasions of Sin, Jamie called them.

So that was that. Jamie had to quit the swimming too.

September 1948

L AST June the fellows had whooped with joy as the bus took them off for the summer hols. They weren't whooping now, September 5, as they climbed slowly from the bus in front of the wide oaken doors of Cock.

Jamie felt strange and self-conscious in his first pair of long corduroys, so it was a relief to see that all the others seemed to be in longers too.

The long, tiled corridors still had that ancient aroma left from generations of boys, mingled with some harsh disinfectant that wafted from the jaxes. And the Middle-Cock dormitory, to which Jamie found himself promoted, smelled like that same coffin he remembered.

Well at least he'd be leaving Smegs behind with the Bottom Cocks, Jamie consoled himself, as he emptied his suitcase onto the bed.

He had hardly thought it when he heard Bentley talking to a crony a couple of cubicles away: 'Y'hear we got Smegs again? He's been moved up – taking over Middle Cock this year.'

Jamie's heart turned into a stone. First dread, and then the red mist came back – the red mist of his hatred. He closed his eyes and hated with his whole soul.

He came out of his cubicle and walked down the long dormitory to the notice board to find where McArdle and Dempsey had their cubicles. They weren't exactly friends, but at least they talked to him and he could walk the track with them.

But their names weren't on the list. No, they must be – he scanned it again. No – they weren't there. That could only mean one thing: McArdle and Dempsey had been left behind in Bottom Cocks. That must be because they were a class behind Jamie. The boys in Middle Cock weren't allowed to talk to the boys down in Bottom Cock. So for the coming year he would only see them from a distance – maybe on the Bottom-Cock rugby fields, or as they marched in silent file to the chapel. And be walloped within an inch of his life if he ever tried to talk to them.

Thank heavens at least Cairns's name was on the list. Jamie liked and admired Cairns, and Cairns was fairly kind to him. But Cairns was too popular, too successful, too remote, to really be a friend of Jamie. In a different league altogether.

***

JAMIE was now one of the Oddfellows – the fellows who didn't belong. Every morning after breakfast and shitfast the whole school was turned out to walk the tracks for half an hour. A bit like they do in prison. The Middle-Cock fellows had the track around the Middle-Cock cricket crease. The Top Cocks had their own track, around their own crease. They swaggered a bit: that was because they were Top Cocks.

All the fellows who didn't belong had to walk alone. One was called Larry the Leper, because he had terrible acne. Another was Pisser Bates, who was so holy that you couldn't talk to him. He walked always with his head bowed and his hands joined down near the crotch. If you said anything to him he would turn his big cow's eyes on you and make no reply. The fellows thought he was a scream, and Smegs hated him because he was useless at rugby, and leathered him incessantly because of that.

Now Jamie too walked alone, because of McArdle and Woods being left behind in Bottom Cock. And since Jamie had the face of a fellow whose mother was in Hell, he didn't make new friends. The other fellows seemed to back away from him. Maybe they found him a bit turned in on himself, with him having to deal with every one of those mortal sins he might be committing.

Once Jamie tried talking to McArdle going into the refectory and Smegs had him up for twelve handers. Somebody said McArdle got twelve too, but Jamie couldn't ask him because he didn't dare talk to him again. Besides, they lived in separate buildings. You could only get a glimpse of McArdle across the refectory or across the study hall.

There was one freezing morning when you could see your breath as the boys streamed out to the track. Jamie was rubbing his hands together to warm them when Mortimer came by with his two pals. Mortimer captained the Junior Cup Team. He gave Jamie a cheery grin and said, 'That's a cold one, eh, O'Brien?'

'Certainly is, Mortimer,' Jamie said, flattered, and came across to join the group.

'Oho, no!' Mortimer said. ' Don't attach yourself!'

ONE day there was a new name on a confession box – *Rev. R. King* – so Jamie went in to him. It was printed on a piece of white cardboard hung on the confession-box door, so the man inside would probably be only temporary.

The voice didn't seem impatient like the others, and listened quietly as Jamie went down his list of sins and probable sins and possible sins and the possibility that he might have taken pleasure when his willy stiffened while he was having a shower, and the possibility that he might have entertained an impure thought about Little Mo or Ann Morgan, or about Ann's mother's knickers – Ann's mother was amazingly good-looking, well, for a mother, anyway – and then there was the possibility that Jamie had allowed a doubt about his Faith to linger for an instant, but he wasn't certain so he wanted to confess it as a mortal sin just to be sure. He was starting to worry as much about Doubts Against Faith as he worried about Filthy Thoughts.

'How old are you?' the voice asked. It seemed interested.

'F-fourteen, Father.'

'And how long have you been worried about this life of sin?'

'For ages, Father.'

'Try to think how long.' The voice was persistent, but gentle.

'Since – since the beginning of last year.'

'Have you ever heard of something called *scruples*?'

'No, Father.'

'It's when you start thinking everything is a sin. When it isn't. You've got a bad dose, little brother.'

'But –'

'Yes, I know. Maybe I don't understand – that's what you're thinking, isn't it? Isn't that it? Actually that itself is a part of scruples. Maybe I'm really sinful – isn't that what you're thinking? Am I right?'

'Yes, Father.'

'Now listen carefully. You don't know me, but do I *sound* as if you could trust me?'

'I suppose so.'

'*Will* you trust me? Will you take a leap in the dark, and just trust me?'

'I'll try, Father.'

'No. Don't say "I'll try". Say "*I will*, Father".'

'I will, Father.'

'That's good. Very good. What's your name, by the way?'

'Jamie, Father.'

'Well now, Brother Jamie. First, I want you to put all this thing about sin out of your mind. Completely out of your mind.'

'But – '

'Just listen to me for a minute. How about I take full responsibility for your doing that? Do you understand?' The voice spoke with deliberation. '*I – am going to take – responsibility – for your putting – all sin – out – of – your mind.* It's going to be *my* responsibility. I will face God today and tell him I told you to put sin out of your mind. I'll do that in my prayer today. So that even if you *have* committed a sin – which I very much doubt – God could hardly hold it against you if your priest in confession told you not to think about it. So will you do as I say?'

'I'll try, Father.'

'Not good enough!'

'I *will*, Father.'

'That's better, Brother Jamie. Now I'll give you absolution, and you come back to me on Thursday so we can see how you get on. All right? *Si teneris aliqua vincula...*' A hand rose in blessing behind the grill. God, what a blessing it was.

***

TONIGHT in confession Jamie was going to have to tell the priest about something that had happened in the past. He had only just thought of it. That time years and years ago when Trevor had pulled out Jamie's willy and made it stand up. Jamie remembered now that he hadn't confessed it properly. He had been afraid to say exactly what happened when the priest had asked him. That meant he had made a bad confession, and thus had been in the state of mortal sin for years. For years. Jamie shivered at the horror of it.

The lights were on above two of the confession boxes, and Fr King's name was on the temporary white card outside one of them. About five of the fellows were waiting in the benches: word must have got around that this new man King wasn't so bad.

By the time Jamie's turn came there were four more waiting behind him. That meant he wouldn't be able to take his time – if he was too long they'd start shuffling and coughing, and maybe even muttering remarks.

So Jamie'd have to hurry. There was a kind of doctor's surgery smell in the dark box when he got inside. The slide clunked back.

126

'Bless me, Father, for I have sinned.'

'Brother Jamie, isn't it?'

Jamie gasped. 'How didja know, Father?'

'You've a fine distinctive voice, Jamie. It'll stand you well.' The priest blessed him.

Jamie tumbled out the whole cock-and-Trevor story as he had rehearsed it, ending with how he had run home to his mother afterwards. 'Well, no, I thought she was my mother but she wasn't. She isn't.'

'Wait a minute. So where is your mother?'

'She's in Hell, Father.'

'She's *WHAT?*'

'She's in Hell, Father.'

There was a long silence. Then: 'Young man. Could you tell me, please, what makes you believe your mother's in Hell?'

'Father D'Arcy-Matthews told us at the retreat, Father. And I saw her face for myself.'

Another silence. Jamie could hear Father King shifting in his seat. The coughs and shuffling were starting outside. Stale incense from the chapel mingled with the peculiar surgery smell.

'Listen, little brother. We need a bit of time to deal with this. I would like to meet you tomorrow. Outside of confession. What's your last class tomorrow?'

'Fourth year tops – Latin. But you're not allowed to talk to us outside class.'

'Leave that to me. Now forget that thing with your friend – it was just children horsing around. Exploring themselves. But I'm giving you absolution for everything – everything – you ever

127

did wrong. Do you understand? Now I'll see you tomorrow. All right? *Si teneris aliqua vincula excomunicationis a quo possum te absolvere...'*

As Jamie stumbled blinking back into the yellow chapel light, Bentley's face sneered up at him. 'Y'must be at it the whole fuckin' night!' Bentley said.

Jamie didn't know what he meant.

***

AT breakfast the fellows were talking about Father King. Not that they bothered speaking to Jamie, but he eavesdropped with interest.

'He's back from the missions,' Bentley said. 'An' he was a chaplain in the war. An' Hitler chopped the head off his best friend, an' King's never got over it.'

'How d'y'know all that?' Cairns asked. 'C'm'here, Bentley, were y'ever wrong in your life? Even *once*?'

'I was once, yes.'

'Oh, you were, were you? Well, tell us, willya? We can't wait to hear it.'

'That was the time I thought I was wrong. An' then I found I wasn't!'

'Oh, for God's *sake*.' Cairns couldn't help but chuckle.

'Maybe that's why King's got more cop than the rest of them here,' someone else said. 'Being on the missions, like. And him being a chaplain.'

Obviously Father King was helping more people than Jamie. Jamie felt a tiny bit jealous.

He suddenly realized he didn't even know what the man looked like. And Father King wouldn't know what Jamie looked

128

like. Still, all he had to do was wait outside the classroom. They'd find each other.

Jamie hoped the boys would be all gone before Father King came. He didn't want them to see him going back into the room with a priest.

'Brother Jamie?'

'That's me, Father.'

'Come on in. I got permission from Father Provost to talk to you, by the way. We'll leave the door open, if you don't mind. Anyway there's no one out there to listen – they're all gone to recreation, I believe.'

Father King was tall and quite thin, but it was the smile you saw first. It sort of lit the room. And the eyes seemed to be part of the smile. They were light grey, with little lines at the sides, and they sort of looked at you over the top of the rimless glasses. Jamie thought he looked a bit battered, though. Maybe the missions do that to you. Or the war.

'So now, my new little Brother Jamie,' Father King said, brushing chalk dust off the lid of a front desk and sitting down on it. 'Tell me about your mother. And sit yourself down.'

There wasn't that much to tell, as Jamie didn't know much. He told how all his life he hadn't remembered a single thing about his mother, and then how Father D'Arcy-Matthews had told them in the retreat about the face of a woman whose soul was in Hell, and how it had all come back to Jamie then, and he remembered being there after his mother died, and he had seen his mother's face. And her terrible teeth bared at him.

Father King listened to every word, and kept nodding encouragingly. So Jamie told him all he could remember.

'What did your mother die of, Jamie?' Father King asked when Jamie had finished.

'I don't know, Father.'

'Did she suffer long before she died?'

'I'm really only starting to remember a lot of things now, Father. But I think she was upstairs a long time. For ages, Father.'

'And she'd have lost a lot weight before she died?'

'I suppose so.'

'Jamie, I cannot be sure, but I'd hazard a guess your mother died of cancer. And that all you saw was the face of a cancer victim. Someone who had suffered terribly and gone to skin and bone. I can't be sure, of course. But this I can be sure of – there is no such thing as the face of a person whose soul is in Hell. That is utter and complete rubbish, and Father D'Arcy-Matthews should have had more sense than to frighten boys with such tactics – don't repeat that, by the way.'

'But – '

'Listen to me, Jamie. Your mother's not in Hell. She's suffered all she's ever going to suffer. She's with God, and she's praying for you every day. Can you believe that, Jamie? Can you trust me? It was her prayers that sent you to me. She's looking after you, Jamie. This very minute. And it will be her prayers that will bring you through these terrible scruples that are crucifying you. And that will bring you out into the light of day, a strong and well-balanced young man. Can you believe that, Jamie? Will you trust me?'

'Yes.'

'Now tonight, before you go to sleep, I want you to pray for your mother. And then I want you to pray *to* her – thank her for all she did for you when you were a child, and ask her to go on looking after you now. Will you do that?'

'Yes, Father.'

'Promise?'

'Yes, Father.'

As Jamie climbed the stairs up to the study hall after recreation, Smegs crooked his finger at him. 'Where were you after class?'

'I – I was down with Father King. In one of the classrooms.'

'What were you doing there?'

'We were talking. He was helping me. He – he had the Provost's permission to talk to me.'

'*You* didn't have *my* permission. Go up to my room and wait for me there.'

***

IT took months, but Father King was patient.

At first Jamie would relapse after a few hours, and his worries would start gnawing at him again. It would usually start after some particularly awful thought that simply had to be a sin, and Jamie would feel that if Father King knew he had harboured such a dreadfully evil thought, then he would have agreed it was a sin and would actually have wanted Jamie to worry about it. Like the time he got a sort of a twinge looking at O'Neill, because he looked so much like a girl. And walked like one. Sort of waggling his bum.

But Father King never wavered. No it wasn't a sin, he'd say. Trust me. And no, you are not to think about sin, no matter

131

how certain you are that something's a sin. Trust me again. 'As long as your general direction is towards God, everything else is all right. And isn't your general direction towards God? Of course it is.'

Father King wanted Jamie to think of God as a father instead of an accountant. Whereas Jamie kept coming back to that picture in the Long Corridor of Michelangelo's *Moses* – ferocious fork-bearded face, veins standing out on the back of hands poised to shatter into smithereens the tablets of the Ten Commandments. That was God for Jamie.

But it wasn't the God of Father King. 'Think of *your* father, Jamie. Isn't he kind to you?'

'He's dead. I'm adopted.'

'Oh.' A pause. ' Well, at least you have an adopted father. Is he kind to you?'

'He doesn't notice me much. He – I think he has a lot of problems.'

'Oh. Well, let me ask you this. Would a father stuff his child into a furnace and burn him? No matter what that child had done? No. And God wouldn't do it either – he's the greatest of all fathers. And can you imagine a father jotting down everything a child does wrong, and holding it against him? No. It's a father's nature to cherish and forgive – to come running to the child. God's like that – he even told us as much in the gospels. Remember the Prodigal Son? How the dad came running to meet him?'

Father King paused for a moment. 'You know, I've been thinking. God's actually both father and mother to us. Did you ever think of that? All motherhood comes from God, as well as fatherhood. So you can think of God as a mother if you want. I bet if you do that, you'll find a softer, gentler more loving God than you could ever have imagined.

'Did you ever try to pray to God as feminine? As mother? I do sometimes, and it really works. It's really different. Try it.'

***

JAMIE tried, but the Moses God was too strong for him. Maybe some day he'd reach a mother God. But not yet. Besides, Jamie was mostly preoccupied concocting some convoluted new problem for the next confession.

It was always the same. And Jamie could come up with some humdingers to feel guilty about. How that man ever put up with it.

There was one point where Jamie told how he hated Smegs – that was after Smegs had given him twelve handers and had seemed to enjoy doing it – and wasn't hatred one of the worst of all sins?

That was the only time Father King had seemed hesitant. So maybe it really must be a sin this time, Jamie thought. And then he got the absurd notion that maybe Father King didn't exactly like Smegs either. Which would have been preposterous.

Anyhow Father King explained the difference between dislike and hatred. You can't help disliking some people – it's because of *them*, not because of you. Some people simply aren't likable. It's something in *them*. But hatred is different – it's inside *you*. It's you wishing bad things to happen to someone.

Which set Jamie off on another chase – hadn't he often imagined Smegs getting pushed over those Cliffs of Moher by a crowd of the fellows? And clinging to the edge and bellowing for mercy.

'Would *you* have pushed?' Father King asked him at the next confession.

'I'm not sure,' Jamie said. 'I think I might.'

And then for some reason Father King seemed to be holding his breath. And sort of half coughing. Very quietly.

No, trying not to laugh.

'You know, Jamie, that's as near to a sin as you've ever come!' Father King said, and started to shake again.

For some reason Jamie started to giggle too. They both laughed and laughed, with that grill between them. And when one stopped the other would start again. And that would start the other laughing once more.

It was so long since Jamie had laughed that it was a strange sensation for him. His whole insides felt massaged and his body was thrumming as he left the confession box. It was a fantastic feeling.

That was the point where his scruples started to lift ever so slightly. It was still to take a long time, but the cure seemed to begin from that moment of laughter.

January 1949

CLASSES began the second day back – the first day being all about gathering textbooks for the various classes, and assigning the fellows to the various rugby divisions.

'Rugby is the soul of Woodcock College,' Smegs announced at his opening *oratiuncula* – his spiff, in other words. 'There is no place here for any so-called gaelic football. That is a game of peasants, invented by peasants, *for* peasants. And we shall leave it to the peasants. God knows there are enough of them in the country.' The thick lip curled. 'And let hurling not be as much as mentioned among us. This is – and always has been – a conservatoire of rugby, a seminary of the Great Game. And always will be.'

***

THE fellows couldn't believe their eyes when Father King walked into English class that second day, instead of old Muggins.

'Father O'Dea hasn't been well over Christmas,' he told the class. 'So you're stuck with me, I'm afraid, Brothers.' He smiled and brought his hands together. 'So, Brother – eh, who have I –?'

'Bentley, Sir.'

'Well, Brother Bentley, perhaps you'd tell us where we are in the curriculum? It's the Inter Cert, isn't it?'

'We were doing *The Last Duchess*, Sir. Just before we broke for Christmas.'

'Ah, my last duchess, indeed ... "painted on the wall, looking as if she were alive." Anybody know what Browning was really on about?'

'The duke had his missus killed, didn't he, Sir?' Cairns spoke up. 'For smiling at fellows.'

'He did indeed, Brother Cairns. A somewhat drastic remedy, wouldn't you think? "Then all smiles stopped together." But what's the poem really about? Brother O'Brien?'

Jamie sort of liked being called Brother. Everywhere else he was just O'Brien. 'I think, Sir, the duke was jealous of his wife – wasn't that it?'

'Insanely jealous. But the poem is surely about something more than that. Any other ideas?'

'He was warning his next wife, Sir,' a fellow said. 'Telling the ambassador to let her know what to expect.'

'Getting there, I think, young man. What is your name, by the way?'

'Gordon, Sir.'

'Good, Brother Gordon. Well, here's what *I* think the poem is really about. It's about what absolute power can do to a man. To anyone. This duke – Duke of Ferrara, wasn't it? – had absolute power over his subjects. Life and death. Could have you snuffed out in an instant. On a whim. As he did to his wife. Can you imagine what that kind of power does to anyone who has it? Absolute power corrupts absolutely, as I think Lord Acton said.

'His actual words, if I remember rightly, were: "Power tends to corrupt, and absolute power corrupts absolutely. *Great men are almost always bad men.*" A terrible thought, isn't it? Indeed something similar was said a century earlier, by William Pitt. "Unlimited power," he said, "is apt to corrupt the minds of those who possess it."'

King sat down on the windowsill and took out a handkerchief to cough. 'I once saw for myself what absolute power can do. I was actually one of the first people into Belsen. As a military chaplain. There was an SS woman there – Irma Grese was her name – who used to set her dogs on the prisoners and have them tear them to pieces. When I asked her why – I was acting as an interpreter too, you see – she just looked at me blankly and shrugged. She did it because she could, she said. She had the power. So why not use it?

'Why not, indeed? There is really only one thing can stop such use: that the one with the power also has compassion. Or better still, *empathy* – in other words, feeling what the victim is feeling. I think that's the lesson of *My Last Duchess* – the Duke of Ferrara had no empathy for his wife. So he killed her simply for smiling.

'So now, Brothers, if *My Last Duchess* comes up in the exam this summer, that's what you could write. Something along those lines. It might get you good marks, for that's I think what the poem is really all about. Any comments, Brothers?'

The fellows just sat there, eyes sort of wide. This was a different kind of class from old Muggins's.

One of the fellows raised a hand. 'Is it only absolute power that corrupts, Sir?'

'Good point, Brother, eh – ? '

'Devlin, Sir.'

'Good point indeed, Brother Devlin. Let's go back to Lord Acton's first words – "*All* power tends to corrupt." So that includes limited power, doesn't it? And there's plenty of that all around us here, is there not? Can anyone here think of the limited power that you yourselves can exercise? And that can corrupt you?'

The fellows were silent.

'Bullying, Brothers. That's the limited power that schoolboys can exercise over one another. And indeed sometimes it can become absolute power, as you must have witnessed here in Woodcock. And you all know how it can corrupt.'

King stood up and brought his hands together. 'Now, before this class ends, I want to say a little about *my* power here. To put it briefly, I am setting much of it aside. While I am among you, no one will be sent out for punishment.'

There was an intake of breath from the class.

'I will trust you to honour my decision, and behave accordingly. I shall try to have empathy for each one of you, and I ask that you in turn try to have empathy for me. In other words, I shall try to understand your feelings, and you will try to understand mine. That way none of us will grow corrupt. Agreed, Brothers?'

As one man the class murmured, 'Agreed, Sir.'

'And now, for your weekend essay – you do have one each weekend, don't you – ?'

'We do, Sir.'

'How about doing it on those words of Lord Acton?'

***

'SO what d'you think, O'Brien?' Cairns fell into step beside Jamie as they walked from class. Jamie felt flattered that Cairns would do so. People didn't usually.

'About what?'

'King, you eejit.'

'He's different, isn't he? I'm kinda glad we have him.'

'Me too.'

'Bentley says he was a psychopath before he became a priest.'

Cairns hesitated. 'Y'mean a psychologist?'

'Well, psycho something, anyway. Bentley was telling the fellows –'don't know where he gets his information from. But he's usually right. Says King studied in Zurich under some famous git before the war. Somebody called Young. Or somewhere in Switzerland or Germany – he wasn't sure. Come to think of it, that's why he was an interpreter. Like, in Belsen. He'd know German, wouldn't he? Y'know what, Cairns, maybe he'll use some of that psychology on us. In class, I mean.'

'I think he already did. Sure even Bentley was quiet. C'm'ere, did y'ever think of joining the aero club?'

'Would they have me?'

'They would if I asked them.'

'But I've no model plane.'

'You could send off for one. There's a Keilkraft kit for seven and sixpence. It's the *Ajax* they call it, I think. You'd have it in a few days.'

'All right, Cairns. I'll give it a go. Cairns – thanks. Thanks very much.'

**

ALL that term Smegs seemed to indulge in an orgy of leathering. As duty punisher he leathered all day, dealing with those sent up to him from the classrooms with their chits for four, six, eight or twelve.

But he leathered away with gusto besides that. One night he walked up the chapel during Rosary, and spotted Hutchinson without a rosary beads. He beckoned him out, and the whole chapelful of fellows faltered in their recitation of the Rosary, as the twelve thunderclaps of the leather reverberated from the marble corridor outside the chapel.

As usual there was never enough time to shower or shit. Both had to be done on the run, at least in a manner of speaking. Although Revvo Fitz didn't lock the jaxes immediately after shitfast any more – he still yelled, 'Come on there, get a move on,' while banging on the cubicle doors.

But nowadays Jamie just ignored it and took his time. He got unfriendly looks at times but the Fitz never said anything to him. Perhaps he knew what had happened.

It was different in the showers, though. After rugby the first batch would be in the shower cubicles while the others waited outside, towels around their waists. Revvo Fitz would suddenly shout, 'All right! All out!' and march down the tiles, pulling open one door after the other, leaving the naked boys exposed. Anyone still covered in soapsuds had to report for a walloping. After two such wallopings Jamie learned to handle soap with dexterity.

140

Jamie couldn't forget the day young Armstrong was in the jax doing his business. He was one of Bentley's regular victims, and Bentley had him persuaded that the jaxes were haunted, and that ghosts flushed the toilets when you least expected it. Bentley had managed to connect a string through the outside window, so that when he pulled it the toilet flushed underneath Armstrong. The poor kid rushed out, tripped on his lowered pants, and sprawled right at the feet of Revvo Fitz.

He was duly leathered for that.

***

THE aero-club became a haven from Smegs and Revvo Fitz. It was the one magical place in all of Cock. When Jamie went into the club room up in the attic, the very first day Cairns introduced him, he met the heady odour of balsa cement – a bit like the smell from a garage where they're repainting a car – which mingled with the deliciously pungent exhaust smell of a model-aeroplane engine being run in on a bench beside the open dormer window.

Those model engines fascinated Jamie, with their finned cylinder heads like tiny motor-cycle engines. Some were diesel, and roared like racing cars; others were petrol or glow-plug engines and these had a smoother, more elegant purring sound.

Cairns owned one of the engines, and he cut the engine and let Jamie flick the propeller to start it again. It was a diesel – compression-ignition, Cairns called it – and you had to tighten a screw at the top of the cylinder head to make it run smooth. It was marvellous being in control of something like that – someday Jamie would have one of those engines.

141

But he was content with his rubber-powered model kit when it arrived in the post: if he built it right, a big elastic band inside would turn the propeller and the plane would take off from his hand and fly like a silent bird. Jamie could hardly wait. But for now, he had to open the box, tape the plan to the bench, pin down the slender strips of balsa wood, and start building the fuselage.

The atmosphere seemed easy in here. The six or seven fellows were more interested in the model planes than in bullying or tormenting anyone. Although they did swear a bit. Maybe one of them could be Jamie's friend. Maybe even Cairns.

***

IT wasn't that the aero club could always take Jamie's mind off his scruples. It worked sometimes, but there were lots of times when King had to help him get through the weeks and months. It was easier now that King was taking English class and they could meet afterwards. And he helped him in the confession box too.

There were relapses of course, when Jamie was convinced he was going to Hell if he died and that he had to wrestle with his latest mortal sin so as to know whether or not he had actually given in to the temptation and whether Father King had properly understood him and maybe he hadn't so maybe Hell really *was* waiting for him.

Most of that anguish came after the Sunday morning sermons, which were invariably about succumbing to temptation and 'the yawning abyss, boys, the yawning abyss of eternal Hell that awaits every single one of you if you abuse the sacred temple of the Holy Ghost that is your body.'

It was after these sermons that Father King had a hard time getting Jamie right again in confession. Sometimes he seemed to get angry, but not so much with Jamie as with the sermons that had set him off.

But the one thing that made all the difference was Jamie's acceptance that his mother wasn't in Hell. He was sure of that now. And at night in bed he prayed for her and found he could even pray *to* her, as Father King had told him to. He felt she was looking after him and would help him through his scruples and his misery.

For now at least he knew it really was scruples. Father King had helped him realize that all this hang-up about sin was not straight thinking. So if it wasn't, then at least he could work towards straightening it. But it was going to take time with all those relapses. And there were many.

But if the scruples receded, the loneliness could sometimes take their place. Those far-off days among the gang back home seemed a time of contentment now gone forever. Some of the fellows here, with their strange drawled accents, seemed a different species from the boys back home, and with an arrogance and a coldness he had never before encountered.

Not all of them, of course, and some of the decentest were in the aero club. The fellows there seemed different from Bentley's crowd. Not out to get you. Especially Cairns. If only they wouldn't crack those jokes and then snigger. Jamie didn't understand most of the jokes, but he knew they were sort of dirty. And when he tried to snigger too he just felt embarrassed.

But the fellows themselves were decent. So Jamie tried to laugh at the jokes anyway, so as to be part of things.

*****

THE rugby remained a powerful outlet for energy. It was only second division, of course, but Jamie was fast as ever. If he got the ball at all he seemed to be able to weave through for a try. And the feeling after that, while you waited for Murray to convert the try, was the mightiest feeling in the world. Especially if someone said, Good man, O'Brien.

Trouble was, Jamie's eyesight was as bad as ever. And of course you couldn't wear specs on the pitch. So the dread was the ball coming out along the line to you, and you fumbling the catch and giving a knock-on. Or you running for the line and trying to avoid a tackle and passing the ball back to the centre but giving a forward pass because you couldn't see properly, and then the whistle and everything stopping and Bentley saying Ah-God-you-fuckin-eejit-O'Brien.

The tackling was still the thing, though. It could go wrong, of course. One time Jamie took a fellow below the waist and was sliding down nicely and then the fellow let such a screech out of him, and Jamie realised he was gripping something dreadfully soft that maybe could've come away in his hands but didn't, thanks be to God, and the fellow lay curled up moaning on the sideline for a half hour, 'in the foetal position', whatever that was – well that was what Bentley called it later. That was when Smegs, who was refereeing, had stood over the fellow and said, 'It's a man's game, Moloney.' That was one of his favourite sayings.

***

'A WORD with you, Brother O'Brien. A few moments of your time, if I may?' King had just finished English class and the fellows were filing out.

It was easier nowadays for the two to talk, as they just remained on after class for a few minutes. Smegs could hardly object to that – teacher and pupil conferring. Bentley had tried to call Jamie a suck, but Jamie had ignored him and Bentley left off after a while.

'Well, Jamie,' King said, dropping the formal Brother O'Brien when they were alone, 'this is one of the best essays I've read in a while. In a long while. You have a gift, do you know that? You could be a writer.'

'Thanks, Father. I have to say I enjoyed doing it.'

'But that's not quite what I want to talk to you about. If you can write like that, you could speak like that.'

'How do you mean?'

'You know I'm introducing a weekly debate here in Woodcock? As English master I got Father Provost's permission. Would you think of taking part in the first one, next week? I'd like you to put your name down.'

'Oh God no, Father. I could never face them. You know what they think of me.'

'All you ever show them is your mournful face, Jamie. Can you really blame them? How about showing them your other face – the one I see in this essay? Your wit, your insights, your way with words? They never hear that, because you never get

145

to talk to them. But let you get up there in front of them, in public, and they'll have their first chance to really hear you. And I guarantee you they'll listen. You've a gift with words, and a voice that will take you far.'

Jamie pondered. 'You know I once knocked a woman off her bicycle with words.'

'You what, Jamie?'

'It's a long story, Father. They were sinful words that I couldn't ever repeat now.'

'Tell me anyhow, Jamie. You don't actually have to say the words.'

So he told King about once learning the word that rhymes with duck, and how it had knocked Mrs McAteer off her bicycle. And King got such a fit of chuckles that he ended up coughing.

***

JAMIE threw up twice the day of the debate. And when that evening all eight debaters took their place on the stage in Grand Hall, he thought he might throw up again. But he didn't.

'Mr O'Brien, next, please,' said the voice from the presiding chair. King's voice.

As Jamie stood up he thought he might faint as the sea of three-hundred-plus faces came and went before his eyes. The notes in his hand shook as he walked to the lectern. What if his heart started to thump, so that his voice failed? But that didn't happen either.

'Mr President, Gentlemen...' It was as if someone else's voice was ringing out.

He spoke from headed notes, as King had shown him. Some of the other fellows had written full speeches and had learnt them off by heart. But King had said the effort to remember the speech took away the spontaneity. Better just use headings, and let the words come.

Well, come they did. They flowed.

Start with a brief story that grabs their interest, King had said, and use it to draw them in. Then bring them with you to where you want to take them – the point you want to get across. Fix your eyes on one face, and then another. Then another. Range around.

What happened was magic. Lips that had mostly curled in contempt now opened wide in wonder at the words that Jamie uttered.

King was right. It was a gift. One that Jamie never knew he had. Well, he knew now.

***

THAT was when things began to come together for Jamie. At least a little bit. He was still a bad mixer, and still regarded as odd, and had never recovered his childhood facility for making friends. But the regular debates he now took part in gained him some sort of respect from the fellows. He remained adequate at rugby in spite of his bad eyesight, although he now realized Smegs was never going to let him on to the Junior team. He hated that man, and knew perfectly well that Smegs hated him.

And it seemed that Cairns might be beginning to offer something vaguely like friendship, even if Jamie could never believe that anyone could possibly want to be a friend. Especially someone as eminent as Cairns.

The aero club was undoubtedly the best place to be. Jamie had never in his life built anything, and now, over a few weeks, to see an aeroplane literally growing under his hands, strut by tiny balsa-wood strut, was a joy. His first experience of creativity. And when he finally attached the three-foot-wide wings to the fuselage with a rubber band, and held the finished plane in his hand, the unbelievable lightness of it, the sheer elegance of its upturned wings, the delicacy of the thing, like a giant insect, the way it balanced when you held it with just two fingers – made him murmur exultantly, 'Hey Cairns, this thing just couldn't help flying.'

'Come on,' Cairns said. 'You and I'll try it right now.'

***

AS they walked out to the cricket crease Jamie felt pride for perhaps the first time ever – in his hand this beautiful white bird that he himself had created, fellows looking at it admiringly, or at least with curiosity. And Cairns walking beside him.

'We'll glide her first,' Cairns said, when they got to the cricket crease. 'Launch her gently, nose slightly down. *That's* it, yeah. Needs a bit of packing under the tailplane. Ok, try again.'

This time the little plane glided smoothly downwards. A few of the fellows gathered around to watch.

'Now wind her,' Cairns instructed. 'But not too much – if the rubber snaps she's finished before you start. It'll unravel and tear the guts out of her. Two hundred turns – that'll do now. Now, launch her, slightly nose-down. Go!'

The little plane seemed to falter momentarily, like a young gull leaving the nest for the first time. Then the propeller bit the air, the plane grew confident and rose above the fellows and up and up until it could have been a soaring seagull. And Jamie suddenly remembered that man Mitchell, watching his first Spitfire leave the ground, and finally vanish into the clouds. He knew now how Mitchell must have felt.

'*And touched the face of God*,' Cairns murmured.

'What?'

'It's a poem. About an airman. Tell you it later.'

Jamie understood: you couldn't talk poetry in front of too many fellows. Somebody might snigger, or think it sissy. He felt a sudden anxiety as the little plane seemed to be heading for the trees. Then the breeze took it, and it came around in a graceful curve, descending towards the far end of the cricket crease.

It touched the grass and went over lightly onto its back. Probably no damage. Then another twinge of anxiety as Bentley and his cronies moved towards it. But Bentley lifted it gently and carried it carefully down the crease.

As he reached Jamie he appeared to stumble, and the wing snapped in half in his hands. 'Sorry, O'Brien,' Bentley said. 'These things will happen.' His face had a smirk on it.

***

YOU can feel euphoria and hate at the same time. Well, Jamie felt both when they got back in the aero club with the broken plane. There was no one there but himself and Cairns. He hated that bastard Bentley more than ever, but there was hardly time to feel it. For he was thinking that for as long as he lived he would never forget the joy of that little plane leaving his hand and lifting into the sky. Maybe Robin Hood had felt like that as a boy, as his very first arrow left the bow.

'What was that poem?' Jamie asked Cairns. Shyly, as he was still a bit frightened of poems. Fellows like Bentley would laugh at poems, and regard poets as sissies. Poets wouldn't be much good at rugby, would they?

But none of this seemed to bother Cairns, and he certainly was no sissy – hooker for the JCT and all that goes with that.

'Some pilot wrote it,' he said. 'Fellow called Magee. It's a terrific poem. "Oh I have slipped the surly bonds of Earth, and danced the skies on laughter-silvered wings..." Wait now – the whole thing's here.' He lifted down a tattered copy of *The Aeroplane* magazine and flicked through the pages. Here it is.

'Oh! I have slipped the surly bonds of Earth
Sunward I've climbed, and joined the tumbling mirth
Of sun-split clouds, – and done a hundred things
You have not dreamed of – wheeled and soared and swung
High in the sunlit silence. Hov'ring there,
I've chased the shouting wind along, and flung
My eager craft through footless halls of air. . . .

'Up, up the long, delirious burning blue
I've topped the wind-swept heights with easy grace
Where never lark, or ever eagle flew –
And, while with silent, lifting mind I've trod
The high untrespassed sanctity of space,
Put out my hand, and touched the face of God.'

There was silence after Cairns had finished reading. Jamie had never heard a fellow read a poem before, except for some sullen reciting of Shelley or Keats during class. And that was mostly sissy stuff about 'the sweet buds every one' – that sort of rubbish.

But this was different, and Cairns had read it as if he were up there among those sun-split clouds.

Done a hundred things you have not dreamed of.... A tear touched the corner of Jamie's left eye, and that wouldn't do at all. To break the spell he lifted the broken wing of his plane: 'Could this be fixed, Cairns?' he asked.

'No problem there. Balsa sticks easy. Come on – why don't we start right now? We'll have her flying again in no time.'

***

THE little aeroplane flew again, after Cairns helped Jamie cement its broken wing. And somehow that seemed to cement something between the two boys. The word friendship would still have frightened Jamie had it been uttered, but at least there was someone with whom to walk the track after breakfast each morning.

And someone to fly the little plane with. Indeed it flew many times, and Bentley never bothered it again. Maybe Cairns had had a word with him, Jamie thought – Cairns was growing fast, and was now taller than Bentley. But Jamie didn't ask.

Finally one afternoon the plane flew into a tree on the edge of the cricket crease and, since tree climbing was forbidden, there was no way to get it down. It stayed there until it became a skeleton flapping in the wind. Like a dead crow, Jamie thought. Maybe my next plane will have an engine. A glow-plug engine. Maybe they'll give me one for Christmas.

Sometimes Cairns helped Jamie with the finer points of rugby. No one at Cock ever bothered teaching you anything about it unless you were on the Junior or Senior Cup teams – the rest of the fellows were just herded out to get on with it, refereed by bored revvos who didn't want to be there and had no interest in teaching the game or just didn't understand it much themselves.

But Cairns showed Jamie how to catch a ball, dig in the heel and shout *Mark*, and how exactly to hold the ball to throw it in for a line out, which wasn't as simple as it looked. 'It's a pill, not a ball,' he'd remind Jamie. 'A rugby pill. Remember that. You have to *say* as well as *do*!'

And at recreation Cairns would help Jamie with his tennis. The two now played together regularly, and Jamie just loved the game because he could wear his glasses and actually see the ball, which didn't happen at the rugby. Cairns showed him how to go up for the serve to get a higher angle, how to make a serve go zipping in a straight line diagonally right into the far corner, missing the net by an inch, and he showed him how to use his thumb in the backhand, and how to put a spin in a ball so it hardly bounced at all when it hit the court. And Jamie began to realize that being a *citóg* – a left hander – gave him a distinct advantage, especially with the backhand.

***

THE aero club, too, remained an escape from everyday life at Cock, and the five or six fellows there were kind. But when they would start to talk about sniggery things, or use that word that rhymes with *duck* – the one Jamie had learned way back years ago, but had never uttered for years, the one that had knocked Mrs McAteer off her bike – he could sometimes feel uneasy. Mostly because he didn't understand much of what was being said. But also because of all that misery he had gone through – about sin and Hell and his mother and things. So he would stay silent. But nobody seemed to mind.

Cairns never said much at such times, but sometimes he'd have a good laugh when somebody said something obviously funny. Jamie would be dying to ask Cairns afterwards what the joke was, but never could bring himself to do so.

'D'y'know the Facts of Life?' Cairns asked Jamie one day when they were working alone in the club.

'Course I do, Cairns.'

'How much d'y'know?'

'Everything.'

'Y'don't, y'know.'

'Yes, I *do*.'

'So tell me then, how'd your mother get *you*?'

'All right, you tell *me* then!'

'No, I won't. It's not my place to. But it's daft you don't know the whole thing. At your age, I mean. It leaves you a fucking freak.'

'Please don't use that word. Anyway, who's to tell me?'

'Look, when you go home for the hols, why don't you ask that uncle of yours?'

'Oh, he'd just head for the sideboard if I asked him anything like that.'

'Well, look, find somebody, will you? Would your aunt tell you? You do have one, don't you? Look, you'll have to ask *somebody*. Promise me you'll ask her. Go on. Promise. Will you?'

'All right.'

'Gimme your word, O'Brien.'

'All right.'

'Your word?'

'I promise.'

Cairns held out his hand. 'Shake on it?'

The two boys shook on it.

*****

JAMIE was in a daze all that Easter break, from the moment his aunt had explained the Facts of Life. He could hardly believe what he had heard.

Aunt May hadn't been too bad when he asked her. She had even skipped her canasta to talk to him. 'It's your uncle's job to tell you,' she said. 'But you know what he's like. That man would run for miles. Or head for the sideboard. Anyhow he's got a lot on his mind these days.' A sigh. 'So I suppose it's up to me.'

And then she went straight at it. About things getting stiff, and why. And about sperm and eggs – it sounded to Jamie a bit like ham and eggs. But it was when she got to the bit about – about – things – things being pushed into – things, that Jamie's imagination failed him.

'And if you don't like it, you've got to put up with it,' Aunt May had concluded.

Jamie was in a daze for days. He just could not imagine his mother and father having ever done anything like that. And he certainly couldn't imagine his uncle doing it to his aunt. Jamie didn't know the word 'boggled', but if he had, he'd have known that his imagination boggled at the whole idea.

Finally he settled on Cairns's mother and father. Since he didn't know them, and had never met them, he tried to imagine *them* doing it. Do they take off their clothes to do it? Are they *naked* together? *NAKED?*

It got worse and worse, the more Jamie thought about it. It was horrible. It was terrifying. And worse, when he kept thinking about it, his thing started stiffening.

But wasn't that a sin?

And wasn't it a mortal sin to think about things like that, anyway? That's what the priests had always been on about, but now at last he understood. Now Jamie understood at last why 'bad thoughts' were bad. So he was back in a state of mortal sin. For thinking about things like that. He'd have to go down to the cathedral for confession before he died in the state of mortal sin and went straight to Hell.

Jamie went down town to confession a lot of times during that Easter break. And he had to quit going to the tennis club again, just like the last time, as it was again an occasion of sin, for all the same reasons. To go into an occasion of sin was itself a mortal sin. Only now he really understood why.

April 1949

'WHAT are we going to do with you, Jamie?' King took out his handkerchief to cough. 'What to do with you? Back in the state of mortal sin again. All set for Hell once more. Oh Jamie, you're a caution.' He sighed. 'But at least you know the Facts of Life, now. High time, if you don't mind my saying so. How old are you, now?'

'M-more than fourteen, Father.'

'Well now, you must admit you were getting a bit long in the tooth to be that innocent. Not many your age are. And none of it's so terrible once you know it, is it? The Facts of Life, I mean. They're not that awful, are they?'

'They are, Father. They scare me.'

'Well, you're stuck with them, Brother. We all are. Under the Like-It-or-Lump-It Act. Way of all flesh!'

'That's what my aunt says, too. That I've no choice.'

It was after the first English class of the summer term, and Jamie had been telling King about the goings on over Easter.

'Well, Jamie, to change the subject, I've a bit of news for you. Father Provost has just asked me to stand in as Spiritual Director for the next while – Father Harding has been moved unexpectedly.'

157

'Shittles is gone?'

'Father *Harding*, Jamie. You're worried about bad language, aren't you? Well, you've just used some. The only real bad language are words that put somebody down. Cruel language is bad language.'

'So will you be moving into Shittles' – uh – Father Harding's room, over on our side?'

'That's the whole point. I'll be accessible, and the one single privilege the spiritual director has is that he can talk to the boys at any time.'

'So I can go up to you whenever I want?'

'That's the way of it, Jamie.'

'But then so can all the others.'

'That too.' King chuckled. 'By the way, Jamie, jealousy's another of those sins you'd want to be watching.' He stood up and stretched. 'Don't worry, laddie. There'll be lots of time for all of us.'

'And Smegs won't be able to stop us going to you?'

'Bad language again, Jamie. I think you were referring to our beloved dean. No, he won't have any say in whether or not we meet.'

***

'HEY, fellas, notice who's not back after Easter?' It was just before maths class, first after lunch, and Bentley rubbed his hands as he regaled the fellows with his latest bit of gossip. 'Morton and Keane-Johnston. Anybody seen 'em around? No, 'cause they're not back.'

'Come on, Bentley. Spit it out,' someone said.

'Well, they won't *be* coming back. They were at it last term, y'know, and either they were caught or somebody squealed.'

'At what?' Jamie asked.

'Aw for Christ's sake, O'Brien, grow up, willya!' Bentley rubbed his hands together and wet his lips. 'But that's not the whole story. Wanna guess who else's not coming back?'

'Aw for God's sake, Bentley. Tell us, willya!'

'Make a guess. C'mon.' He rubbed his hands together again. 'C'mon! C'mon!'

'Well, who else is missing?'

'Crawford's not back,' somebody said.

'Due back tomorrow. Abroad with his people. Rome, for Easter. No, it's not Crawfie.' Bentley paused, relishing the effect. 'Anyway, who said it was one of the fellows?'

'Jeeesus. Y'don't mean – y'don't mean – not Shittles?'

'The very one.'

'Aw go on, Bentley. You're havin' us on.'

'I swear to God. He was at it with those two, and maybe some others' – Bentley looked around to see if any face reddened – 'and they decided to move him. Not sure where, but sure he'll be at it again wherever. That's how these eejits here solve things: they just keep moving the creeps on. Spreading their charms around, like.'

'So who'll be taking Shittles' place as SD?' Cairns asked.

'*I* can tell you that.' Jamie was chuffed that for once he had something to tell, and that everyone turned to listen.

'So tell us,' Bentley commanded.

'King. He's Spiritual Director for the interim. Until they get a permanent one.'

'How d'y'know that?' somebody asked.

'He told me himself.'

'*I* believe you,' Bentley said. 'Even if thousands wouldn't. Sure aren't you King's suck?'

'What about English class?' Cairns asked. 'Will he be giving that up now?'

'Sure didn't he have us today?' McCann said. 'And didn't he promise us notes for the Inter? Cripes, I hope they don't change their minds on that. We need him for the exam.'

There was a murmur of assent. And Jamie sensed considerable interest among the fellows in the fact that King was now acting spiritual director. He hoped he wouldn't have to start booking his time with the man.

***

THAT brief summer term was as near to bearable as Jamie could remember in his two years at Cock. There was the Inter Cert coming up, but King's English classes were master classes in both essay writing and poetry appreciation. And Jamie felt adequate with the other subjects, except perhaps maths. Smegs of course leathered away from morning to night, but that was simply the suffering that is part of life. The way night and darkness are part of each day. You just accepted it. There was nothing else for it.

But there seemed to be a slightly different atmosphere in the place. Not quite a caring atmosphere, but one where bullying was not as much to the fore as it had been. It seemed to start from a talk King gave in the chapel during Sunday Mass. He didn't climb up into the pulpit and orate like all the rest of them did: instead, he came out of the sanctuary and sat down among the fellows. And just talked. And asked questions, and let fellows answer if they felt like it. Just like it was in English class.

Only here it wasn't about poetry or essay writing. It was about how fellows should treat each other.

'Try asking yourself a couple of questions,' King said. 'The first one might be, how would you like people to treat you? Say if you were hungry – and I know you are often hungry here – and another fellow had a cake out of a food parcel from home.'

'Give us a scrounge!' someone piped up.

'Exactly. You'd like him to share, wouldn't you?'

'Second question is this: So if you'd like someone to share, would you do the same? Would *you* share? *Do* you share? As a habit? Incidentally, Brothers, some anthropologists have concluded that the human race became human at the very moment they started to share food.

'But food is just the most basic sharing of all. There are other things need to be shared too. Contentment, for example, needs to be shared. Yet how often do we do the opposite – taking away someone's contentment or peace of mind by teasing, or humiliating, or mocking? Just for the fun of it. To increase our own happiness by taking someone else's away.

'It's all summed up in the word *bullying*. We've all done it. And yet, bullying can destroy another person. It can sometimes even kill. Let's think for a moment about that.'

There was silence in the chapel for a few moments, as the fellows pondered King's words.

'There's nothing new in what I'm saying. It was said a long time ago, and you know who said it – anyone know what I'm referring to?'

'*Do unto others...*' someone said.

'Exactly. *As you would that men should do unto you, do unto them in like manner.* Not as easy as it seems, but there's a secret to making it work. The secret is to get inside the other fellow's head and imagine how he feels about what you are doing to him. It takes effort, of course, but it's crucial to life. It goes by a very simple word – *empathy*. It's actually the key to all human relations. The key. But it takes effort – constant unremitting effort.

'But this I promise you, Brothers: if you make that effort, you will never be a bully. And you will be happier than you have ever been in your life.'

***

THERE were more talks like that during April and May. There was one talk where he reminded them of their privileged position as scions of wealthy families.

'There are colleges like Castleknock and Clongowes and Newbridge,' he told them, 'where the whole emphasis is on the obligations that follow from privilege.' In those colleges, he told them, the boys are reminded day in, day out, that a life of service to others must be the natural outcome of the very special start in life which those boys have. *And unto whomsoever much is given, of him much shall be required: and to whom they have committed much, of him they will demand the more.* Christ's words, Brothers, not mine.

'I myself went to Clongowes as a boy, and I remember how clearly they spelt out what our future should be. We knew we would mostly become professionals, but we were to become men whose first duty was service. It was all about vocation. The vocation of a doctor was healing, not growing wealthy. Indeed, it's why I became a psychiatrist – to heal minds. Solicitors, barristers, were to ensure that justice was done and that people were secure from unfairness and exploitation. Bankers were to facilitate growth and honest commerce. Even politicians were to be dedicated to the community, not to their own enrichment. And if you look around, you'll see that most of them have lived up to those ideals. Ideals of service.'

While King never actually said it, the fellows got the message – that somehow, the ethos at Cock had been somewhat different from Glenstal or Newbridge or Clongowes. Perhaps the school motto, *Conquer for Christ*, had something to do with that. Perhaps there ought to be more *Christ* and less *conquer*. The crusaders had shown a good while back what too much conquering can lead to.

That was when King told them how his best friend had given up his life rather than go conquering. He was an Austrian priest who had studied with King before the war. And, when called up to fight in the German army, he had refused, saying it was an unjust war and that Hitler was evil. He was executed for it.

The talks didn't work miracles, perhaps, but Cock College seemed a more tranquil place during that brief time. Or at least Jamie's class was more tranquil, but that could have been because they were all working towards the Inter Cert exam. As

King himself was heard to say, wryly quoting Doctor Johnson, 'The prospect of immediate execution concentrates the mind wonderfully.'

***

THAT summer term was a time of sunlight and blue skies flecked with little lazy clouds. The forest bordering the playing fields shimmered iridescent green, with the occasional copper beech slowly darkening to its final rich hue. The grey limestone Burren beyond the trees, glimpsed from the upper windows, seemed sometimes to vibrate in the sunlight.

The cricket creases, elegant with their white figures, resounded to the mellow *tock* of bat on ball, the occasional clapping of hands, and the outdoor cries of youngsters. Of course the inner regions where Smegs lurked still resounded to the less-than-mellow crack of leather on flesh, but somehow that summer it didn't seem to matter quite as much. Just the shadow you get in every bright day.

Even preparing for the Inter Cert exam was no great shakes. Jamie was learning that he could concentrate, and he even began to enjoy the extra hour of night study that exam candidates were permitted.

It was also a time of tennis and swimming. Play against someone better and your game will improve, was the advice he had always heard at the tennis club back home, and that's what happened now from regularly playing against Cairns. Cairns was a natural and always stayed ahead, but Jaimie's skill level rose during that summer. The game would sometimes go from deuce to van and back so many times that you couldn't but improve with the rhythmic practice. And

164

fellows from the aero club might join to make up a foursome, and Jamie began to think that maybe he was beginning to be accepted at last by at least some of the fellows.

It was also the summer when Jamie learned to play chess. Cairns taught him, and showed him how chess was the one chance to be as cruel as you ever dreamed – you get a man down, and then you hound him and harry him until death. Death of the King, that is. No quarter, given, ever. No other game like it – a game without mercy. Jamie just loved it.

In the matter of swimming, there was no coaching at Cock unless you were on a team, so Cairns more or less became Jamie's coach. The two would go down to the swimming pool every morning before the rising bell – for some reason that was permitted (probably because the pool was dreadfully cold and thus was the equivalent of the cold showers that are supposed to make a man out of you) – and Cairns helped him get beyond his breast stroke and mediocre side stroke.

The crawl was the bugbear – keeping the legs straight but flexible (should they move in time with the arms or not?); curving each arm diagonally into the water at just the right angle; getting the head around to breathe (should the body turn or just the neck? – and should it be between every stroke or every second stroke? – and should it be to the left or the right, seeing as Jamie was a left-hander?). For a long time it was a flounder of limbs amid gasps of air and gulps of water, and Jamie would be exhausted and panting after just one length. But Cairns was patient. Patience was Cairns's second name.

Then one day it all came together. That first moment when Jamie found legs and arms and lungs all working in unison, and found himself moving gracefully down the pool with hardly a ripple, was a moment he would remember for the rest of his life. Like that first time years ago when he learned to ride a bike, only way better. This was like flying.

***

ALL that summer term King's tall reassuring figure seemed to be everywhere. He'd be out watching the cricket and applauding a good couple of runs; you might hear a 'Well-done-Jamie' as you backhanded a ball low across the net (King would often watch the tennis, and even played once or twice until the coughing stopped him); and you'd often see him sitting on one of those white metal garden seats with a couple of the fellows, and a few others sitting on the grass around him.

Sometimes it might be a bit of leisurely coaching for Inter-Cert English – he could make those poems come alive for you – other times he might be talking about how easy it is to pray, or about what's really worthwhile in life.

'It's like keeping your eye on the ball in rugby,' he told them once. 'Keep your eye on what's really important in life – like caring and being generous – treating people they way you'd want to be treated. Remember what Paul Claudel said – or was it John of the Cross? – I can't remember which. Anyway, whichever it was, said, *In the evening of your life you'll be judged on your love.*

'That German friend of mine who went to the guillotine – he did that out of love. He wouldn't wage war on his fellow man.

166

You know, I only found out after the war what had happened. I'll tell you the whole story sometime.

'Think about it, Brothers. By the way, don't be afraid of the word *love*. All it really means is wishing the best for someone else. Or wanting to ease someone's suffering. And doing what you can to make it happen, whenever the chance offers itself. It's as simple as that. It's what Christianity is really about. The rest will take care of itself.'

And it's not just Christianity, King told them. It's what the other great religions are about. 'One of the five duties of every Muslim is to give alms – in other words, compassion. You know the poem, *Abu Ben Adam*? No? It's not on the course! Who cares, if it's not on the course! Right, Brothers? Anyhow, Abu woke one night and saw an angel writing down the names of those who love God. "Is mine there?" he asked. "Nay, not so," the angel said. So Abu said, "Well, write me as one that loves his fellow-men." And the angel wrote and vanished.

> 'The next night it came again with awaking light
> And showed the names of whom love of God had blessed.
> And lo! Ben Adam's name led all the rest.'

***

SMEGS must have hated King's relationship with the fellows, but there wasn't much he could do except keep on leathering, which he did. And lurking. He sort of seemed to lurk indoors, as if he didn't like the light, or as if he didn't want to come out when King was around. It was just a feeling Jamie had. And he was beginning to suspect the two men mightn't exactly be keen on one another. But no one said anything.

And yes, Jamie did sometimes have to wait his turn for King's room, and he didn't like that one bit.

'What's this glum face all about?' King asked him one day. 'Something bothering you?'

'It's not glum,' Jamie said glumly. 'An' nothin's bothering me.'

'Something is, y'know, Jamie. And I know what it is. So do you, by the way.'

'I dunno what you mean.'

'Remember what I said about sharing food, Jamie? Well, sometimes you have to share people too. I know we're friends, Jamie, but there's brothers out there that maybe need a bit of my time too. Maybe some of them suffer from scruples, just like you. Or depression. You're not the only one, you know, Jamie. Far from it. Or maybe some of them just want to learn how to pray. Or how to deal with bullies. There are a lot of needs out there.'

'Hinph!' Jamie said. A little snort through the nose.

'*Jamie!*' This was a new stern King. 'I'm surprised at you. Almost a man, and sulking like a child. I thought you'd do better than that. Now do you know what I want you to do? For your penance – I know it's not confession, but I'm giving you a penance anyway. D'y'hear? I want you to go down to the chapel for the next half hour and thank God that you're beginning to get a handle on the scruples, and ask Him to help you with those relapses. And then I want you to ask His pardon for being a selfish little git. Go on, now.'

***

JAMIE stayed away from King for a week, and the latter simply let him cool his heels. And then Jamie couldn't stand it anymore and tapped on King's door. There had been a twinge of the old scruples and that had helped him swallow his pride.

It was as if nothing had happened. King was warm as ever and soon put the scruples to flight. Then he said something unexpected.

'I'm not your father, Jamie. I know you don't have one at home, and I know how much that hurts. And how much you need one. But I can't be your father – if only because I mightn't be around for too long.'

'What?'

A pause. 'Well, you know how they move us around. *Know not the day nor the hour*, eh?'

'They'll never move you from here. They couldn't. They wouldn't dare. Not after what you've done for us all.'

'Well, maybe not. Not for the moment, anyway. We'll see. But to get back to the father business, what I'm really saying is not to get too dependent on me. You're growing into manhood, and my task here is to help you become strong and independent. Free of fear – fear of God or fear of other fellows – and able to think for yourself. And above all, able to love. And share, of course, which is a very big part of loving.

'In that sense I *am* your father – your spiritual father. That's my official title here, actually – *Spiritual Father*. And I'll keep helping you go on growing, like you are right now. And then one day soon I'll set you free, as every father has to. They've a saying in Germany: *Wenn man etwas wirklich liebt, dann sollte man es frei lassen...* "If you love something, set it free. If it comes back to you it's yours; if not, it never was."

'Jamie, some time, sooner than you think, you'll come back to see your old mentor. And I'll be so proud to see the man you'll have become. Because you're going to be a fine one. Now be off, like a good man. There's one or two brothers waiting out there.'

As Jamie left, he thought he saw a tear in the man's eyes. But that could just have been the light from the window.

June 1949

THAT summer vacation was the best of times and the worst of times. The very best time came towards the end of the hols, after Jamie got a letter containing his Inter Cert results: seven honours with a mighty mark in English. And better still when a card came from Cairns inviting him for a week to his family home in Limerick. There was a PS that read, 'Do you realise you got first in the school in the Inter?'

Even Uncle Henry seemed pleased, and patted Jamie on the back. 'Well done, old chap,' he said, before his tired eyes wandered to the sideboard. 'Jolly good, indeed. I think perhaps I'll drink to that.'

The worst of times came earlier. At least there was a hint of them at the very start of the hols, as Jamie lugged his suitcase and tennis racket in through the front gate.

Sheila the maid had spotted him from the window and came running down the steps to give him one of her magnificent soft hugs. 'Oh, Master Jamie, you don't know how good it is to see you. You've no idea. Oh, Jamie, my little Jamie.' And then, unexpectedly, uncharacteristically, Sheila began to cry.

It took Jamie back quite a bit, but Sheila quickly reassured him. 'It's just – I'm so glad to see you, Master Jamie. We're all so glad to see you. You've no idea how much we've all missed you.'

Things were fine for a while after that. Jamie was quickly into a regular round of tennis and swimming, with only an occasional twinge of scruples occasioned by short skirt or bikini. Well, not exactly occasional – quite frequent in fact, but they stayed just twinges because King had him well grounded by now in a phrase from Saint Augustine: *For in passing hither and thither it is not forbidden to see women.* The bold King had wisely omitted the second part of that utterance – *but to desire them or to wish to be desired by them is wicked.* That was because the second part had been aimed at monks and nuns.

'It's natural to have feelings like that,' King had said. 'And it's healthy. In fact, the time to worry would be when you don't get those feelings. Many an older man would give his right arm to feel as you do.'

Fifteen is a wonderful age to be, for a young fellow in the full of his health. To find your legs stretching; your chest broadening; your voice deepening; to wake up in the morning and feel your limbs vibrant and buzzing; to feel an energy seemingly without limit that is the true ecstasy of youth; to feel sea water in your nose and mouth as you plunge from a diving board; to feel your muscles sing as you backhand a ball across the net; to feel a belly yawning with hunger and then to fill that belly; to get your first admiring glances as you stride down Hill Street.

All of course provided that your head is right. Because if it isn't, all this can pass you by. Thirteen and fourteen could have been wonderful ages too, but they had both passed Jamie by. Like ships in the night. And what a night it had been. No, not a night but a nightmare.

But things were different now.

Different, that is, until Jamie found Sheila at the kitchen table, head in her arms, sobbing. It was the evening before he was to visit Cairns in Limerick.

'Oh Sheila. *Sheila.* Tell us what's wrong. For God's sake, what's happening? Sheila, love, what's happening?'

Eyes red with weeping looked into Jamie's. 'They're letting me go, Master Jamie,' Sheila whispered.

'They're *what*? But you're family, Sheila. No they're not letting you go. They can't.'

***

YES they can. And yes they must. And yes they will. This Aunt May explained, when Jamie ran upstairs to the lounge to tackle her.

'We have simply no option, Jamie,' she told him. 'Money's tight at the moment. Don't ask me too much – just take my word, we have to economise just now. We – just – don't – have – any – option. Take my word, please, and leave it at that for the moment.'

'I won't leave it at that. I've a right to know. Sheila has a right to know.'

'She doesn't, Jamie. She doesn't have any right. She has no rights at all in this house.'

'But she's been here all our lives. All *my* life. You can't do this. You can't *do* it.'

'Let me tell you something, Jamie. We're put to the pin of our collar just to keep you at school right now. No, you didn't know that, did you? Well, it's time you did.'

'But what's *happening*, Aunt May?'

She sighed. 'Look, Jamie, there are a couple of things that aren't quite right at the moment. To begin with, your Uncle hasn't been too well. And – and things are not going well at the office at the moment. Nothing that can't be put right, of course. But it's going to take a little time.'

'He's drinking, isn't that it?'

'That's unfair of you, Jamie. Anyway there's a lot more that you simply don't know. Look, you're going to your friend in Limerick tomorrow. Why don't you forget about things while you're there? Let's leave it at that for the moment, shall we?'

September 1949

THE first week back at Cock started with something of a kerfuffle, when Bentley slipped into one of the confession boxes and heard the confessions of about twenty of the fellows. There were ructions of course, and the whole school fell apart laughing, except of course the twenty fellows. But they couldn't do too much to Bentley, really, as he now knew pretty well everything they had got up to during the summer.

'Knowledge is power,' Bentley was overhead saying to a crony.

It also was the first time Jamie hadn't been sick at the prospect of going back to Cock. At least here was better than the gloom that had descended on his home after the departure of Sheila.

Usually those grim limestone buildings, which darkened in every rainstorm, had seemed part prison, part convent, part reformatory and, as you climbed out of the old blue bus below the clock tower, you felt like a prisoner returning to finish his sentence.

But not quite so this term. There was no doubt that King's presence had something to do with how Jamie felt. And Cairns too. Just the fact that both would be there made a difference.

And if King was still acting as spiritual director – it might make a very big difference indeed.

It turned out that he was.

A day or two into the term Jamie found Cairns with some of the fellows clustered around the SD's notice board.

'C'm'here till you see this, O'Brien,' Cairns said. 'Gettin' a bit of culture in this nest of philistines. Whatcha think of that?' He pointed to a typed notice pinned to the green baize behind the glass:

CLASSICAL MUSIC CLUB
Those wishing to hear some
classical music this term
please give your names to
me by Friday evening.
            – Fr R King

'Flutes for fuckin' fruits,' Bentley was heard to jeer. ''Suit you down to the ground, O'Brien.'

***

IT was a small group that gathered in the big visitors' parlour for that first music-club meeting the following Saturday afternoon. Jamie really didn't know what to expect, and wasn't even sure what exactly classical music was, since he hadn't ever heard any in his life.

There certainly had never been any at Cock College up to now. Jamie had heard mention of names like Beethoven, Mozart, Wagner from time to time before, mostly on the wireless – but had never paid any attention to them, as they had seemed so remote, so meaningless, so irrelevant to ordinary life, certainly nothing to do with life at Cock.

Jamie guessed that this classical music would have to be different from *Irene Goodnight* or *Cigareets an' Whiskey an' Wild Wild Women,* and that it probably didn't quite fit into the ethos of Cock, the same way that poetry didn't quite fit. Was it really just for sissies? Would real he-men have any time for it? Could classical music and rugby go together? Like, could *men* actually take to it? Like, without becoming sissies?

Well, Cairns was here too, and he was tops in rugby and no sissy, that was for sure. And some of the other fellows here could hardly be called sissies either. And there was nothing sissy about King himself. On the contrary.

Two fellows carried in a large black shiny box and put it on top of the piano. Behind them came King, with some brightly coloured square folders. There was a bit of fussing as things were plugged into the wall, and then the lid was hinged up off the box, revealing a gramophone turntable.

King broke them in gently. 'This, Brothers, is the revolutionary Decca *Black Box.* It's a new kind of gramophone, for a new kind of record that most of you have probably never heard of – one that can play for half-an hour each side instead of just three minutes. And that won't smash to pieces if you drop it' – he smiled – 'rather a bonus among you lot, I should imagine!

'But there's much more to it than that. Together this box and these special records – they're called *long-play* records – can produce a kind of sound that you will never have heard

177

before in your life – a very wonderful sound called "high fidelity". This, take it from me, is a revolution.'

The fellows looked at one another hesitantly. All this was a bit different from the usual Cock.

'Tell you what,' King said. 'I'm going to throw you into the deep end right away.' He took a black disc out of its elegant blue-and-gold folder and put it on the turntable. 'When you listen to this, I want you to imagine a crowd of terrifying giant women in armour, all with Viking helmets and horns, riding huge horses down from a mountain top, but galloping across the sky and coming ever nearer and nearer.'

'*Ghost Riders in the Sky,*' someone said, with an embarrassed giggle.

'The very thing, Brother Bowen,' King said. 'But – a bit different from that particular song. Let's just listen, shall we?'

Jamie had never heard anything like it. The sound rolled around the room, reverberated off the walls, assailed his ears. *Dah dah-dah-DAH-dah, Dah-dah-dah-DAH-dah* – Jamie closed his eyes and could almost see those monstrous steeds bearing down on him. He opened his eyes and looked around: most of the fellows had eyes closed and mouths open in a sort of awe.

When it was over, there was silence, except for fellows exhaling. This was different – this was a different world altogether. A glimpse of a world beyond Cock.

***

THE following Wednesday King took them through *Scheherazade*. The fellows felt more at ease when he told them it was just the Arabian Nights set to music. Then he went to the piano and picked out a few notes: 'That's Sinbad's theme –

his signature tune if you want. Listen for it when it comes up on the record. And here is Princess Scheherazade's own theme.' He picked out a few more notes on the piano.

When the record began, Jamie felt joy as he realized he could distinguish the masculine metre of Sinbad, and the ethereal theme of Scheherazade, as it wove in and out like a diaphanous veil. Indeed it was as if some veil was being lifted from his eyes as he listened. A spigot removed from his ears.

It seemed to mean something to Cairns as well. And as the weeks went by Jamie gradually became aware that both of them were looking forward to the Wednesdays and Saturdays of the classical music club.

There was one wonderful moment when Jamie heard a sound that brought him right back to when he was very young during the war. *Dah dah-dah-DAH*. That V-for-Victory sound – the morse *dot-dot-dot-dash* – that used to come out of the wireless after Alvar Liddell had read the BBC News, announcing allied landings in Sicily or Salerno, or sometimes sadly having to say that 'eighty-three of our bombers are missing'. But now that sound grew and swelled into a mighty symphony where the horns moaned it and the trombones and trumpets finally blazed it until you wanted to stand up and cheer like you were on the sidelines cheering on the Senior Cup team against Glenstal.

***

AS the leaves thinned on the trees and carpeted the ground around the playing fields, during those few months of autumn and early winter, King's presence continued somehow to temper life at Cock. It had no effect of course on Smegs or his sidekick Revvo Fitz, who clattered their bells and blew their whistles and rattled their keys and locked their doors and battered bare bottoms to their hearts' content. (Fitz had even devised a new form of punishment which he called 'six each way'. That meant six wallops on each hand and six on the bared bottom. He was really proud of his invention.)

Nor did King's presence have any effect on the men whose black cassocks swished into the classrooms each day and swished back out again as they headed off to Lahinch to play their golf.

No, the effect was on the fellows, and it was subtle. There were fewer fights. Fellows seemed to share things more, and when some hungry wretch said 'Give us a scrounge' in the tuck room, he was at least as likely now to be given the scrounge as to be told to fuck off. People even mostly left poor Pisser Bates alone, letting him shamble around wrapped in his cocoon of impenetrable piety.

Even Bentley and his cronies seemed relatively subdued.

Those preachers no longer came up from Limerick to deliver their 'Sunday thunder', as the fellows termed the weekly sermon. It was King who now took the Mass each Sunday, and after the gospel would come down among the fellows to talk to them.

Jamie would always remember that Sunday morning in November when King told them to forget about God as an oul' fellow with a beard glaring down from above, with a notebook in his hand taking down everything.

'You saw the sky these last few nights, didn't you?' King said. 'Remember all those stars? And some of you who got to use my binoculars couldn't believe the billion more stars you saw in one tiny bit of that sky. Who was it I heard say they were as dense as the sago we had for dinner?' He chuckled. 'I think I'd prefer to think of sand on the seashore. As many stars as grains. And more again.

'Anyhow, think of the power that put them all there, and holds them all in place. And then tell yourself it's the very same power that holds you in place and keeps you breathing. The same power that fills this chapel, fills you with life, and runs through your very blood and bones and mind and soul.'

There wasn't a sound in the chapel. The candles on the altar hardly flickered.

'Now,' King went on, 'I want you to imagine that power, which flows through all things *including you*, as a living thing. A living being. Which it is. A being that lives, and thinks, *and loves*. Now a being that lives and thinks and loves is called a person.

'And a person is someone you can talk to. This particular person is very easy to talk to. This person is present here, right now. *Right here among us*. Listening to us right now. We call this person God.

'So next week, if you like, we might look at how we can talk to this person.'

***

JAMIE had never before in his life looked forward to sermons. Well, not exactly sermons, as King didn't get up into a pulpit and rant. Conversations – that's all they really were. Maybe it was the way he came down among the fellows and sat with them while he talked. No, it was more than that. It was what he said.

Anyhow the next Sunday King told them about *I and Thou*. 'When you're talking to another fellow,' he explained, 'you're not just throwing words at him. Or if you are, then he's just a thing you are throwing the words at. Talking *at* him, not *to* him. No, if you really want to reach him, he has to become a real person to whom you are actually relating with those words. He has to become truly a *You* – or a *Thou*, as many prefer to call it – so that you and he are linked in a real relationship, as *I and Thou*.'

Some of the faces looked a little blank, and King chuckled. 'Maybe I'm not quite relating as *I and Thou* to some of you right this moment. But let's not worry – it takes time and effort for all of us, but it's well worth it. Anyhow, what I'm getting at is this – remember what I talked about the last time, about that power that runs through us all, and that is a living thinking loving thing – the person we call God? Well, that's how we talk to God – as *I and Thou*. You just go quiet, and concentrate on God as a real person who is actually listening. A *Thou*. Then talk to him – say thanks for today; say sorry for what you got wrong; and ask him for what you need. That's it. Then let your mind go completely blank and let him talk to you. Easy, isn't it?'

'Easy when you know how,' Cairns said.

'Absolutely right, Brother Cairns. It takes some learning, some trying. But it could become the most worthwhile thing in your life.'

***

THEY say example is better than words, and word spread among the fellows that King spent a lot of time every night in the chapel. But there was no way of knowing if it was true. How could anyone know, anyhow?

Be that is it may, there was one night around three o'clock that Jamie lay awake. Smegs had been battering bare backsides for over half an hour, and the bangs echoing down the dorm, and the whimpering from the beds after the fellows came back with buttocks aflame, had left him sleepless. It was something you could never get used to.

Jamie was brooding over why they had to bare the fellows' backsides to wallop them. People said it was tradition, but Jamie thought it was just sick. It could hardly hurt any more than being walloped through the cloth. So there had to be another reason: the men who continued the tradition must be getting some sort of jollies out of it. And wasn't it obvious to anyone that both Smegs and Revvo Fitz just loved doing it?

The curtain rustled and the shadowy figure of Cairns came in, with a finger to his lips. He was barefoot, but dressed in vest and trousers. 'Shh. Fitz forgot to lock the dorm, an' the east door's open. Let's go and check out the chapel. 'See if King's there.'

'But Smegs? If he caught us?'

'Sleeping it off. Worn out from all the buttocking. And the brandy. We're safe as houses. Hurry, pull something on.'

The two boys crept past Smegs's room, down the stairs, and down the long corridor to the chapel. The stained-glass door opened without a creak. It was hard at first to see anything but the tiny red flicker of the sanctuary lamp. There was the faint smell of quenched candles.

As Jamie's eyes got used to the darkness, he discerned a silhouette against the faint glow of the lamp. It was King, seated in the very front seat, in front of the altar rails. The two boys stood watching in silence.

Then suddenly King murmured something.

'What was it he said?' Jamie whispered as they crept back up to the dorm.

'Something about a chalice – *let this chalice pass*, I think. Something like that, anyway. But I wouldn't be too certain.'

***

THAT autumn term of 1949 wasn't such a bad time for Jamie, in spite of the gloom he had left behind at home. Indeed it was good to be away from that. It was good to be growing an inch taller now than Bentley, who never bothered anyone bigger or stronger than himself. And then there was the music, and the aero club, and the debating, and the rugby. And King to turn to when the twinges of scruples came, as they still occasionally did. That is, if Jamie managed to get to see King, as you nearly had to get in line to see him nowadays.

Nothing is perfect, of course, and Jamie could get depressed at times, especially when he was left playing rugby in second division, and realized that Smegs was never going to move him up to first. How he hated that man. How he hated the rolling, belly-out swagger of the bastard, and the uppity creamy voice and the way he wet his lips when he walloped you. Above all he hated him for what he had tried to do that awful night, which Jamie could never tell to anyone.

The hatred surfaced one day shortly before the Christmas break, when Jamie was talking to King in his room, and grumbling about being left playing in second division.

'So why don't you talk to Father Smith about it, Jamie? Ask him to move you up, for a trial anyhow? I hear you do a pretty good job out on the wing.'

'Never. I'd never ask Smegs for anything. Bastard.'

'Jamie. Respect, now. C'mon.'

'I hate him, Father. I *hate* him. I hope he dies.'

'Well, now, Brother Jamie, that's as near to real sin as you've got in a while. That's where the real trouble might be – not in the bad thoughts. That hate is something you might want to work on.'

'I'll always hate Smegs. How could I help it, after what he did – what else could he expect?'

'What did he do?'

'Uh, uh, what he's always doing. Beating the lard out of us.'

'I'm aware of that, Jamie. And I keep trying to get something done about it. But it's not just Father Smith. It's built into the way this place is run – it's run on fear instead of care. And that goes back a long way.' He sighed again. 'And we're supposed to be the Fathers of Compassion. There's something very wrong in this place.' King ran his hand through his wispy hair. 'I've even written to Rome about it – twice, as a matter of fact – but keep that to yourself.'

'What did Rome say?'

'They said they'd look into it. But they said each province has its own customs and methods and it's better to leave it that way.' Another sigh. 'I'm talking out of turn, Jamie. I should never have said any of this to you. Keep it to yourself, will you? Promise?'

'Promise.'

'Meanwhile, what about a little forgiveness?'

'For Smegs?'

'For Father Smith.'

'Oh no! *No*. I hate him. I just *hate* him. I want him to suffer.'

'Well, Jamie, a psychologist called Melanie Klein says you've got to hate before you forgive. So maybe we should leave it at that, for the time being. But I'll tell you this – the moment you do learn to forgive, that's when you'll really become a man. Keep that in mind, Jamie.'

'I'll try.'

'Do. By the way, I'm going to be away for a while for a checkup. Look, it's only for a short while. I'll be telling the class tomorrow. And Jamie, take that mournful look off your face. I'll be *back*.'

January 1950

IT was the first day back after Christmas. English class was at 11.30, after the piss-break. Jamie could hardly wait to see Father King come in. And it seemed the other fellows were looking forward to him as well.

Five minutes went by, and no one came.

Then along the corridor came the gentle sound of a mincing gait. It certainly wasn't King. Into the room, black robe aflutter, glided old Muggins.

At lunch that day, word went round that King was still in hospital and wouldn't be coming out for a while. A lot of the fellows seemed disappointed.

'Something he picked up in the war,' Bentley said. 'Probably the clap.'

'Shut your filthy mouth, Bentley,' Cairns said.

Jamie wasn't sure what the clap was, but it didn't sound too nice. And anyway he was sure it was something Bentley had made up.

'An' are we going to be stuck with Muggins for the year, then?' Fitzroy-Carter asked.

'Sure why would you complain?' Bentley gave a guffaw. 'Sure aren't you his sort?'

Fitz bit his lip and turned away. The other fellows laughed. Jamie didn't know what was going on. But the main thing was, steer clear of Bentley and his cronies, because they could always find some way to embarrass you.

Worst of all, King was gone from Cock.

***

ONE week before the annual retreat, a large rack of Catholic Truth Society pamphlets appeared at the end of the Long Corridor. They had titles like *Mystical Rose* and *Joyful Martyrdom*, and *Saints for Six O'Clock*, and there were covers with pictures of St Joseph looking like an effeminate grandfather in a pink dressing gown, a lily in one hand and a blond curly-haired child in the other. Each cost sixpence. There was one particular title that sold out within the first hour. Its title was *Dirty Stories*.

There was considerable grumbling among the fellows when the pamphlet turned out not to contain any dirty stories – they should have guessed, for God's sake – but was all about the danger of *telling* them. It was written by some priest called Father Daniel Lord. However the sixpences had all gone through a tiny slot in the rack, and there was no way to get them back. And you could hardly ask Smegs for your money back.

Dirty stories indeed was the theme of much of the retreat that followed. It was the same Father D'Arcy-Matthews who gave the retreat, looking more cadaverous than ever. And cadavers were what he went on about – 'cadavers in stench-filled coffins, cadavers with rotting lips – rotting lips that had once been used to fashion filthy words, and rotting tongues

188

that had once rolled around the vowels of foul stories. Stories that had already brought to Hell the onetime possessors of those lips.

'But whoever listens to such stories, and does not rebuke those who utter them, bears equal guilt and shall merit an equal place in Hell. For all eternity, mind.

'Remember boys, your very silence itself can take you to Hell. Your silence, when you fail to rebuke the filthy utterances which emanate like foul gases from the open tombs that are the mouths of many.

'Speak up; speak out; or forever be still. Yes, and it will *be* forever, but it will be the stillness of damnation. *Rebuke*, or you will go to Hell....'

For three long days Jamie brooded about the dirty stories he had so often failed to rebuke. Those mysterious, awful stories that had set fellows sniggering, and that he now knew were taking them and him to Hell. Them for telling the stories; him for failing to rebuke. Failing in his bounden duty to warn them of their eternal peril.

His life would have to change from this moment.

***

THE fellows in the aero club were working quietly on their models when Moloney suddenly piped up. 'Hey fellas, did y'hear about the Scotsman that bought the roll of tartan cloth?'

Jamie tensed. Was this going to be one of those dirty stories, because if it was, he'd have to protest. Or merit Hell.

'Go on, tell us,' Cairns said.

'I got it off Bentley,' Moloney said. 'Anyways Hamish brings the roll of cloth back to his mum, an' gets her to make a kilt for him. But there's lots left, so he gets her to make a panties to go under the kilt. Ones to match, like.'

Jamie's heart started to speed up as the story developed. It was getting dirty, and Moloney was making a meal out of it, and Jamie was in agony that if the story got any worse, he'd have to speak up. He'd have to protest. Or go to Hell. But he dreaded having to speak up.

'Anyways,' Moloney goes on, taking his time so as to savour the dirty story, and Jamie's heart thumping away worse than ever. 'Anyways, yer man Hamish is walking along by Loch Lomond with the girlfriend...'

Oh, this is getting dirtier by the minute. Once girlfriends come into it, it always gets real dirty.

'...Now Hamish's a bit absent minded, so he's forgotten to put on the panties under the kilt. Anyhow yer one looks down an' sez, "Och, Hamish, I really like yer new kilt."

' "Y'haven't seen the half of it yet," sez Hamish. And he lifts up the kilt to show her. "Whaddya think o'that?"

'She looks down and goes all red. "I'm sure it's verra nice, Hamish," she says.

" I've another five and a half yards o'that back at the house!" sez Hamish.'

The fellows just roared. Jamie felt dizzy, and his heart was going like hell – like the Hell he was surely going to. He tried to speak, but couldn't manage it. The fellows laughed and laughed. No, it wasn't laughing – it was sniggering, Jamie thought. That's the way you laugh at dirty jokes. But he just couldn't open his mouth to protest. He was paralysed. And those words of the preacher ran around his mind, *Your very silence can take you to Hell. Speak up, or forever be still...*

'Hey, *do* they wear anything under the kilt?' Cairns asked.

'Jesus, I don't really know,' Moloney said.

God, now they're using the Holy Name, in the middle of a dirty story.

'Know what?' Smith said. 'I bet it's like those Franciscan monks. I bet they wear nothing either.'

O God, now they're bringing priests into it. Isn't that what sacrilege is?

'Hey, remember yer woman asking the monk if there was anything worn under the habit? "No Ma'am," sez he. "It's all in perfect working order."'

I must. I have to. I must speak up. Jamie's voice shook as he spoke. 'You know, fellows, you shouldn't be going on with talk like this. It's just filthy. An' it's a sin.'

Everyone stopped and stared at Jamie. His hands shook as he bent over the new plane he was building – the one that would have a real engine in it.

'What the fuck's got into you?' Moloney asked.

'I can't stay here with all this filthy talk,' Jamie said. 'If you all want to go to Hell, I can't stop you. But I'm not. So I'm walking out.'

'Fuck off, so,' Moloney said.

Cairns didn't say anything.

***

THERE was no sleep for Jamie that night. He tossed and turned and thought of Hell. And he could never go back to that aero club again – although he really liked the fellows there, it was an occasion of sin, and it's a sin itself to go into the occasion of sin.

The next morning after breakfast Cairns joined Jamie as he started around the frosty track. Their breath came white in the cold air.

'So what got into you last night?' Cairns sounded cross.

'You know right well, Cairns.'

'I don't. So tell me.'

'I have to speak out when sin is being committed.'

'Are you out of your tree? What sin?'

'There was filthy talk going on there. Filthy sinful talk, that'll take you all to Hell. An' *you* never spoke up against it.'

'For Christ's sake, O'Brien. The fellows were just sharing a joke. What was wrong with that?'

'There you go again – taking God's name in vain. Listen, it was a dirty, filthy joke. It was a sin to tell it. It was a sin to listen to it. An' an' it was a sin not to speak out against it. A mortal sin, Cairns, that'll take you to Hell. An' all the rest with you.'

'Know what? I can't believe you're so narrow minded. So, all right, it was vulgar. But, sure, fellows are always vulgar. Vulgar isn't sin. Surely you know that.'

'Father D'Arcy-Matthews warned us about filthy talk. You heard him yourself.'

'That oul fart?' Cairns gave a snort. 'Sure nobody minds him. Just a right oul woman. Anyway they're all just trying to control us.'

'You're just going on like this now, because you hadn't the courage to speak up when you should.'

192

'That's fucking well not true!'

'There you go again. Filthy language again.'

'O for God's sake. You narrow-minded little bastard. You know something, O'Brien? You're quite repulsive when you get all self-righteous like this. No wonder the fellows don't like you.'

Jamie was close to tears. 'That's a rotten thing to say, Cairns. A rotten thing. And you know what, Cairns? At least I'm not a coward like you. At least I spoke up when you stayed silent. You were afraid to protest. You're just a coward, Cairns – a coward, d'y'hear?'

'An' do you know what *you* are?' This was a new steely Cairns. 'I'll tell you what you are. You're a fucking, miserable, narrow-minded little cunt, that I wouldn't want to be seen dead with.'

Cairns stalked off, leaving Jamie to walk the rest of the track alone, before the eyes of all the fellows. It was the humiliation a fellow might feel if a girl abandoned him in the middle of a dance floor, only Jamie didn't know that yet.

***

FOR weeks after that, Jamie walked the track alone. Walked everywhere alone, experiencing a sensation where everything was grey and dreary and there was nothing to hope for and nothing to look forward to. Where horizons closed in around him, and the nimbus hung low in his personal sky.

He couldn't go back into the aero club, for that would have been an occasion of sin. He did go in once, but his presence seemed to bother the fellows. Not that anyone was rude to him, but Jamie was tense in case they'd start telling dirty stories, and of course they were tense around his tension. And of course Cairns wasn't speaking to him.

So Jamie started going into the chapel during recreation periods. He began to realise that there were other fellows doing the same thing. They were always the same fellows, and some of them spent a lot of time going in and out of confession. They were mostly fellows that nobody bothered with, who walked the track by themselves, or fellows whom Bentley and his gang picked on. Fellows like Pisser Bates.

Bentley mostly concentrated on Pisser these days, which at least was a relief to Jamie. Pisser was holy, and Bentley's gang loved baiting him.

'Hey, Pisser,' Bentley would say, after gathering a crowd around Bates. 'Hey, Pisser, tell us why you're wearing that Pioneer pin.'

Pisser's long pimply face would grow more solemn than ever, and he'd extend his hands as if he were about to bless the fellows. 'When the Lord Jesus hung on the cross for me, for three long hours,' he would intone, 'the least I can do is make the sacrifice of never knowing the taste of spirituous drink.'

And the fellows would get into paroxysms of guffaws, and Pisser would stand there with his head bowed. He would be offering the humiliation up to God.

'Hey, Pisser,' Bentley would say. 'Did y'ever hear the one about the fellow that fucked a sheep?'

Pisser would put his hands over his ears and stand there with head bowed so that he couldn't hear the rest of the joke, and the fellows would laugh their heads off, both at the joke and at the spectacle of Pisser looking like the third monkey in *See no evil, speak no evil, hear no evil.*

Jamie of course would move away if he happened to hear Bentley at it, because he knew it was going to be a dirty joke, even if he didn't understand it (wasn't *fuck* just a swear word? – did Bentley mean the fellow said *fuck* to the sheep?). Well, it was dirty anyhow, or Bentley wouldn't have bothered telling it. But Jamie would never have dared to rebuke Bentley – his courage didn't extend that far. So of course he'd have to confess it that night, that he had failed to rebuke filthy talk.

So Jamie was in and out of confession an awful lot, and so was Pisser. There was always at least one priest hearing confessions each night, and Pisser and Jamie were regular customers along with about eighteen or nineteen others.

But there was no way Jamie and Pisser could be friends. Once or twice Jamie tried to talk to him, but Pisser just joined his hands and gazed at him with his cow-like eyes and didn't reply.

Smegs of course hated Pisser because he was pathetic at rugby. When a ball would land at Pisser's feet, he would just look at it and cringe as if the ball was going to bite him. Consequently Pisser was forever being hauled up for a walloping, for standing or walking during rugby, when he should have been running. Pisser would bow his head and hold out one hand after the other, for nine on each. A bit like that Dinny McCracken back in primary school, who'd hold out his hand every morning for Mr McGuchan to wallop him, and bow his head like a dumb animal.

Smegs had a few things to say to Jamie too. He didn't relish Jamie's mournful face, and suspected, rightly, that Jamie hated him.

'O'Brien! Come here!' he commanded one morning, as Jamie was heading for the track. With sinking heart Jamie crossed the corridor and stood before Smegs.

'You hate me, don't you, O'Brien?'

'N-no, Father.'

'That's a lie, O'Brien. I know you hate me – it shows in your face whenever you pass me. Of course I don't give *that* for your hate' – he snapped his fingers at the word *that*. "Let them hate..." – come on, give me it in Latin, O'Brien.'

'*Odiunt*, uh, *dummodo timeant.*'

'Precisely, boy. "Let them hate, provided that they fear." Don't you ever forget it, O'Brien. But I'm not prepared to look at that miserable face of yours any longer. From now on, O'Brien, you smile whenever you pass me. D'y'hear me? A smile, O'Brien, *every time you see me.* Or it's up to my room. And you know what that means, don't you, boy?'

***

THE morning of the Senior Cup quarter final against Christians Cork, Jamie headed out as usual for his solitary walk around the track. The sun was just up over the trees, and the sky promised a vivid winter blue. Little clusters of fellows were walking the track ahead of him, striding out with an air of elation for the coming hols. Jamie felt no elation, and his personal sky was black and low. Ahead of him loped Pisser, head down and also alone. There were a few other solitaries on the track, mostly the fellows who frequented the chapel.

Cairns fell into step beside Jamie. Jamie's heart tightened, but he said nothing. The two boys walked for a few minutes in silence.

Cairns seemed to be trying to make up his mind to say something. 'Will you be coming to the match, O'Brien?' he finally said.

'I will.'

'Good. I was hoping you would.'

'And you have a great game, now, Cairns.'

'Thanks, O'Brien. Thanks. I'll try. I really will.' He kept staring straight ahead as he walked.

The two walked together in silence. Then the whistle blew for *All In*.

'Hey, did y'hear anything about King?' Cairns asked. 'Heard he might be back soon.'

'Well he's back in Barrington's – I just got a card from him. And I'm going to see him after the match, so I'll let you know what he says about coming back.'

'Great. You do that.'

As they headed back into the building, Jamie's personal sky began to lighten. Cairns was walking with him, and there was a chance King might be back. Maybe they'd have him for English next term. And maybe they'd have a spiritual director again. God knows they needed one.

'Give King my best, will you?' Cairns said.

***

KING certainly looked thin when Jamie went into his room at Barringtons's Hospital in Limerick. But when he smiled you felt warm all over. Same as ever.

Soon Jamie was telling him how after the match a crowd of the fellows had gone into a sweet shop near the stadium and, while a couple of them distracted the old lady behind the counter, the others stuffed sweets and chocolate bars into their pockets until nearly everything was gone. The old lady was in tears when they were leaving.

'So it's come to that,' King said. 'You know, Jamie, I'm not in the least surprised. One thing leads to another, so now we have thieves and robbers, as well as bullies. There's simply no morality left.'

'Why don't they preach about things like that, Father, instead always about – about – y'know – ?'

'Sex, Jamie?'

'Uh, yes.'

'These one-track minds have bothered me for years, Jamie. I'm tired saying it. Sometimes you'd think there was only one kind of sin. Some of those preachers seem obsessed with it.' He smiled gently. 'A bit like yourself, Jamie.'

'I suppose I am, Father.' And suddenly he was telling King about the row with Cairns, over the bad language.

'Your friend was right, you know,' King said. 'Being vulgar isn't a sin. It's just something maybe you mightn't say in front of a lady.'

'But, but if it's about – about – uh – '

'The Facts of Life?'

'Yes.'

'Well, at least you know them now. And high time too. Now, would you accept that God designed you? And girls too?'

'I suppose so.'

'So the whole thing must come from God, all right? Now think along with me for a minute. God must have thought the whole thing up, right? So either God had a dirty mind, or the whole thing is good and beautiful. Agreed?'

'I suppose so.'

'So it's good, isn't it? And beautiful?'

'Yes.'

'All right. Now, like any other good thing, people can use it wrongly, or hurt each other with it. Or fill the place with babies that nobody wants or that have no one to care for them. That's really why we surround it with so much caution.

'But to tell the truth, I think we've gone a bit overboard with that – if it gives young fellows all that guilt and misery that you've been through, then we certainly have gone far too far.'

'But those jokes, Father. The ones I have to rebuke, or go to Hell.'

'Who told you that?'

'Father D'Arcy-Matthews. At the retreat.'

'Oh, for God's *sake.*' King sighed. 'Look, Jamie. Young fellows your age are trying to get used to the whole idea. So they need to talk about it. Also, they're still embarrassed about it – so they deal with that by cracking jokes. Can you see much harm in that?'

'I suppose not.'

'So I'd just forget Father D'Arcy-Matthews for the time being. Look, why don't you go back to that aero club? Just be yourself – the warm, caring young lad that I know you are, deep down. Don't let the jokes bother you – you don't have to tell them yourself, but you don't have to yell at someone for telling one.'

'Maybe I'll try it, Father.'

'One other thing, Jamie. Would you mind if I wrote to the Provost about that shop being robbed? I mean, the college really should reimburse that poor woman. I wouldn't say where I heard it, of course.'

'I don't mind, Father. Just as long as I'm left out of it.'

'Good, Jamie. Now be off with you. I don't want you to be late for your bus.'

'When will you be back to us, Father?'

'Not too sure, Jamie. But when I do get back I'll have something to say about robbing and stealing. And with the help of God it will be soon. '

***

BUT it wasn't soon. Then some of the fellows began saying King might never be back, but Jamie couldn't accept that.

'He's just – *needed*,' he said to Cairns.

And indeed King was. And Jamie felt grief as he watched things slide, and saw the old Cock College slowly emerge once again. Like the dreary steeples of Fermanagh and Tyrone, as Churchill once said.

It showed most of all in the renewed bullying. In particular the fellows turned more and more on Pisser Bates – egged on by Bentley, of course.

They put toothpaste in the crotch of his pants, and Pisser walked around all day with the pink stuff oozing through the grey fabric. He was offering it up.

They spread Golden Syrup on his chair in the refectory, and there was a cheer when Pisser sat down on it. Pisser just joined his hands and prayed. There was another cheer at the end of the meal when Pisser stood up with the chair still stuck to his bum. He stayed standing there with the chair hanging off him, his hands joined in prayer, offering it up, and the fellows in fits of laughter, until Smegs came down the aisle and ordered Pisser up to his room for causing a disturbance.

Old Muggins, back taking English class, had no control at all and, whenever he'd call on Pisser Bates, the fellows, egged on by Bentley, would whisper, in unison, "Mister Bates, *Master Bates*; Mister Bates, *Master Bates*; Mister Bates, *Master Bates*.' They'd whisper it rhythmically, then gradually get louder and louder until nearly the whole class – except for Cairns and Jamie and a few others – would be chanting it. Pisser would have his head down and his hands joined, and old Muggins would be bleating, 'Stop it now, stop it – 'pon my word I don't know what's got into you boys.'

They didn't stop, of course, and they'd continue until the fellows got tired of it.

Then Bentley invented a variation, and it became – 'Missus Bates, Mister Bates, *Master Bates*; Missus Bates, Mister Bates, *Master Bates*.'

It only ended when one day Cairns, Jamie and another fellow pushed Bentley into a corner after class, before his cronies could notice, and Cairns said to him, "They do that one more time, Bentley, and you're the one that's going to get it. Just once more, d'y'hear?'

A tiny bead of sweat came out on Bentley's fattish face and he wet his lips. Jamie wondered if that was all he wet. Jamie was beginning to realise it might be helpful to be growing a bit faster than Bentley.

And that was the end of that.

***

AT the end of the Long Corridor was an alcove, where stood a smallish statue of the Sacred Heart. It was the usual pathetic plaster thing, complete with effeminate face, blue eyes, blond beard, and long nordic fair hair, the whole thing wrapped in a pink plaster dressing gown. If the real Jewish Jesus was aware of it, he must have been either embarrassed or furious, or more likely both. But of course that never occurred to Jamie or the other fellows, or to the priests either.

Anyhow, there came a day when somebody broke the head off the statue. One day the head was where it should be; the next day, there it was, *gone.*

Smegs was fit to be tied. 'It's clear from the break that force has been used,' he announced in his Saturday *oratiuncula.* 'Which means that someone deliberately broke the head off. Now I am about to count to ten, during which the culprit will own up. One – two – three…'

The fellows sat in silence as the countdown ground to its inevitable and fruitless close. Then Smegs too sat in silence, motionless. The only sounds were a fellow clearing his throat, and someone else swallowing.

Finally Smegs spoke. 'Very well. The following is now in force. Until the culprit is identified – whether by himself or by others – the snooker room will remain closed – the recreation rooms will remain closed – the library will remain closed – the gym will remain closed – the aero club will remain closed – the tuck shop will stay shut. And of course the classrooms and dormitories will be out of bounds as usual. The playing fields will only be used for rugby – otherwise you will not go out of doors.

'However you will still have the Long Corridor to yourselves, where, may I remind you, there are neither chairs nor seats. Any boy caught sitting on the floor will be severely punished.

Of course you will also have the chapel. However the following rule will hold there: you may kneel, but you may not sit. I assure you, I shall inspect the chapel regularly.'

***

FIVE days went by, and tempers shortened within the Long Corridor. Fellows took it out on one another.

Bentley especially took it out on Pisser. 'Tell us, Pisser, d'y'hold it when you piss? That could be a sin, y'know. Hey, tell you what – we'll hold it for you. We're sinners anyway.'

Pisser hung his head.

When the fellows went up to the dormitory on the night of Day Five, someone had pinched the curtain off Pisser's cubicle. So Pisser knelt by his bedside the whole night, because it would have been immodest to take his clothes off with the curtain gone.

Next morning Bentley was chanting, 'Relics of Pisser's curtain, thruppence each! Relics of Pisser's curtain, thruppence each.'

The next night Pisser was kneeling by his bedside again. At three in the morning Smegs came around with a flashlamp and found him. On the pillow in front of Pisser was the head of the Sacred Heart statue. Pisser was praying to it.

From the interchange that followed, eagerly eavesdropped by nearby fellows, it emerged that Pisser had been carrying the

Sacred Heart head in his trousers pocket, in the hope that its proximity would quell his constant erections.

'Go to my room,' Smegs then said.

The whole dormitory, now wide awake, counted together in gleeful unison as the twenty-four massive bangs reverberated through the building – that unforgettable sound of leather slamming into naked buttocks at eighty miles per hour. At the eleventh bang, Pisser roared in anguish. That would be about when the blood would be coming.

***

NEXT morning when Jamie and Cairns came out after breakfast, no one was walking the track. Instead crowds of fellows were silently hurrying across the playing fields towards the line of trees. There was something inexorable about the way they walked – as if they were all in a trance.

Two of the revvos raced past, carrying a ladder. One had robes flapping, like a black crow; the other was in shirt and pants.

Jamie and Cairns joined the crowd and followed it through the trees, to the clearing where a massive oak tree stood. Its branches, still devoid of leaves, were like arms raised to heaven in supplication.

Pisser hung from one of the branches.

That evening the snooker room was open again. So was the recreation room, and the gym, the library, the aero club and the tuck shop.

April 1950

COCK College was a place of gloom when the fellows got back after Easter. The memory of Pisser seemed to haunt the place. The trees beyond the playing fields, full of the promise of fresh green though they were, seemed just to screen that massive oak from which Pisser had hung.

In the dormitory, Pisser's cubicle lay open and empty, its curtain never replaced, so that the fellows could see the empty bed as they tiptoed past. But mostly they didn't look. There was something awful about it, especially after the fellows heard Bailey's bit of gossip:

'Did ye hear they buried him in a field back home? Just stuck him in a corner behind a hedge?'

'What'd they do that for?' Cairns was shocked.

''Cause he killed himself. They wouldn't let him into a graveyard because he killed himself. That's because he's damned – he's in Hell, y'see, for committing suicide, so they couldn't put him in consecrated ground.'

'That's a load of rubbish,' Jamie snorted. 'I don't believe a word of it. Poor old Pisser had his Hell right here. I bet he's at peace now.' Jamie was surprised at his own vehemence. He wished King were around: he felt sure King would agree with him.

Jamie felt he had passed from one place of gloom to another, for things had not exactly been cheerful at home. The Rover was gone, and in its place was a ramshackle fifteen-year-old Ford Ten. Jamie felt ashamed to see Aunt May climbing out of it. Especially when the Watkinses were swanning around in a brand-new Humber Hawk.

And the home was mostly empty, with Sheila gone and Aunt May out at canasta or whatever. And Uncle Henry not back mostly till after midnight. No marks for guessing where he was, either.

Bentley was strangely subdued. Some of his cronies seemed to have dropped away, and he walked the morning track mostly with Hutchinson.

Smegs leathered away but his heart didn't seem to be in it, and Revvo Fitz rattled his keys and locked his doors in a sort of a trance.

And still King stayed away.

**

D'ARCY-MATTHEWS, up from Limerick for the Sunday Thunder, was the only one who seemed to have any enthusiasm for what he did. The chapel echoed to his warnings against the wiles of women – women that fellows never even got a glimpse of in that all-male establishment.

'Never ever *ever* forget the warning words of Saint Augustine, my dear boys – "For in passing hither and thither, it is not forbidden to see women, but to desire them or to wish to be desired by them, is wicked. And even if you be seen not by your brethren, you cannot escape that Eye which is above, from which nought can be hid."

'Remember that Eye which is above, my dear boys. It watches your every move and sees your most hidden thoughts. And remember above all what the Fathers of the Church have to say about women. There can be good women of course – your mothers, for example – but nevertheless women can be the greatest danger to your souls.

'It was a woman who caused the fall of man and deprived him of paradise. Listen, dear boys, to what the great Church Father Tertullian had to say to all women: "Do you know that you are Eve? ... You are the devil's gateway ... How easily you destroyed man, the image of God. Because of the death you brought upon us, even the Son of God had to die."

'And Saint Jerome, dear boys, says even more: "Woman is the gate of Satan, the path of wickedness . . . a perilous object." And St. Thomas Aquinas tells us precisely why: "If a female is conceived," he says, "this is due to a defect in the mother or to some external influence like that of a humid wind from the south."

'Listen to me, dear boys, before it is too late. Or if not me, hear Saint Jerome – *women can bring you to Hell.*

'There is, however, one way, my dear boys, in which you can free yourselves from all such dangers to your soul. And that way is called a vocation. A life lived in holy purity; a life of virginity. The perfect life that God longs for you to lead. Remember what the early Church Fathers said again and again – *that the chief function of marriage is to give virgins to the Church.*'

'GOD, Cairns, I never heard such a load of horse shit in my life.' Jamie was angry as they walked the cricket crease after the Sunday Thunder. 'That fella hates women.'

'Know something, O'Brien? I believe you're starting to think for yourself at last.' He clapped Jamie on the back. 'You're growing up, d'y'know that? Never thought I'd see the day.'

'Maybe I am, an' maybe I'm not. But I'm – I'm fed up with that eejit's notions. Virginity – what's he bloody well on about? He said nothing about what real priests do out on the missions – feeding people, digging wells, teaching about God. King was telling me about it. Helping people get a decent life; helping them to die – King even helped those Germans they hung in Belsen after the war. Helped them face God before they died. He told me about it. Even stood with them on the gallows.

'Now *he*'s a real priest – King, I mean. You saw yourself what he did here – what just one man could do in this asylum. Oh God, I wish he was back with us, Cairns.'

'Don't we all!'

'An' I don't think King was ever that pushed about women being dangerous. I'd say he likes them, whaddya think? Hey, know what? I wonder did he have one during the war?'

'God, O'Brien, you're getting real wicked. Never thought I'd hear you say a thing like that. Well, if King did have one, he won't be tellin' us, that's for sure.'

***

THE classroom vibrated as the great bell in the tower rang out the Angelus. Revvo Cleary glided into the classroom as the last tremors died. He stood by the rostrum, consulted his roll book, and looked around. 'Your turn, I think, Hutchinson. The Angelus, please.'

The class waited for the Hutch to recite: *The angel of the Lord declared unto Mary, and she conceived of the Holy Ghost...*

But nothing happened.

'Hutchinson, please. We haven't all day.'

Still there was silence.

'Hutchinson! *Boy!* We're waiting.'

'I can't, Sir.'

Cleary stared at him. 'You've forgotten it?'

'No, Sir.'

'Well what, then? What the devil's going on?'

'I just can't say it, Sir.'

'And why, pray, can you not say it?'

An agonizing pause. Then: 'I don't believe it any more.'

There was total silence as the class held its breath.

'*What – did – you – say?*'

'I – I don't believe in it any more, Sir.'

There was a collective exhalation of breath, then total silence again. It seemed to Jamie like an eternity, but must have been just a few seconds.

'Would you repeat what you have just said?'

'I said – I said I don't believe it any more, Sir.'

Another silence.

'I think you had better leave the room, Hutchinson. *Now.*'

Hutchinson looked as if he was going to cry as he shambled out.

***

THERE was so sign of Hutchinson during that afternoon's cricket. Jamie's side missed him as he was one of their fastest bowlers. But there was very little enthusiasm for the game anyhow: everyone was both subdued and agog at what had happened at the Angelus. And everyone was wondering what would happen now.

They were soon to find out. As the fellows traipsed in after cricket, word was passed along that study had been cancelled. All were to assemble immediately in Main Hall. The house bell began to clang in the Long Corridor to summon the whole school.

As the fellows waited in Main Hall, the murmur of conversation rose like a kettle coming to the boil and, just as a kettle does when it boils, suddenly dropped to a whisper. That was when the black-robed college staff filed up the centre aisle, climbed the steps and moved to either side of the stage. Two of the revvos laboured in with a heavy upholstered leather armchair that looked very like Smegs's, which they placed on the centre of the stage. Something tightened in Jamie's solar plexus when he saw the chair. The two revvos then went back down the centre aisle and out through the door.

Some minutes later the Provost came slowly up the aisle, followed by Smegs and Revvo Fitz. The Provost's tall gaunt figure was almost never seen, except when he presided at High Mass on special feastdays. He seemed permanently holed up in the admin building, as though familiarity might somehow take from his authority. It seemed strange now to see him in ordinary black cassock instead of the robes of High Mass. He ascended the stage, nodded to the assembled fathers, and moved to the right hand side.

There was a pause. The Provost clapped his hands.

Hutchinson came slowly up the aisle, flanked by the two revvos who had carried in the armchair. Hutch was in a white shirt and dark grey trousers. He was without his blazer, so you could see the braces that held up the trousers. He looked pale. The three figures climbed to the stage, moved to the centre, and the Hutch was turned around to face the assembly with a revvo on either side of him.

The Provost mopped his brow and cleared his throat. 'There stands here before you,' he said, '*an apostate*. One – who – has – renounced – the – Faith. A young man who has given himself over to Unbelief, and thus to Satan.

'Such a creature has no place among us. Such a creature will not be allowed to defile this hallowed place, or to corrupt you who were once his fellows, but are so no longer. He will therefore leave our company forthwith and forever.

'But before he does, he must be made an example of before this house. An example he will remember for the rest of his life, however long that may be – a memory that might, in the years to come, cause him to reflect on the terrible consequences of his apostasy. Father Smith, if you please...your duty...'

Smegs moved forward and bowed slightly to the Provost (as if it was a High Mass, Jamie thought), clicked his fingers to the revvos, who manoeuvred Hutchinson over to the chair, turned him around, bent him across one of the arms, and held him there with his backside facing the assembly.

211

Smegs approached the chair. There was a gasp from the hall as he undid the boy's braces and buttons, and pulled down the grey trousers. A slight sigh of relief, then, as the exposed white underwear was left in place.

'Proceed, Father,' the Provost said.

Jamie wasn't sure where it came from, but in Smegs's hand there suddenly appeared the huge buttocking paddle so familiar to its victims. Maybe it had been lying on the seat of the chair, or lying beside the chair. You couldn't be sure.

When the first bang came it reverberated through the hall like the crack of a gun. Hutch lurched upwards, but was held in place by the two revvos. Eighty miles an hour closing speed, Jamie remembered.

After the first six bangs, Smegs rested briefly (like God at Creation, Jamie thought). Then he resumed, resting again at twelve to wipe his brow. It was obviously strenuous work.

The blood appeared after the seventeenth bang. Not a lot, but it was clearly visible on the white underpants.

Smegs stopped at twenty-four. By then Hutchinson's eyes were closed and he was curled up like a foetus, and quivering like an aspen. He remained curled up when they lifted him to his feet, so the revvos could hardly pull up his trousers for him.

'Your taxi is at the door, Sir,' the Provost said. 'Go forth from this place, and never, ever, return to defile it with your ungodly presence.'

***

JAMIE was expecting the following Sunday's Thunder to be about *losing the Faith*, but old D'Arcy-Matthews mustn't have heard about what happened. Word obviously had not reached Limerick. Or maybe it had all been hushed up.

Anyhow, what D'Arcy-Matthews thundered about this time was the foulness of fellows' bodies. 'Your bodies are made from mud, my dear boys. Mud. *Dust thou art*, Holy Scripture says. And what is mud but dust and water? *From the slime of the earth are you made*, as the Book of Genesis says. And your bodies have all the tendencies of slime and mud – a drive towards filth and foulness. Yes, you may be soul and body, but to your detriment are you so made. The soul is destined to see Almighty God, whereas the body is destined to rot within the grave. But long before it rots below the ground it can rot above the ground, with foul diseases brought on by wicked and filthy behaviour. Diseases, boys, which, if you were to see them, would make you abstain forever from the evil and filthy coupling of bodies.

'And even if the body be not a prey to such rottenness, it is still the heaviest burden upon your soul, because its main function is to pull the soul downwards and prevent it rising towards God. Your body is Satan's gift to you. It is only when the soul is loosed from the body by death, that it becomes free to fly up to Almighty God.

'There are parts of your body you must never deliberately gaze upon, because of their especially evil inclinations. And you know well what parts those are. When I studied as a young man in Rome, we were given a black substance similar to an Oxo cube to dissolve in the bath water, so that we should not be tempted to gaze upon our own bodies.'

Bentley let out a long slow murmuring fart, and the stench that filled the chapel bore ample witness to the bodily foulness under discussion.

Some of the gas must have ascended unto the pulpit, for the voice rose in pitch and emphasis. 'Remember, always, that your bodies are made from mud – mud, dear boys, no matter how elegant you think them now. And unto mud they shall and will return. And that mud that is your body makes you deaf to the call of God. Remember the words of Shakespeare: 'Such harmony is in immortal souls, but whilst this muddy vesture of decay doth grossly close it in, we cannot hear it.'

The sermon ended abruptly shortly after, and Jamie wondered if it was Bentley's fart that had driven D'Arcy-Matthews from the pulpit. If so, Jamie felt a grudging gratitude to Bentley. And a grudging admiration for Bentley's quite astonishing mastery of the art of the fart. Bentley had developed proficiency far beyond that of ordinary mortals. It was obviously a gift of nature. He could summon up a fart like a genie out of the air – well, hardly quite out of the air; he could select its intensity and even its aroma; he could spread a fart far and wide or project it in a narrow cone towards a selected target. He could use his farts for offensive or defensive purposes and regularly did both. The man was a genius at it.

As good as any skunk.

***

JAMIE had never seen King so angry. It was a shock to see him almost speechless with anger, sitting in a chair by the window in Barrington's, after Jamie had told him what they did to Hutchinson.

'Are they – are they out of their goddam minds? The *f...* – the *idiots. Arschlöcher*. Absolute, bloody *idiots*. Have they learnt *nothing*? Sorry, Jamie, but these people are mad. I shouldn't be saying it to you, but they're quite out of their minds.'

He rubbed a hand through his wispy hair. 'Do you realise what they've done? Young fellows will be terrified to talk about their doubts now. About their worries. They'll be turned into hypocrites. Dissemblers. And, you know what, Jamie, that poor boy they flogged will never get back his Faith now. The most precious gift of all. He will hate and detest everything to do with it. And can you blame him?'

'Maybe he's better off without it, Father. It only ever gave me grief.'

'It wasn't the Faith gave you grief, Jamie. It was the nonsense those idiots fed you down the years. Since you were a toddler. I don't suppose you've ever read *Barchester Towers*? Trollope?'

Jamie shook his head.

'No, I thought not. There's a scene there where Archdeacon Grantly is asked what Jesus Christ would think about some Church shenanigans or other. *This has nothing to do with Jesus Christ*, is his answer. Well, he's absolutely right. Now, the stuff you've been fed – about repressing sex, about conquering, winning, about guilt, virginity, about your body being evil, has precious little to do with Jesus Christ either. These people haven't an idea.

'When do they talk about love – the only thing that matters? *By this shall all men know that you are my disciples, that you love one another?* When do they talk about joy? About

215

forgiveness? Feeding the hungry? Visiting the sick, like you're doing right now? That's what Christianity's about.' King stopped for breath. 'I'm sorry, but I'm very angry, and I just have to say this.'

'Well, if Christians are like that, what's the point of belonging?'

'Fair point, Jamie. But remember Jesus said the net caught good and bad fish.'

''Seem to be lots of the bad ones, Father.'

'The *Apostles*, Jamie. The very first Twelve – they were a pretty flaky bunch. One was a traitor and hanged himself. The top man renounced Jesus – simply denied that he followed him. Remember? – *And then the cock crew.* And every single one of the rest were cowards. Remember that? – *And after they laid hands on Jesus, all the disciples left and fled away.* ALL of them. What do you make of that?'

'That Christians are pretty flaky. Like you said.'

'We're all sinners, Jamie. *Like you and me.* Sinners, and idiots, Jamie. *We're* what Christianity is about, Jamie – it was made for the likes of us. And it's what will bring us to God in the end. And find us forgiveness for all our madness. And badness. But above all, *it will bring us to love.*' King sighed. 'That's why I stay a Christian, Jamie.'

Jamie could see how thin King was when he stood up – how his dressing gown seemed far too big for him.

'Now will you be off, young fellow-me-lad, and stop making me angry. It's tiring me out.' King smiled and stretched out his hands. 'Come here till I give you my blessing.'

***

'THEY'RE taking names for the FCA for next year,' Cairns said to Jamie as the two headed out to cricket. 'The notice just went up. We'll be in Top Cocks next year, so we'd be eligible. Wanna put your name down?'

'Whaddya think?'

'I think it'd be great. Local Defence would get us out of this lousy dump every Sunday – there'd be the manoeuvres and route-marches, and we'd have our own rifles. And we'd get up to the firing range in Galway. And there'd be summer camp if we want.' Cairns chuckled. 'To say nothing of the free boots. And the uniform – jeez, we'd cut a right dash, wouldn't we? Of course there's no bloody girls here to see us.'

'That's for sure, anyhow. Know what – maybe there'd be some might see us on the route marches.'

'You're coming on, laddie. It wasn't so long ago that you'd run a mile from a girl. Occasions of sin, and all that. Remember?'

It was Jamie's turn to chuckle. 'I think it must be D'Arcy-Matthews's sermons that's doing it. They're so full of nonsense that they just drive me to think the opposite. Such as, that girls are OK.' He sighed. 'Not that I know many, of course. Well, one or two mebbe back home. But I don't know them well.'

'*Tiocfaidh do lá*, laddie!' Cairns rubbed his hands. '*Tiocfaidh* all our *lá*'s.'

***

IT was two days before the summer holidays, and Jamie and Cairns headed out the door for the morning walk around the track. Whether it was the sparkling morning sunshine or the prospect of immanent release from confinement, but Jamie felt that the gloom of the hanging and the flogging somehow had lifted off at last.

But on the steps the two boys stopped. No one was walking the track. Instead, everyone was headed straight for the woods, walking trancelike as they had on that morning of the hanging. And they were headed in exactly the same direction as the last time.

Oh God, not another one – Jamie's heart tightened and he could hardly swallow.

'C'mon,' Cairns muttered.

The two hurried down the steps, across the track, straight across the Top-Cock cricket pitch, past the pavilion and in among the trees. There was no sound except the crunch of many feet on twigs. Slender sunbeams slanted down through the forest mist, and tiny flecks of sunlight dappled the red blazers of the boys as they walked.

Jamie just knew it had to be that tree again.

And so it was. Already a silent crowd of red blazers filled the clearing, and Jamie and Cairns had to push their way through to get to the tree. When they got through, they too stopped and stared.

Smegs was completely naked, his back to the crowd of boys, his arms embracing the massive trunk of the oak tree. Handcuffs had been clamped on each wrist, and a rope linked both pairs, encircling the trunk of the tree. The rope was evidently hooked over a branch at the back of the tree, to prevent Smegs from sliding downwards. Another rope bound the ankles tight to the bottom of the tree trunk, keeping the legs together.

Jamie was surprised at the size of Smegs's backside. He was even more surprised at the state of it. It had been beaten raw and purple like meat in a butcher's shop, and blood was still trickling down the backs of the man's thighs. Wedged between the thighs, held in place by another piece of rope, protruded the huge leather buttocking paddle so dear to Smegs. It slanted upwards from the red backside like the tail of some horrible ape. It too was bloodied.

You couldn't see Smegs's face. It was pressed into the ivy that covered the trunk. But you could see the shoulders rise and fall as the chest heaved for breath.

The fellows just stood and stared. No one said a thing. Jamie felt slightly dizzy. He didn't know whether to laugh or cry. The silent gazing went on for some minutes.

'Make way! *Will ye for God's sake make way!*'

The crowd parted reluctantly as two revvos pushed their way through. One produced a blue dressing gown which he hooked over Smegs's shoulders, but then removed it again to pull away the paddle. The other produced a kitchen knife, and started sawing at the rope that bound the man's feet. Once they were free, he cut the rope that had held the paddle in place, and only then severed the rope that linked the handcuffs. As the rope gave, Smegs slid slowly to the ground. The revvos lifted him up, one under each arm, fumbling to get the dressing gown around his shoulders. No one offered to help. The revvos closed the dressing gown with its girdle, turned Smegs around and the crowd of boys parted to let them through.

As the three moved slowly past Jamie, Smegs's bare feet hardly seemed to touch the ground. His eyes were closed – and his head hung down with the chin on the dressing gown. The handcuffs still dangled from each wrist.

June 1950

SCHOOL holidays that summer was a time of white fluffy clouds sailing day after day across blue skies, of glimmering girls in summer dresses, of sun tan and whites at the tennis club, of sparkles dancing on a Carlingford Loch that was blue as the Bay of Naples, and of seawater gently warm as you plunged into it at Warrenpoint.

People were to remember it as 'the Spanish summer', for its warmth and its dazzling brightness. Except at Jamie's home. Jamie was to remember that summer as a time of closed curtains, shut windows, sighs and silences.

He sensed it the moment he carried his suitcase and tennis racket in through the door of his home. Aunt May was just coming down the stairs. She smelled ever-so-slightly old as she kissed him on the check.

'Gosh, Aunt May, I thought you'd be out when I saw the car gone,' Jamie said.

'There isn't any car, dear. We're between cars at the moment. We're all walking, and – and I do believe it's doing us a lot of good.'

'Uncle Henry at the office?'

'Oh yes. And he probably won't be back till late. He's pretty tied up these days.'

'Is he drinking?'

'Jamie, that's unfair of you. And it's really not your place to make a remark like that. Actually things are difficult at the office at the moment, and your uncle's very bogged down. You're going to have to be patient with him. And show a little understanding. Come on and we'll make a cup of tea together, before I go out – I've a committee meeting at four. Why don't you get some tennis in this afternoon? Weather's so lovely.'

'I'll do just that, Aunt May.'

***

IT really was a relief to get out on the club's sunny centre court, where the red *en-tous-cas* surface reflected the warm sun into Jamie's face. Ann Morgan, leggier than ever, had just been taking her racket out of its press when Jamie came into the club house. There had been a screech of welcome – Ann in her teens had become given to screeches – and Jamie was treated to an enthusiastic hug and a kiss. The centre court was free, and the two went out to play singles.

Jamie won the first set and drew the second. Ann was good and put up a right fight. As they headed in to the club house, a tall, fair-haired young fellow in whites passed them on his way out, carrying a racket. He smiled and nodded as he passed. He looked vaguely familiar. There was a boy and a girl with him, both in whites as well.

Ann turned to watch his easy stride to the now-vacated centre court. 'Isn't that some hunk, Jamie? Nearly as good looking as yourself.'

222

'Who is it, Ann? I think maybe I know him from somewhere, but I can't place him.'

'He's new here. Family just bought a holiday home in Warrenpoint and he comes in here most days with a couple of friends. He's got one of those motorbikes with a sidecar. That's it over there. Somebody said his name is McCracken.'

'God. I – don't – believe – it. *Dinny McCracken*. Couldn't be.'

'You know him?'

'We go back a long way, Ann. That's if it *is* him. And I think it might be.'

'Has to be. His name's Dinny, all right.'

***

INDEED it had to be Dinny McCracken, whom Jamie had last seen as ten-year-old urchin being carried screaming out of the classroom with blood pumping through his ragged cut-down trousers.

After Ann had gone home to her tea, Jamie went out to the centre court to watch the young man play. It was a foursome, three fellows and a girl. And could that Dinny play. His serves zinged just across the net without the tiniest curve. He spent a lot of time up at the net and could smash the ball down into the tramlines, yards from his opponents. He moved with astonishing grace and sureness.

It was Dinny McCracken, all right. Seven years makes a massive difference when it's between ten and seventeen, but still the face was the same. The flaxen hair; the slight turn up at the tip of the nose; the blue eyes. And with a twinge of annoyance Jamie realised that Dinny McCracken had been good-looking even then. Or might have been, except for the shaven head with the flaxen fringe in front, the ringworm on the scalp, the hungry chicken-chest, and those awful cut-down trousers.

***

JAMIE watched the foursome finish their game. And then he watched Dinny McCracken climb onto a gorgeous maroon and silver Triumph motorcycle, driving off with a girl in the sidecar and a fellow on the pillion. He didn't know why he was so disturbed by Dinny's reincarnation. He hadn't wanted to speak to him. He couldn't have spoken to him.

Sure what could Jamie say? Remember me, who gagged at the smell off you? Remember me who sniggered when fellows kicked you? Remember me who called you an animal, well at least inside my head?

For much of that night Jamie tossed and turned. It was just hard to handle – one day a creature you had learnt to despise; seven years later someone you might find yourself having to look up to. Or at least an equal anyway. This wasn't going to be easy.

And what might Dinny McCracken think of me? Here's one of those bastards that sneered at my shaved head and cut-down pants and my ringworm. Well now it's my turn.

And how in hell did he get to where he is? Some bloody fairy godmother? That only happens in fairy tales.

Jamie stayed away from the tennis club for several days. He just couldn't face meeting Dinny McCracken. For some reason it was that motorbike that had disturbed him more than anything.

224

For the next few days Jamie cycled to Warrenpoint to swim. It was a lot better than having to meet Dinny McCracken. A sparkling tide was in and there were no jellyfish around, so he swam off the shore. Slamming into those rolling breakers with the foam up your nostrils, and the freshness of the water as you did the crawl away out as far as it was safe to go before turning back, would help you forget anything. As close to flying as a fellow can get.

***

'HELLO. It *is* Jamie O'Brien, isn't it?'

It was Dinny McCracken, standing beside him on the pebbled shore, just as Jamie was pulling up his pants beneath the towel. He had come up without Jamie noticing. Jamie was furious at being caught in such an undignified posture. But Dinny didn't seem aware of any indignity.

'It's – it's me, yes,' Jamie said, hoping he wasn't blushing. 'And – and you're Dinny McCracken, aren't you? I saw you at the tennis club.'

'You did? But whyn't you say hello? When was that?'

'A few days ago. I – I was in a hurry. Had to get home to my tea.'

'Well, d'y'know something, it's grand to see you.' Not a hint of rancour. 'C'm'here – would you like an ice? Or a mineral? Malocca's is just down the street.'

The voice was pleasant; not quite posh but what Jamie's aunt would have called 'a nice accent'. Not *vin ordinaire*. And certainly not the accent of one of those Animals. Then Jamie felt a momentary shudder at having ever thought of people as Animals.

225

'N-no, I have to be going,' Jamie said. 'I – I have to – to – Och, sure why not? Why not an ice?' He couldn't think of a way out.

The two young men strolled the promenade and Jamie noticed a few heads turning as they passed. Some of the heads young ones. Female ones.

'So tell us, what've you been up to this past while?' Dinny asked.

'Och, just the usual. School, an' exams, an' things. Sports. The usual. What have *you* been up to is more to the point. We haven't set eyes on you since – uh – since –'

'Since I got that pencil up my arse?' Dinny chuckled ruefully.

'Uh, yeah. That.'

'It's a long story, Jamie.'

'Wouldn't mind hearing it. That's – if you wouldn't mind telling us.'

'Aye, all right, so. What y'having, by the way? Mine's an ice-cream soda.'

'I'll have that too.'

The two were settling themselves in one of the booths at Malocca's. Jamie fiddled with the menu for a moment, conscious that the other lad was looking at him.

'So?' Jamie said.

'The story?'

'Aye.'

'So where do I start?' Dinny thought for a moment.

'Start from when they did that – did that thing to you.'

'No, I'll go back earlier than that. Did you know my mother was a Protestant?'

'No, I didn't.'

'Well, she was. A Presbyterian from Bangor. The family cut her off when she ran off with my father. For him being a Catholic. And drinking too much. But even if he didn't drink, they'd have cut the pair of them off for him being a Catholic. They just wiped them out of mind. They didn't exist any more.

'Anyhow the pair of them ran off to England, but they soon came back and settled here in Newry, where my mum died when I was four. So I hardly remember her much.'

'So did mine,' Jamie said. 'Died when I was four, I mean. But I remember her, all right. Well, some things, anyway.' *The Face on the Pillow*, he thought.

'Bit of a coincidence, isn't it? So you know what it's like, then. Anyhow my dad couldn't cope after she died. He tried for a wee bit, but he just couldn't hack it. Drank and drank and drank. Drank himself to death, actually. Well, died of a stroke brought on by the drink. Anyway from the minute my mum died I had to cope on my own. From the age of four. Can you believe it? All those years. And as you remember, I didn't cope so very well, did I?'

'I think you did just great, Dinny.' Suddenly Jamie felt tears starting, but didn't let them. 'You did great, considering. Selling those papers, an' all. I couldn't have done like you.'

'Thanks. Thanks, Jamie. I really appreciate that. Anyhow, my dad died while I was still in hospital that time. So there was nobody after that. Will we have another?'

227

'Aye. But I'm paying this time.' Jamie hoped his few pence would reach to it. 'So what happened then?'

'The hospital chaplain got on to the RUC, and between them they found my mother's people in Bangor. They couldn't have been that hard to find.'

'How did they take it?'

'They nearly died when they heard all that had happened. They'd no idea. They thought we were still in England, y'see. They were absolutely horrified when they found out. And especially at the state I was in. My mum's sister just came and got me out of the hospital, took me home, and took me in as one of the family. And that was that.'

'Boy oh boy, so it *is* a fairy-godmother story. Never thought things like that really happened. An' you lived happily ever after. That it?'

'Just about. Until now, anyhow. Actually they were very decent about things: they're strict about principles, and they decided I must be brought up Catholic, since I was born one. So they sent me to Catholic schools all the way. Primary and secondary. Couldn't have been easy for them.'

'So what school are you at now?'

'I'm away at Clongowes. You know, down in Kildare. Must be costing them a bomb.'

'I'm at Woodcock. Costs a bit there, too.'

'What's it like?'

'Don't even ask. What's Clongowes like?'

'Och, it's not so bad really. Couple of decent men there, who help you through things when you need them.'

228

'We've one man like that too. Except he's in hospital a lot of the time. Actually he's just been moved back to Dublin – a hospital there – and I'm going up to see him next week. You want to come?'

'I wouldn't mind. Let me see if I can. I'll check at home.'

***

THE friendship between the two young men began from there. It brightened that summer and was a refuge from the gloom of the house in Dromalane. There now was a further source of gloom there – the fact that Rafferty's fields – those lovely fields across the road, fields that sloped down to the canal and the river, had been bought by the town council for the purpose of building 500 working-class homes.

'It's quite simply *the end*.' Aunt May was aghast. 'It's for families with six children or more. Hideous people – the sort who'd keep the coal in the bathtub. And riddled with TB – that's for sure. I've heard about people like that.'

Some of the neighbours were already selling out and scurrying off to more salubrious neighbourhoods like the Belfast Road, far from the expected madding crowd. But the awful thing was – and Jamie was just starting to suspect it – that probably aunt and uncle might like to move too, but might not be able to afford it. Jamie suspected that that was behind the intensity of Aunt May's grief.

Jamie stayed out of the house as much as he could. So that, in spite of the gloom at home, there was joy that summer. There were trips through the Mournes with the motorbike and sidecar, and together the two explored the leafy lanes around

Slieve Gullion and the Cooley Mountains where Cuchulainn had fought his battles.

Dinny took Jamie to Warrenpoint to meet his people. Aunt Heather was an ample motherly soul in a big floral dress, given to clucking and fussing, and she quickly set about getting food into Jamie to fatten him up.

'Och, aren't you the thin wee man, surely,' she'd say from time to time.

There were a grown-up son and daughter both working in England who wrote regularly and seemed to be well loved. Aunt Heather's husband had a furniture business in Bangor, and came down to the holiday home at weekends. Jamie liked his sense of humour and he seemed to like Jamie. He was delighted to find that Jamie could play chess. 'I need a partner, Jamie. I can get no good out of this here lot. That there Dinny is hopeless! D'y'hear that, nephew?'

Dinny just grinned and shrugged his shoulders.

Jamie found it hard to reconcile the warmth of these people with the hardness with which the same family had cut off Dinny's parents in the bad old days. He said as much to Dinny.

'It was my grandfather did that,' Dinny explained. 'It was a case of never-darken-this-door-again. He was one of the old school: signed the Ulster Covenant in 1912 – *with his blood!* A right old patriarch, I believe – rod of iron and all that.' He chuckled. 'But the oul bastard was dead by the time the family came to get me. And thanks be to God he was, or I'd not be here now.'

There were several trips to Dublin for Jamie to visit King at St Luke's Hospital, and mostly they used the motorbike for that. Jamie began bringing Dinny in to see King, and the two got on wonderfully. So well indeed that Jamie had to pinch himself so as not to be jealous.

King was fascinated by Dinny's rags-to-riches story, once he had persuaded him to tell it. 'So what are you planning to do with yourself, young brother?' he asked him.

'Not sure, Father, but I think it'll be medicine at Queens.'

'And what would you do then as a doctor?'

'I'd like to work in some clinic for poor people. Like my mum and dad were. A doctor might have saved them – well, saved my dad anyway – if they could have afforded one.'

'You wouldn't make much money at that.'

'I've had a bit of practice at that, Father. Not making much, I mean. Remember I sold papers. Wouldn't be anything new to me.'

***

IT was that same evening, towards the end of the summer, after Jamie arrived home from Dublin, that Aunt May sat him down. She had something to say to him, and came straight to the point.

'Have you ever thought of the Bank, Jamie? Becoming a bank clerk, I mean?'

'*What?* Indeed I haven't. An' I wouldn't like it at all. I'm going to university, like Dinny McCracken. What put that idea into your head?'

'It's just, dear, that nice Mr Kerin – you know, he's manager at the Munster & Leinster – he told me he could put in a word for you. He said you'd be certain to get it.'

'But I don't *want* it. I'd hate the bloody Bank.'

'Don't swear, please, dear, in my presence. I hope that McCracken boy isn't teaching you to swear.'

Jamie was outraged at this ridiculous Bank suggestion. 'Listen, Aunt May. I don't know where you got this notion. I've a year to go anyhow, before I make any decisions. And I can tell you, it won't be the Bank. Counting other people's money for the rest of my life? You must be joking.'

'Jamie. There's something else I've got to say to you.' Aunt May sighed. 'There are money troubles – well, you know that already. But – look, I know you've a year to go. But – I've been trying to get up the courage to tell you this – you'll not be going back to Woodcock next month. And I'm afraid there won't be any university either. There's just no more money.'

'Oh my God. Oh – *God!*'

'Come on, now dear. Pull yourself together. Your uncle hasn't been well. Far from well. He'll be going into hospital for treatment in a couple of days.'

'Is it Purdysburn?'

'Yes.'

'Then it's for the drinking, isn't it?'

'For *treatment*, dear. But they say he many not be able to work again. And there's been a tiny bit of trouble with the Law Society. Like there was in Enniskillen. Nothing much but – what I'm trying to say is, you may have to be the man of the house fairly soon.'

JAMIE wandered in shock for several days. Shock and anger. Aye, and envy too. Envy of Dinny McCracken, swanning off to be a doctor and leaving Jamie behind to count other people's bloody money.

Should have seen it coming, he thought. Sure weren't all the signs there? Sure hasn't it been coming for years? Oh fuck. Well, at least I can swear now, and it helps.

Jamie couldn't face the tennis club. He couldn't face swimming either, in case he ran into Dinny. How could he ever tell him? He had lately had visions of himself and Dinny together at Queens, Dinny doing his medicine and Jamie doing – well, whatever. He wasn't sure yet what he'd be studying there. Maybe Cairns with them too. What a threesome they'd make.

And now it's not going to happen. How can I tell Cairns? But I won't be seeing Cairns. *I'm – not – going – back – to – Cock.* And I won't be seeing King either. I'll be stuck in this godawful place, slaving in some godawful bank. No way. It's unthinkable. Well, think it, son. It's how it's going to be. Oh God. Oh *God.*

Jamie cycled and cycled, the highways and the byways of south Armagh, high above Camlough Lake without ever seeing its beauty, across the border into Louth, down past St John's Castle in Carlingford, all the way around to Dundalk and back through Ravensdale. For much of that week he'd leave home early and come back late, with only a bottle of water clipped to the handlebars and a hastily-made sandwich oozing inside greaseproof paper in his blazer pocket. There were occasional thoughts of just wading into Camlough Lake, thoughts speedily banished because that way lay Hell for all eternity, but thoughts that came back nevertheless.

And then – it must have been the Monday of the following week – as Jamie's bike came up along the Dromalane Road, there, standing in the middle of the road in the twilight, outside Jamie's house, was Dinny McCracken. He just put out his hands and gently grasped the handlebars of Jamie's bike as it rolled to a stop.

'You don't have to tell me,' Dinny said gently. 'I got it all out of your Aunt May.'

Jamie started to cry, which is an awful thing to do in front of a fellow.

'You're coming home with me tonight,' Dinny said. 'Just for the night. I asked your Aunt May, and she has your toothbrush and things packed. C'mon. Go and get them. I've the motorbike here.'

Jamie wept convulsively. Quite irrationally, he whispered, 'Dinny, when I think of the things we did to you....' He couldn't finish. The weeping stopped him there.

'*You* never did them. You were never one of them. I always knew that.' Dinny put a hand around his shoulder. 'C'mon, now, y'boyo. Snap out of it.'

***

THAT evening Dinny's Aunt Heather clucked and fussed and fed the two boys like turkeys being readied for Christmas. And the two stayed up till the wee hours talking and talking endlessly about Jamie's predicament.

'The one thing that's for sure,' Dinny said. 'You *must* finish school. You must get your Leaving Cert.'

'But sure how can I now?'

'There has to be a way. You'd be mad to pass it up. And you'd spend your life regretting it. C'm'here – couldn't you go back to the Brothers here? They'd take you back for the year, wouldn't they?'

'I suppose they would, but – '

'Course they would. There'd be different textbooks down here, but you'd catch up pretty quick. I remember you as pretty bright.'

'Dinny. Willya listen to me. What I'm trying to tell you is, it's not as simple as that. You heard what I said – Aunt May wants me to go for the Bank. Right away, she says.'

'Och, for God's sake, what's the woman on about? That's out of the question, Jamie, and you know it. You effin' well finish school, d'y'hear?'

'She says there's no money, and she says I'm going to have to be man of the house.'

'So what's gone wrong? No, don't tell me – I think I know. It's that Law Society thing – story's all over town. So they want you to go out and work. Is that it?'

'Seems to be the case.'

'Couldn't your aunt go out and work?'

'Gee, I never thought of that. She never suggested it.'

'No, she wouldn't, would she? Why don't *you* suggest it?'

***

AUNT May was outraged. '*Me?* Behind a counter in Quinn's? In a brown shop coat? And a pencil behind my ear?'

The thought of a pencil behind Aunt May's ear gave Jamie a momentary urge to giggle. But this was serious.

'Besides, I'm far too busy.' Aunt May sniffed. 'Do you know how many committees I'm on? There just wouldn't be time to go out to work.'

'How much do the committees pay you, Aunt May?'

'That's not the point, dear. These are social duties – expected of someone in my position.'

'Your position could be changing, Aunt May.' Jamie was suddenly shocked at the hardness he was finding in himself. He didn't like it – didn't like himself for it – but he kept on anyhow. 'People might have more respect for you if you went out and earned your living. Given the circumstances.'

'To think you could say a thing like that to me, after – after all we've done for you. I can't believe it. I just –' She dissolved into tears, and put her head in her hands.

Immediately Jamie felt ashamed of what he was doing. *After all we've done for you*: indeed they had done so much for him. Everything. How could he be so selfish? So cruel? He sat down beside her on the sofa, and put his arms around her. While he felt the sobbing ebb and flow, and the narrow shoulders shaking, he suddenly realised the misery this woman must have been going through for months. Perhaps years.

They sat together on the sofa. Neither said anything for what seemed an age.

***

'I'VE put myself down for the Bank exam, Father. It's next week.' Jamie was sitting with King and Dinny on the veranda of St Luke's Hospital in Dublin. It was a warm afternoon, and King was in his blue dressing gown.

'I've begged him not to, Father,' Dinny said. 'But he won't listen. Maybe he'll listen to you.'

King's chin was in his left hand, and he looked at Jamie over his glasses. The face seemed thinner. 'You're sure it's the right choice, Jamie?'

'There *isn't* a choice, Father. There's no money at home. My uncle's drying out, and they say he'll never work again. He's lucky he's not in jail, I'm told. And my aunt can't work. So it's time for me to grow up and be the wage earner. That's if I *get* the Bank. Otherwise – God knows.'

'I hate to see you miss out this last year at school, Jamie.' King leaned back and tucked his thumbs into the cord of his dressing gown. 'It's so important. Vitally so.'

'I know. *I know.*' Jamie was exasperated. 'But for God's sake, I don't have any *choice*. There's no point in going on about it.'

'It wouldn't matter where you'd finish school,' King continued as if he hadn't heard him. Or as if he was thinking out loud. 'In fact you might be as well off out of Woodcock with the way it's going down the tubes. The Christian Brothers would be fine, if they'd take you back. Do you think they would?'

'Father, did you *hear* me? There's – no – *money*.'

'There has to be a way.'

'That's what I said,' Dinny interjected.

'Oh shut up, Dinny. It's all right for you. I just said there's no money.'

'Temper, Brother.' King looked across the glasses. 'Don't lose it now. Tell me – you said your aunt can't go out to work. Why?'

'She just can't handle it, Father. She goes all to pieces when I mention it. I don't think she'd be able for it. And I think she'd feel humiliated in front of the town, having been so prominent. The thought of standing behind a counter kills her. It would be utterly selfish of me to push that on her.'

'Who mentioned behind a counter?'

'She did. Said she couldn't face it.'

'Could she handle – doctor's receptionist, maybe? Something genteel like that? Or work in a law firm? – there'd surely be contacts there through your uncle.'

'God, maybe – I never thought of anything like that.'

'I imagine she didn't let you. People can control the way you think. One thing, by the way – you said you'd be selfish if you sent her out to work so you could finish your schooling. That it?'

'Suppose so.' A shrug.

'Just a question, mind. Could your aunt be selfish, asking you to quit your schooling so she doesn't have to work? Will you think about that?'

***

THERE was no feeling of elation when the results of the Bank exam came in and Jamie learned he had passed. Well, no elation for Jamie, anyhow. But Aunt May seemed pleased.

'A door opening for you, Jamie,' Mr Kerin the bank manager had said when he stopped him in Hill Street to congratulate him.

More like a door slamming shut, Jamie thought.

As usual, he had got nowhere with Aunt May. The face would tighten up and the lower lip start to quiver at the very mention of work. And it wasn't that she lacked energy: she flounced from golf to hospital committee to *feis* committee to library committee to her bridge and her canasta. Are there many people like that, Jamie wondered, who will do work galore as long as it's voluntary, but run a mile from work you get paid for? Do they find it demeaning or what? It was certainly hard to understand.

Depression hit when 5 September came and Dinny went back to Clongowes and presumably Cairns went back to Woodcock and every day Jamie saw the fellows walking up William Street to the Abbey Christian Brothers. The longing for school was a lump in the solar plexus and a thing that went round and round inside his skull. Not unlike the scruples of old, except it wasn't guilt now but yearning.

How could he be yearning for Woodcock, where he had endured such misery? Well, there'd be Cairns and the FCA and being a Top Cock this year, and being tall enough now so Bentley wouldn't dare bully him, and having a good chance for the debate medal, and being able to finish his schooling with a flourish – a good Leaving Cert result that would sweep him into university like a surging wave carries you onto the beach at Warrenpoint. Sweep him *where?* Not to university. There was to be no university. None. And no school either.

Hate came back. Jamie had a lot of hate in him. Hate this time for Aunt May, and her fucking golf and committees. Well maybe not exactly hate this time, but acute resentment.

Especially at her nagging: 'When are the Bank going to send for you, dear? I wish you'd go down and see that nice Mr Kerin. He'd be sure to know. Or he could arrange something. Money doesn't grow on trees, remember.'

And hate too for the banks themselves down the town – he felt their dank shadow every time he walked past the gloomy Munster & Leinster in Margaret Square or the hungry door of the Bank of Ireland on Trevor Hill. Shades of the prison house were closing.

When Jamie returned from one of his mournful walks through the town, he found two letters on the mat inside the front door. It was 20 September. The first letter was from Cairns. Part of it read:

> ...Where the Hell are you, anyway? Why didn't you tell us you weren't coming back? We miss you, you hoor you. It's depressing here without you. There's no one to help me keep Bentley in his place.
>
> No sign of King either. We miss him too. God do we miss him. Now they're saying he might never be back. Nobody really knows. And there's no sign of Smegs either. But we don't miss him I can tell you.
>
> The place is falling apart here. Maybe you're as well off out of it. I don't know how it will all end. Anyhow, stay in touch, will you? Just one letter wouldn't kill you. Come on, write, you hoor.
>
> Yours
>
> *Jeremy Cairns*

I'll have to write to him now, Jamie thought. Haven't had the courage to do it so far. Couldn't think what to say – how do you tell about life going down the tubes? And what's the point in keeping in touch anyway? It'll only make things more depressing. Especially with our lives heading in such different directions now.

The handwriting on the second letter looked vaguely familiar. Then Jamie recognised it from the corrections on the margins of his English essays. King had written:

> A little bit of news for you Jamie. I did not mention this before, because I was unsure of the outcome. It's this: the Old Woodcocks (that's what they call their past-pupils' union) have a fund for members who have fallen on hard times. And for their dependants, in certain circumstances.
>
> Although an Old Clongownian myself, rather than an Old Woodcock, I have long been a member of their fund committee, and I managed to do a bunk from the hospital for long enough to attend its meeting last Friday. I put your circumstances to the meeting (as you know, your uncle is an Old Woodcock). To make a long story short, the committee has now agreed the following:
>
> Your final year at Woodcock College is to be funded by the committee. The committee will not fund a course at university, but has agreed that a loan be offered, covering university tuition and upkeep, which you would be expected to pay back, interest free, over the 15 years subsequent to your graduation. Finally, a fairly small monthly stipend

is to be made available to your uncle, in view of his current ill health and financial situation. It will not be enough, however, unless your aunt takes up some kind of work.

I urge you to take up this offer. I think it is time to tell your aunt that your education is paramount, and that, if she wishes to continue to live in the state to which she is accustomed, or near to it anyhow, she will simply have to take up work.

This may seem harsh, but as a psychologist I have seen similar cases, where people are frightened to go out to work yet eventually have to do so out of necessity. In almost every case they adapt quickly and end up enjoying their work. Indeed they often express regret at not having done it sooner.

May God bless you, Jamie, and guide your decision.

Yours affectionately in Jesus Christ

Ralph King

Could a man's chest burst with joy? Jamie's came close.

September 1950

'DID your oul fella get struck off?' It was Bentley, of course. On Jamie's first day back at Cock.

Jamie put a finger to his lips conspiratorially. 'C'm'here till I tell you, Bentley,' he whispered.

Bentley came close to hear what Jamie was going to whisper. Jamie shot his left knee up into Bentley's crotch and, as Bentley lay curled up and moaning, Jamie leaned over him and whispered, '*One.* He's not my oul fella. As you should know. *Two.* He was never struck off, you little fucker. *Three.* If you ever, ever, say that again, Bentley, *ever*, it's those balls of yours'll get struck off. Y' hear me, now?'

The Cock College to which Jamie returned for his final year was a different place. Smegs of course was gone: he could hardly have come back after what had happened.

No one had ever found out who perpetrated the outrage on Smegs. The Gardai had been called, and the Top Cocks had all been quizzed, but no one knew anything. Or no one said anything. One theory was that a few of the fellows who had left the previous year, and were now at university, had come down to do the deed. But that was just conjecture.

With Smegs gone there was the relieved sense of a heavy weight lifted off. But in another sense it was as if Smegs had been a lid on a seething cauldron, and when the lid was lifted away the cauldron proceeded to boil over.

And, to mix a few more metaphors, there was also a sense of the authorities kicking for touch, as they say in rugby. It was as though they weren't quite sure what to do next, and were in a state of making do until they thought things out. Things seemed kind of on hold.

***

KING was still in hospital, and there had been no replacement as spiritual director. So there was no one for the fellows to turn to for guidance. It was as if the college had simply forgotten them.

Revvo Fitz had taken Smegs's place as dean but, with his brutal mentor gone, Fitz's swagger was gone too, and he wasn't making much of a fist of discipline. To mix one more metaphor, the fellows were starting to push the envelope.

It showed first in the study hall. There was a new young revvo in charge there – the Rev Charles Chinsworth – promptly nicknamed Chinny, due both to the name and to a notable paucity of that particular facial feature. He also seemed to lack that natural authority needed to keep three hundred plus fellows in check, a lack which was swiftly noted by the fellows with their unerring instinct for weakness.

It was Bentley as usual who started things. When Chinny demanded his name for talking during study, he was heard to say, 'Bentley-ffrench, Sir. Spelt with two small *f*'s, Sir.'

That set everyone sniggering.

The next evening Bentley produced a box of stink bombs he had brought back after the holidays, and now found a marvellous way to use them. The bombs were fragile glass phials which shattered when they were thrown. The fellows were half way through the study period when an evil odour wafted through the study hall, growing steadily more awful until everyone had handkerchiefs to their noses.

Eventually the odour reached the quivering nostrils of Chinny, who came tumbling down from his look-out pulpit, little chin trembling with vexation, and stood arms akimbo in the central aisle, saying, 'All right, now. Whoever perpetrated this will own up. *Now*. I'm waiting.'

A ripple of sniggers came from the desks.

'I said, I'm *waiting*.'

More sniggers.

'Very well, if that's the way you want it. You'll all have to suffer now, for the disgraceful behaviour of a few.' There was a long pole topped with brass hooks for opening and closing the high windows all around the study hall. Chinny grabbed it and scurried around shutting all the windows so as to keep the stink in.

A few fellows showed their annoyance by quietly vibrating the desk lids up and down against the desks. Slowly the vibrations spread until all the desks in the hall were vibrating in unison. Then the vibrations got louder and louder until it was like rolling thunder and the hall itself seemed to be shaking.

Chinny's chin was shaking too, and he looked close to tears. 'If you think you're annoying me,' the shrill voice screamed,

245

'you're not. D'you hear me? You're not. You're *not.*' He scurried back up to his pulpit, where he sat with a white handkerchief to his nose, trying to read a book, or at least pretending to.

It went on for a good few minutes, until eventually the fellows got tired of the rattling, and the stench finally faded.

It was the beginning of a new persecution, with Chinny now the victim. It wasn't that Chinny deserved it, or that there was anything nasty about him: indeed he was probably quite decent. It was just that he was a natural victim – one of those unfortunates whom bullies unerringly zero in on, and whom the general crowd does nothing to defend.

The fellows spread glue on his seat in the pulpit, and he had to stay sitting there until everyone had gone down to supper so that no one could see his humiliation. They crammed shit into the keyhole of the study-hall door, which came out on the key and went all over his hands when Chinny unlocked the door.

Then a quote from Bernard Shaw was writ large and pinned to the study-hall door: *The most ludicrous sight in the world is the weak man putting his foot down.*

And most days, when the fellows had grown bored or frustrated, the Vibration of the Desks would recommence. It would always start quietly and gather strength until it was deafening, and it continued week after week, long after Bentley had used up all his stink bombs. A refinement was now added, in which the rhythm from the Ride of the Valkyries entered the vibrations – *dah-dah-dah-DAH-dah; dah-dah-dah-DAH-dah...*

A variation was the Shuffling of the Feet, during which three hundred and forty pairs of feet would shuffle under the desks, back and forth, back and forth, slow at first, then getting faster and faster, and then the feet stamping, until it was like an erupting storm.

In the end Chinny would just sit in his pulpit with his head down and fingers in his ears.

It was nearly as hard on the fellows as it was on Chinny, and Jamie grew fed up with it as it was impossible to get any study done. He and Cairns even took Bentley aside and threatened to beat the shit out of him if he didn't stop.

'But it's not me,' Bentley stammered, moistening his lips. 'It's not me any more. Nobody knows who starts it now – it's everybody's at it.'

They had to believe him, for it was true.

***

THE whole school seemed depressed. And it quickly jumped to Jamie, his own depression coming back with a vengeance. It wasn't scrupulosity any more: the scruples had well and truly gone, but they seemed to have morphed into a nameless anxiety about the future; about his coming university loan and how could he ever pay it back; about why he had bothered coming back to Cock, when it was such a mess; about Aunt May's letter whining about her new job as a dentist's receptionist and how demeaning it was; about life in general; about everything around him.

It was as if life at Cock was somehow unravelling. Bullying was rife; fellows were nasty and short-tempered with one another; noses were broken and eyes blackened in the rugby scrums – indeed Hancock in first division ended in hospital after a collapsed scrum, with something they said might be a broken back. The fellows were saying he mightn't ever walk again.

Even rugby was losing its attraction for Jamie. He played as well as ever, and with Smegs gone he might have had a chance of getting on the SCT – the senior cup team. But it wasn't that simple – he was still in second division, and the fellows in first division had been at it so long, and together so long, that there would have been no way to muscle in. Cairns did his best to help Jamie, but even he had to admit it was a closed shop.

Indeed Jamie got so fed up that he moved himself down to third division – nobody seemed to care any more what division you were in, since the SCT – the rugby senior cup team – was all that really mattered at Cock. In third division the fellows were allowed to play soccer – nobody really cared what they played – and Jamie took quickly to the soccer. Just the speed of it – which suited Jamie's natural speed – and the long plays between whistles, were exactly what he needed.

Jamie's eyes of course were still against him, and he could only judge by the colour of a fellow's jersey when he went in to take the ball off him. And you still couldn't wear specs because one ball into your face would mean glass into your eyes. Blindness, maybe. Jamie sometimes still longed for those contact lenses that film stars had.

'Why don't you get plastic lenses in your specs?' Cairns said to him one day. 'They'd be quite safe on the field.'

'Plastic lenses? Are you joking? There's no such thing.'

'They're all the rage now. You go ask Dennehy – he's got a pair. Got them last week.'

'Know what – I did see him wearing specs at soccer yesterday. But I only half noticed. God, imagine what they'd do for your game.'

'There's Dennehy now. C'mon and we'll ask him.'

Dennehy was decent enough about it. He let Jamie try on the specs, and Jamie was amazed at how light they were. These would never slide down your nose like his own specs did. He flicked them with his nail: they gave a *tock* instead of a *ping* like glass would.

'Careful, though,' Dennehy said. 'They scratch easy. That's the down side. But they're worth it, I can tell you.'

'Dear?'

'Bit more than usual. But not that much.'

'Your aunt could afford that,' Cairns said to Jamie. 'C'mon – ask her to get you a pair. She'd have your prescription at home. You'd never look back.'

Jamie never did look back, certainly not through his new plastic lenses. Well, not quite plastic – something called *Perspex*, Dennehy had explained. Same as the cockpits in those Spitfires and Stukas.

Packets from home had always been a rarity for Jamie, so when this small packet arrived he knew exactly what it would contain. He could hardly get it open fast enough. Oh, the lightness of these specs. And they weren't those awful wiry round things like the bottoms of bottles that Jamie had always worn – these ones were squarish, with light-coloured horn rims. Jamie even looked good in them when he saw himself in the cubicle mirror. Then just a tiny twinge: vanity's a sin, isn't it? Well, just a tiny sin, then.

But the soccer field was transformed by the specs. Jamie could actually *see* it. See it for the first time. He suddenly realised he had never really seen a playing field before – it had always been a sort of vague blur where figures came and went as if in mist, and you had to judge by the colour of the jersey coming at you: you only saw the line when it was under your feet, and you had to guess in what direction the goalposts were.

Now suddenly that green jersey coming at you had Mahony's face on top of it; you could move in beside Moran and with a little deft footwork take the ball right off him; you could pass to Dennehy with an undreamt-of accuracy; you could swerve just in time as you dribbled the ball up the field; and there up at the end of the field was the hungry goal mouth waiting for you to feed it. And feed it you did. And it longed for more and you longed for more when the whistle sounded for *All In*.

No sport had ever been like this. The sheer downright joy of it. A joy that made even the depression fade away. A sense of physical wellbeing that kept that depression at bay. Sometimes a little thing can transform your life: those specs did.

Even as Woodcock College seemed to be falling apart around him, Jamie's world was beginning to come together. He hoped it would stay that way.

***

THERE was one other source of satisfaction in Jamie's final year at Cock. That was the FCA – the college's company of the Local Defence Force for which Jamie had signed on. So now the whole of each Sunday was devoted to FCA activities.

Putting on the 'bull's wool' – which was the fellows' term for the rough green uniform with its jaunty beribboned shangarry cap and the steel-tipped boots and the ankle leggings and that brass-buttoned greatcoat that made you feel like a Cossack general – it all opened up a new world for Jamie.

You even got a gun all to yourself. Each fellow was issued with a Lee Enfield .303 rifle which he was allowed to keep in his cubicle press for the whole of that year. He was responsible for its maintenance: there was a circular slot in the wooden butt to hold the oil container, and the gun was required to be oiled and cleaned with military exactness.

There was a bayonet for the gun, but the bayonets were kept under lock and key and only issued for special ceremonial drills and guards of honour for visiting dignitaries and sometimes at High Mass. (Somehow bayonets and rifles and stamping boots didn't seem quite to fit with High Mass, but, well, that's the way it was. And Jamie certainly loved thudding up the centre aisle of the chapel as part of the guard of honour.)

Somebody said that fellows used to be allowed to keep the bayonets along with their guns, until one day some eejit ran down the dormitory pushing his bayonet through the curtains just for a lark. Apparently in one of the cubicles a fellow was standing a bit too close to his curtain for comfort. Perhaps just a college legend: no one knew for sure.

There was of course no ammunition. They'd get that later when they went on the firing range at Renmore. But there were a few things to be done before that. Like becoming soldiers.

***

JAMIE would never forget his first day's drill, which actually began without the guns. An officer had come down that Sunday morning from Renmore Barracks in Galway in one of those big wooden Ford station wagons, and with him were a couple of sergeants, who quickly bawled a crowd of scraggy schoolboys into something that looked vaguely like soldiers.

The fellows were lined up in the gymnasium wearing the bull's wool for the very first time. The officer nodded to one of the sergeants and walked to the front of the hall where he just stood and watched for a few moments before going outside. Perhaps for a smoke, thought Jamie.

The sergeant, short, stocky and dangerous looking, with a quivery little moustache, stalked along the line of seventeen-year-olds. He stopped in front of Jamie. "Did you brass those buttons, Private?'

Before Jamie could answer, the sergeant hissed, 'What are you looking at, Private? Don't you eyeball me! I asked you did you clean your buttons – I didn't ask you for a fucking date!'

There was a tiny snort from Cairns, right beside Jamie.

The sergeant moved slowly to stand in front of Cairns. He folded his arms. 'So you think this is funny, Private?' It was uttered in a hiss. Then a roar: 'Fucking well *answer* me, Private!'

'N-no, Sir.'

'*Louder!* Can you hear me, Private?'

'Y-yes, Sir. N-no, Sir. N-not funny, Sir.'

'Gimme fifty. *Now.*'

'F-fifty what, sir?'

'Press-ups, you fuckin'eejit. Down, d'y'hear? *Now.*'

252

'You.' The sergeant turned back to Jamie. 'Start countin' for him. Fifty, y'hear?'

'Y-yes, Sir. One – two – three...'

As Jamie counted and Cairns wheezed up and down, the sergeant continued his inspection. He stalked up and down each line, glaring at each fellow individually and prolongedly, from under a pair of terrifying eyebrows. He seemed to have an instinct for anyone who might be suppressing an urge to giggle, or that might not be staring straight ahead.

By the time he had finished the sergeant had found fault with practically every uniform, and more than three quarters of the fellows were wheezing through twenty or fifty press-ups.

And no one had any further urge to giggle.

When everyone was back standing up again, the sergeant addressed them, this time in a voice now quiet, but laced with menace. 'If I can't trust ye to pass my inspection, ye'll never get past Captain Kennedy's inspection. And that's where *my* reputation is at stake. Y'hear? *My* reputation. So if I have to give each of ye a thousand press-ups a day, ye'll not get near any officer until ye've passed for me. *Do – ye – hear – what – I'm – telling – ye?*'

Just as he was finishing, as if on cue, the door opened quietly and the officer came in. He was tall, peaked cap jauntily tilted, and wore cream-coloured riding breeches and high brown jackboots that glinted in the gymnasium lights. He held a swagger stick under his left arm. He looked magnificent.

The sergeant went up to him, and the fellows saw him salute. There was a brief murmur of conversation. The officer tapped his swagger stick gently on the side of his right boot. He nodded; the sergeant saluted again; the officer returned the salute, turned and walked back out through the door.

Jamie guessed the sergeant had told him they were not ready. Or maybe that they would never be ready. Never be any use.

'Company, *dismiss!*' the sergeant bellowed.

***

THE first few Sundays were all like that. That sergeant was a holy terror. 'You. *You.* God help me, what a useless crowd of fucking country bumpkins I have to deal with. But I'll make soldiers out of ye if it's the last thing I do.'

The fellows simply loved it. It was great to be bawled out. You felt you mattered. But above all, you felt that someone was in charge and was making something out of you, at a time when the school itself didn't seem to have a clue what it was supposed to be making of you.

By the end of the first month the company could march adequately; knew the Irish commands *Seasaíg ar Áis* for 'Stand at Ease', and *Aire* for 'Attention'; could shoulder arms in three smart movements and could present arms (*Táirgíg Airm*) as if they had been born to it. And they had their own corporal – Mortimer – who had been in the FCA the previous year and was now promoted.

The route marches were killing at first. Seven miles out along those little Burren roads lined with hazel; seven miles back, between those endless limestone deserts littered with giant boulders; agony for the first few miles until the rhythm took over and your hips and knees and ankles became limbs of some giant green centipede whose hundred booted feet went

254

tramp, tramp, tramp in unison, as the great beast snaked its way along the roads between the limestone plains and boulders of the Burren.

The blisters were brutal during those first route marches, until you learned to rub soap into your socks, by which time your feet had begun to harden anyhow.

The marches took place in all weathers and in all seasons. There were days when your were half blinded with the sweat running into your eyes; other days when your half-frozen breath shot out like smoke as you marched; days when the rain ran down your neck and you had to cover the muzzle of the .303 to stop it getting into the barrel; there was one day when your footfalls were gently muffled by one of those rare snowfalls; and finally, when spring came, and early summer, marches under cloud-flecked blue skies with the cracks in the limestone plains erupting with astonishing alpine flowers.

Not that Jamie really noticed flowers. Not yet. But something happened during a route march in late spring that changed him, although he didn't realise it at the time. The company was marching on a woodland track through a forest up near Gort, and a halt was called. *Ar Socracht*, Stand Easy, was ordered. Feet apart, gun butts on the ground, everyone breathed and stretched and relaxed. Jamie looked around him, then up at the canopy of trees above him. Sunbeams were driving through the foliage so that each leaf was lit up like a tiny green flame as the sunlight penetrated it. And all those thousands of flames flickered in the breeze as though the forest were engulfed in green fire.

'*Aire.*'

Jamie snapped out of his reverie but, as he came to attention and shouldered arms, he knew that something had changed for him. Later he realised that he had become aware of Beauty.

***

"KNOW something, O'Brien?' Mortimer said. 'You could be a fuckin' great shot. Y'ever shoot before?'

'Well, a catapult? I wasn't too bad with that in the old days. Oh, an' I had an airgun.' Jamie chuckled. 'Until they took it off me.'

'For being too good a shot, was it?'

'Well, I did get Eileen O'Connor's pony in the arse. Boy you should've seen it take off, with Eileen up, too. There was a bit of trouble over that.'

'Bet there was.'

The two fellows were lying prone as they talked, facing one another, with Jamie aiming the empty rifle, slamming the bolt forward and pulling the trigger. Mortimer lay facing him, holding in front of his eye a metal disk with a tiny hole in it. That hole was the target and, as Jamie pulled the trigger, Mortimer could see whether or not the gun stayed on target.

This was the same Mortimer, now corporal, who wouldn't have been seen dead with Jamie a year or two back. Jamie had never forgotten that freezing morning around the track when Mortimer had told him, 'Don't attach yourself!'

Something was changing.

Developing as a marksman certainly helped. From the very first of these exercises Jamie came out continually with full marks. And later, when they got to the actual firing range up at

Renmore, he quickly gained the reputation of being a crack shot. He didn't really understand why it worked for him and not for some others.

It was as if he had heard the commands all his life – *Get ready – Range three hundred – Kneeling position – Three rounds – In your own time – FIRE*. He just lined up the sights, adjusted, gently squeezed the trigger and somehow managed to hit a bull or an inner practically every time.

'You'd make a fuckin' great sniper, d'y'know that, O'Brien?' Mortimer said to him.

Those weekends in the FCA did more than anything in years to give Jamie back that confidence in himself which Cock College had so eroded.

For the first time in years he was experiencing respect, and the comradeship that comes with respect. At the start he hardly understood what was happening.

'Bit of chocolate, O'Brien?' This was Hanley offering him a couple of squares from his Cadbury bar during the halt in a route march.

Things like that hadn't happened much before. But now fellows who would not have bidden him the time of day were marching beside him; sharing water bottles or a couple of fig rolls with him during the halts.

'Try some of that, O'Brien! Great for the blisters.' That was O'Hagan tossing him a tin of Germoline ointment as he bathed his aching feet in a stream by the roadside.

Jamie remembered King once telling him that being unpopular was usually only a temporary condition. He hadn't believed it at the time.

'You can get over it once you learn what's causing it – what you're getting wrong,' King had said. 'And in the end it comes down to caring about the other fellows. Really caring.'

The conversation had begun with Jamie telling King that nobody ever reached out to him.

'Well why don't *you* try reaching out to *them*?' King had replied.

Jamie had tried then, but somehow seemed to have lost the knack. And the boys had obviously developed a contempt for Jamie's introverted face and miserable self-absorption.

Now maybe that knack was coming back. If it was, it came from those moments when you crouched in the firing range along with the other fellows; it was chuckling over smutty jokes that you felt you could now laugh at without going to Hell; it was swearing and grumbling behind Sgt Madden's back; it was having fellows shake your hand and say, 'Good man, O'Brien!' when you came out on top as a sharp shooter.

Jamie's stock went up considerably when he saved Sgt Madden's life. Literally. The fellows were all in the firing range when that eejit Mulcahy found his gun had jammed.

'Look, Sir, me gun won't work,' he said, turning to the sergeant with the gun pointed at the man's navel.

He was just pulling the trigger to demonstrate, when Jamie, right beside him, dashed the gun sideways, which fired as he did so.

***

ALL Jamie's FCA activities, as well as his new-found joy in soccer, were a source of fulfilment, and indeed growth, in those months coming up to Christmas. Probably for others too. They

258

were something to focus on as the school seemed to disintegrate around them. Revvo Fitz had rapidly become a figure of contempt, and that poor creature who tried to control the study hall continued to be a figure of fun.

'Chinny'll have a breakdown if it goes on,' Cairns said one day after a three-hour period that was more bedlam than study. 'But what can we do, Jamie? We've tried yelling at them to leave off but nobody pays any heed.'

'It's mob rule, that's what it is,' Jamie said. 'But why doesn't the Manor intervene? You never even see the bloody Provost, except to flounce around at a High Mass. And as for his sidekicks – '

'Look, the hols are next week. I'll take a bet they'll have Chinny changed when we get back. Maybe they just didn't want to be seen giving in to mob rule. They'll change him when we're away – wait till you see.'

'And they say King'll be back next term. That's what Bentley says, anyway. He might pull things together here. King, I mean, not Bentley!'

259

January 1951

THERE was still no sign of King when the old green bus rolled to a stop on the gravel, and the fellows climbed out to face another term at Cock. King would have been there to greet them if he were in the place at all – he had always made a point of it.

That meant he was still in hospital.

And they hadn't changed Chinny. He was still in charge of the study hall. However things were quiet enough there: it seemed maybe that mob rule had run its course.

'Maybe the fellows forgot about it over Christmas,' Jamie suggested.

'Or maybe the Christmas spirit got to them.' Cairns gave a chuckle. 'Though I'm inclined to doubt that. I'll tell you what *I* think it is. There's exams coming up, and none of us was getting any work done. And maybe the eejits are coppin' on to that. It's hurting them as much as poor ole Chinny. I'd say it's self interest, more than the Christmas spirit.'

'Well, whatever it is, let's hope it lasts.'

It didn't last. Or rather, it lasted until Cock lost to Glenstal in the very first round of the rugby Senior Cup.

***

HOPES of victory had been high all that January and early February. Father Moran, one of the teaching staff, had taken on the training of the team, and was far and away the best yet. But after Glenstal clobbered them 15-8 – in spite of two trys, and a convert by Cairns – morale at Cock plummeted.

All the energy that might have been spent on rugby, or at least on cheering on the team, now seemed to turn inwards. Bullying recommenced with a vengeance, and there was a sense that things were getting more and more out of control. Revvo Fitz walloped and clattered and rattled and locked, but might have been invisible for all the effect he had on discipline. Depression settled on the long grey corridors.

'Jeez, would y'look at the faces,' Cairns said to Jamie. 'You'd think there was nothing more to live for. It's only fuckin' rugby, for God's sake. There's more to life than rugby. You just wait and see – they'll start taking it out on Chinny again.'

And indeed they did. First it was the stink bombs, then the shutting of windows by Chinny to keep in the stench. And inevitably came the rattling of the desk lids, quiet at first like the muttering of a distant storm, then slowly rising to the thunder of more than three hundred desk lids slamming up and down together with all the energy the fellows could muster – bangety-*bang*, bangety-*bang*, BANGETY *BANG*. Then a lull, for a couple of minutes. Then bangety *bang*....

It would mostly lead to Chinny running up and down the study hall, screaming – 'If you think you're annoying me, you're not, *you're not*, *YOU'RE NOT*.' Or sometimes he'd just sit there in his raised pulpit, with his head in his hands, or his hands over his ears.

Then someone broke the study-hall door lock to bring in a roll of barbed wire, which was wound around Chinny's pulpit so he couldn't get up there.

Fellows started firing books at Chinny when his back was turned. Then came catapults, with stones aimed viciously at the back of Chinny's neck. One stone hit him in the face, right beside the left eye, and Chinny was seen to wipe blood away with his handkerchief.

Cairns tried to intervene a couple of times. 'Ah lads, will ye cut it out, now,' he yelled once. 'Ye've gone too far.' For his pains he got a catapult stone into his face too.

No one could get any study done.

'Why doesn't the Manor intervene?' Jamie asked Cairns. 'I mean, they must know what's going on. Sure they must hear the racket from here.'

'They're saying the Provost drinks,' Cairns said. 'An that's why he's never seen around the place.'

'God, I never knew that. Where did you hear it?'

'Bentley, as usual. 'Was saying it this morning. Bastard's usually right.'

'Well hasn't the bloody Provost got a staff? What about those assistants of his? Or administrators, or whatever they are? Can't they do something?'

'Blowed if I know, Jamie.'

'Know what I think, Cairns? I think they're all waiting till King gets back. He's the only one could handle this. I bet they're just kicking for touch till he comes.'

'Aye, but *will* he come? They're saying he's still not well. Well, Bentley's saying it. Of course.'

"KNOW something, Cairns – I just dread going into that study hall any more. My guts are in bits every evening before I go in.' Jamie was fed up with the whole carry-on.

'So imagine how Chinny must be feeling,' Cairns said. D'y'know, I think what we're seeing is mob rule. I remember reading about it somewhere – what the Nazis did to the Jews. If everybody's in it together, people can lose their own minds and become one big animal.'

Jamie slapped his forehead. 'God, you're absolutely right, boy. And d'y'know how I know? Because I was part of a mob once. Years ago. We all ganged up on this little Jewish kid and beat the shit out of him. Could've killed him. God, I haven't thought of that for years. God, it's mob rule, all right. I recognise it now.'

Of course all mobs, whether those in the French Revolution or the Nazi stormtroopers on *Kristallnacht*, grow rapidly more violent and more vicious.

And so it was at Cock.

The end came quite suddenly. That Saturday-evening study had been one of the worst ever, with the hurling of books and stones and the banging of desk lids almost incessant. Just about five minutes before the end of evening study the stench of yet another stink bomb filled the hall, and Chinny went around pushing up all the windows with the long brass-hooked pole, starting at the back and finishing at the top of the hall.

'Right, then,' Chinny yelled as he shambled down the centre aisle between the desks to the back of the hall. 'I'm keeping you all in for another half hour.' He placed himself with his back to the big stained-glass double door, and stood with his arms folded. 'You can just sit in your stink, and your supper can wait until I let you out.' His voice shook as he spoke.

The banging of the desk lids began again, and the fellows began chanting in unison – 'We – want – *out!* We – want – *out! We – want – OUT!'*

The chant became faster and faster, and the banging kept pace with it. Finally it degenerated into *'Out! Out! Out! OUT! OUT!'* roared by more than three hundred throats together, with the desks banging in unison.

The chanting and the banging grew to a crescendo, as eight of the senior fellows went to the top of the hall, took the window pole, levelled it like a lance and, all of them holding it one behind the other, came tramping down the long centre aisle to the rhythm of the chanting, with the brass hook of the pole pointing directly at Chinny's navel.

The chanting suddenly hushed as the crowd of boys perceived what was about to happen, until the only sound was the tramping of eight pairs of boots as the lance came down the hall.

At the last moment Jamie shut his eyes and put his head in his hands. He couldn't bear to look.

When he opened his eyes again the boys were streaming out through the open doorway. There was no sign of Chinny. There was no sign of the lance.

But King stood in the middle of the open doorway, the fellows streaming by him as river water parts to go around a rock.

***

IT had all happened in a very few seconds, but it seemed like slow motion at the time. Cairns filled Jamie in on what had happened in those moments when Jamie had shut his eyes.

'Jeez, Jamie, the pole was just yards from Chinny's navel, and everyone was wondering would he step aside or would the fellows stop coming, or would – Christ, Jamie, it's unthinkable. But like, when there's eight fellows together, who's going to stop? It's a bit like a firing squad – nobody'd get the blame.'

'Will you get *on* with it!'

'Well, like I said, the pole was just feet from Chinny when the door opened behind him and King stepped in. That was it. Everything just stopped.'

Apparently King said something to Chinny who just went out through the door. The eight lancers simply dropped their weapon and merged in among the desks. And the fellows started swarming through the door and down the stairs to their supper.

***

NEXT day King was at the altar for the Sunday morning Mass. He looked thin, and the mass vestments looked loose on him. There was utter silence when he came through the altar rails after the Gospel reading, and came down among the fellows.

Then he gave that smile and everybody relaxed. Same old smile as ever. 'I've missed you, Brothers,' he began. 'I wish you could know how glad I am to see all these faces again.' He paused, and gestured to one of the pews. 'Look, would you mind if I sat down? I'm still a little short on energy. But getting there, thank God.'

The fellows in the pew slid over to let King sit down. Then, spontaneously, all the fellows came out of their own pews and gathered in a circle around King. It meant sitting in the centre aisle, in the side aisles, sitting on top of the back rests, crowding in on top of one another. But nobody seemed to mind the crush.

'So what do you think happened last evening?' King asked.

There was silence.

'Make a guess, Brothers. Brother McArdle? Any suggestions?'

'Were we possessed, Father?'

'Got it in one, Brother. Possessed is the word. Now has anyone any idea what that word means?'

'Something to do with the devil, Father?' someone said.

'I'm not sure we even need him, Brother. We've enough evil in ourselves to be going on with. It lurks inside each of us, waiting its moment to get out. A lot of people call it Original Sin – I sometimes call it our Shadow Side. I learned that phrase from a wonderful man I studied under in Zurich. We're made up of light and dark – like a photograph.'

'So what brought out the dark side last night, Father?' A voice from down the centre aisle.

'Let me tell you something I saw happen in the Rhineland. You know I studied there, as well as in Zurich? Anyhow I was there when the Nazis were coming to power. There were two things they kept saying to young people like yourselves – the young lads of the Hitler Youth – you must dominate others; and you must be without pity. To *win* was everything. Hitler's actual words were, "I want a youth, a cruel, unflinching youth,

267

as hard as steel – Krupp Steel." It took a long time, but eventually he got what he wanted. Those young lads grew up to run Belsen and Auschwitz, and to kill six million Jews.'

King looked into the faces around him. 'You see, it takes a long time to get to that. Like what happened in the study hall last evening – that was Belsen or Auschwitz, just on a smaller scale – it took a long time for us to reach that. It took years of win-at-all-costs, years of bullying – dominating each other – years of cruelty in these corridors of ours, and years of nobody saying stop. You see, Brothers, the Dark takes a long time to fully emerge, but when it does, it can make us into that Thing that I saw last evening. The Thing that almost took a man's life. And may well yet take his sanity.'

King stood up. 'Will we leave it at that, Brothers, for the moment? I'm still a bit tired. Maybe next time we might talk about remedies. I'll try to have a couple of suggestions for you.'

***

IT was a different Woodcock College now. It was quieter, to begin with. Fellows even closed their study-hall desks quietly. The new revvo in charge there, a man called Finnegan, could hardly have known his luck: there was barely a murmur in the hall, ever.

So Jamie could at least get his study done, as could everyone else – after all there was the Leaving Cert coming up in a dauntingly few months. And a lot of time had been lost.

Over the following Sunday mornings, King took the fellows through what could be described as a spiritual rehab course. When he came down to sit among them they would always form that circle around him. Jamie found himself thinking that must have been the way people gathered around Jesus. The talks were always brief, as King seemed to tire easily.

'What we got wrong here at Woodcock,' King told them, 'is, we've replaced compassion with competition. It's all about winning, isn't it, Brothers? No matter what the consequences? Would you agree?'

There was a murmur of assent.

'But what does Jesus say really matters? Anyone remember?'

'*I – I was sick and you visited me...?*' someone ventured.

'Right you are, Brother Kane. *I was hungry and you gave me to eat. I was naked and you clothed me. I was in prison and you came to see me...* What does it all really say?'

'Is it about caring, Father?'

'Got it in one, Brother. *Caring.* Empathy. In the end, really, nothing else really matters. All the other things we're supposed to do, like coming to church today, or saying our prayers, is meant to help us become more caring. More loving, if you like (though that word seems to scare young fellows). Even getting our exams – that's to help us succeed in professions where we can care for others. Even when we are earning money, it's so we can care for our families.'

'There's not much of the caring here, Father, is there?'

'Point taken, Brother Cairns. There's what I call the three Cs of Christianity – Compassion, Caring and Charity. I'm afraid we've replaced them here with a different three – Contempt, Compete, and Conquer. All of us here – we've put Christianity into reverse. And you've seen what that can lead to. What it *has* led to.'

THE following Sunday King took them further through what can go wrong when competition squeezes out compassion. 'We have a long tradition here of producing professional men. And many of you will become lawyers and doctors and bankers. Or perhaps even enter politics. And that's all something we can be proud of. But can it go wrong? Would you agree that there are two kinds of lawyers?'

'Solicitors and barristers?'

King chuckled. 'Indeed so, Brother Dempsey. But it wasn't quite what I had in mind.'

'Crooked and straight?'

'Well, let's say, there are those whose sole aim is justice, and those whose sole aim is money. Two kinds – the men of compassion and fairness, and those who quite simply practise greed. Money at all costs. Selling themselves to the highest bidder. Refresher fees and all that. They're the ones who have dumped compassion and replaced it with competition. Did you ever see pigs at a trough? That's the perfect symbol of competition without compassion.'

'What about doctors, Father?' Cairns asked. 'Isn't that a caring profession?'

'It is, thank God. Thank God indeed for doctors and the caring they give. But they've the same temptation as the lawyers. Greed. Don't we all know the occasional medical man who is just out to get as rich as possible? Who thinks it's his inalienable right? Who demands higher and higher fees? Or did you ever watch the kind of bonuses that some top bankers give themselves? Or the salaries politicians vote themselves?

Or how politicians take bribes instead of serving the people who elected them? Greed, Brothers. Greed.'

'Priests?'

There was a chuckle from the fellows.

'We're the most tempted of all, Brother. With us it's not so much about getting rich – there's few ways we could, even if we wanted to. No, for us the great temptation is power. Our biggest sin of all is seeking power over others. Or misusing our authority to bully others. To hurt them. Even destroy them. I don't know why it is – sometimes I think it's a substitute for the sex we've given up.

'And our second temptation is leading a lazy life, a comfortable life, forgetting the people we were ordained to serve. Indifference indeed is a great sin of the clergy. But it's only trotting after the power thing. And the lack of compassion it brings with it.'

Someone said, 'Smegs!'

'I didn't hear that, Brother. Oh there's lots of ways any of us can forget compassion. And replace it with competition. Actually I think it was Max Weber who said that all professions, all organizations indeed, end up serving themselves instead of those they were meant to serve. That's why we need compassion and the empathy it brings, and God's grace to keep us compassionate. It's a lifelong struggle.'

Cairns seemed agitated. 'Are you telling us, Father, we shouldn't try to win at rugby? That's competition, isn't it?'

'I'm telling you no such thing, Brother Cairns. Of course you try to win – that's what sport is about. But it has to *stay* sport. It's when it becomes *win at all costs*, when it's fists inside the scrum and knees up into crotches, that it's no longer really sport. The sportsmanship is gone out of it. And then of course losing becomes a catastrophe – look at our depression here right now, our devastation just because we lost to Glenstal. Just because we're out of the Cup.

'Actually one of the functions of school sport should be to teach us to handle disappointment – to accept it sportingly and come back up ready to try again. And never stop trying. That's hardly the case here, is it?'

***

SOMETIMES Jamie felt that King was a man in a hurry. Trying to accomplish a lot in a short time. He was forever among the fellows when they were't at class or study or at rugby. Of course as spiritual director he had the freedom to do that.

There was a copper beech at the edge of the Top-Cock crease that would have slowly darkening leaves when spring came. A seat under that tree was King's favourite spot. That's where the fellows would gather around him, often perched on the grass if the weather had been dry.

Not that King talked religion all the time, or anything like that. They'd just be discussing things – anything that came up. Often King would just ask a question and see where the conversation led. And that often led to another question.

'A bit like Socrates,' Cairns said to Jamie.

'Soccer – what?'

'Socrates. Some oul git in Greece, I think, that was always asking questions of young fellows. He came up in Greek class. They had to poison him in the end.'

'The fellows poisoned him?'

'No, eejit. The authorities. Said he was leading the young fellows astray. Something like that.'

'Do you think maybe they're trying to poison King here? He isn't looking that well.'

Cairns got a fit of laughing. 'Well, to tell you the truth, Jamie, I wouldn't put it past the bastards. They'd be capable of it. Or maybe Smegs's sticking pins in a doll, somewhere. *He'd* be capable of that. Any idea where he is, anyway?'

'Bentley says he's in the provincial house in Limerick. They say he never goes out.'

'Bentley say that too?'

'Don't know where I heard it. But I tell you, I'm delighted. D'y'know I still hate that – that fucker. I hate him so much I hope he dies. I hope he dies roaring. God, how I *hate* him.'

'I'll say this for you, Jamie, you're one great hater. Full marks for hating, whatever else.'

***

'*IN the beginning was the Word* – you heard it at Mass this morning. What does the word *Word* mean?'

It was one of those sunny early spring days that can be quite warm, and King was doing his Socrates bit under the copper beech one afternoon. There had been no rain for days, and about fifteen or twenty fellows were sitting on the grass around him.

'Brother Dempsey? The word *Word* – what do you think it means?'

'Something you *say*, I suppose.' Dempsey shrugged.

'Or something you write, yes? So there have to be people around to say it or write it. So, when were the very first words?'

'When the first people came?'

'Indeed, Brother. And when was that?'

The fellows looked at each other.

'Well, I'll tell you,' King went on. 'Some experts say only a hundred thousand years ago. A couple of million at most. So words have existed only since then – spoken words, I mean. And there have only been written words for the last three thousand years. And printed words for only five hundred. But the universe has existed for fifteen thousand million years – *without any words*. What do you make of that?'

'Probably better off without them,' Cairns said.

'Point taken, Brother. Words have done a lot of mischief, as we well know around here. But here's the problem: that line from St John – *In the Beginning was the Word*. In – the – *Beginning*. What do you make of that?'

'Must be God's word, then. Is it?'

'Got it in one, Brother. But is that a word like ours? Just God speaking?'

'So, *you* tell us, Father.'

'Well, the Hebrew for "word" is *Dabhar*, but what it means is God's *creative utterance*. In other words, the divine energy that brought – no that *brings* – everything into being. Because creation goes on every instant, just keeping us and everything else in existence, as right now.

'*Our* words simply represent things that are there. *God's* Word makes them *be* there. When God said, Let there be light, there was light. When God said, let there be Brother Bentley, there was Brother Bentley.'

An embarrassed snort from Bentley. A chuckle from everybody else.

'Which means that Brother Bentley is a Word of God. He has been uttered by God. No – *is being* uttered by God. Right now.'

'Aw, will y'give over, Father.'

The fellows were delighted to see Bentley embarrassed. It was a first, and they loved it.

'That means,' King went on, 'that this tree we're sitting under is an actual Word of God. It is *uttered* by God. So is all that forest behind it. The forest itself is a book about God. Meister Eckhart says every creature is a word of God and is a book about God. Nature is God's first scripture, indeed the first sacrament of all, and Nature loves us. Buadelaire says it beautifully:

> 'We walk through forests of physical things
> That are also spiritual things
> That look on us with affectionate looks.

'God's word is the divine energy flowing to you through all things. That's why you're loved. All you need is a sense of wonder, to see that energy and love everywhere. Come to think of it, one of our own poets said it better than anyone. Anyone remember? – We learned it in class. A patriot who was executed, remember?'

'*I see His blood upon the rose...*' Jamie ventured.

'Right, Brother. Joseph Mary Plunkett, wasn't it? Why don't you give us the whole verse?'

Jamie hesitated, then recited:

> 'I see his blood upon the rose
> And in the stars the glory of his eyes,
> His body gleams amid eternal snows,
> His tears fall from the skies.'

'Good man. Anyone give us the next verse? Brother Bentley?'

'I'll pass, Father.'

'Would you not *try*, Brother? Come on.'

Bentley shrugged. 'OK, I suppose. Here goes:

> 'I see his face in every flower;
> The thunder and the singing of the birds
> Are but his voice—and carven by his power
> Rocks are his written words.'

'Good man, Brother Bentley. Wasn't so bad, eh? Now, who'll give us the last verse?'

Spontaneously, all the fellows began to recite it together:

> 'All pathways by his feet are worn,
> His strong heart stirs the ever-beating sea,
> His crown of thorns is twined with every thorn,
> His cross is every tree.'

***

FROM time to time Jamie found himself still slightly resenting the way the fellows hung around King. Although he might not have put it that way, he sort of had come to regard King as his personal property.

'Are we being jealous again, Brother Jamie?' King said to him one night, up in the spiritual director's room.

'What d'you mean, Father? Why'd I be jealous?'

'Well, you sat there sulking, didn't you, while the other two brothers were here, didn't you?'

276

'I wasn't sulking. I was just waiting for them to go. I needed to talk to you alone. There's things I need to ask you. What's wrong with that?'

'Nothing, I suppose, Jamie. But don't forget that those young fellows need to talk too. You're not the only one here who has suffered scruples, you know – sometimes I think it's endemic here. These lads have things they need to ask, same as you have. And there's not a lot of time left.'

'How d'you mean?'

'Well – ah – you'll all be leaving soon, won't you? We've a lot of ground still to cover, don't we all? Anyhow, there's a few things *I* need to ask *you*.'

'What sort of things, Father?'

'Well, for starters, how do you feel about Father Smith?'

'Smegs?'

'The very one.'

'Was Cairns talking to you?'

'Shall we say, he asked me to have a word with you about Father Smith.'

'The bloody little so-and-so, going behind my back like that. How *dare* he! Wait till I get my hands on him.'

'Jamie. Leave that for now. I asked you a question, and I want an answer – how do you feel about Father Smith?'

'Sure you must know, if Cairns talked to you. I hate him. He's my enemy. I hate him so much, I can hardly tell you. I *hate* him.'

'Jamie. Listen to me. Remember you used to worry so much about sin? And how often I had to tell you to forget it? Well, this is a bit different. This is as close to real sin as you could come. What did Jesus say about enemies?'

'To love them.'

'Well?'

'I can't, Father. *Love* that bastard? After what he *did*? How could I? No, I'll hate him till the day he dies. Till the day *I* die. I hate him. I *hate* him.'

'Where do you feel that hate, Jamie?'

'Right here.' Jamie pointed to his solar plexus.

'And what does it feel like?'

'It's – it's like a sort of acid, burning away inside me, whenever I think about him.'

'You couldn't have put it better, Jamie. It *is* burning away inside you. That hatred will eat away at you, and it will destroy you. Hatred will warp you, warp your whole personality in the end. It will destroy your soul, which will become twisted and ruined by hate. But it will also wreck your body – it's so negative, it even releases things into your bloodstream. Hatred like that can make you ill.'

'You're not just scaring me, now, Father?'

'Far from it, Jamie. Hate can even lead to cancer in the long term. And it does no harm to the man you hate. It harms *you*, not him. Beside, he's not even aware of it. He's forgotten you. Let it go, Jamie. Please, I really ask you, let – it – go.'

'I can't, Father.'

King stood up and went to the window, where he gazed out over the distant Burren, gilded now in the dying light of early spring. He stood there for what seemed ages. Suddenly he turned from the window. 'There's something I want to tell you,

Jamie. Well, actually, two things. I wasn't going to say them, but now I think I should.'

Jamie had never seen him agitated like this. Gone was the gentle, slightly teasing humour that made him so easy to be with. There was a sort of urgency about King.

'Jamie. Maybe I shouldn't say this, but I've loved you from the first time I met you. I know I once told you I wasn't your father but, in fact – I'm not sure why – I've loved you as the son I never had. Why? I'm not sure. No, that's not true: *I do know why.*

'Jamie, once upon a time I nearly had a son. Well, a child, anyhow.'

'How d'y'mean, Father?'

A hand ran through thinning hair. 'This is incredibly hard to say, Jamie. And I've never said it to a single soul until this minute. Not to a soul. You're the first. The first to know, after all these years.'

King was silent for some moments. Jamie just waited.

'I got a girl pregnant when I was a student – a lovely Cork girl. Fiona. And to my everlasting shame I denied it: I said someone else could have been the father. I just – I just didn't want to take the responsibility at the time. O dear God in heaven.'

King put his face in his hands. 'Jamie, she killed herself and the unborn child.'

The silence seemed forever. It looked as if King was going to weep. Then: 'I've had to live with this all my life. My utter selfishness and my cruelty. It's a terrible shadow that's forever there. And God knows I deserve it.'

'Was it why you became a priest?'

'In fairness, no. Maybe a part of it. But I'd seen such horrors in Germany long before the war, and came through scot free myself, that I felt I wanted to put something back in. Do even a little good before I died.'

There was a long pause, during which Jamie tried to come to terms with what he had just been told. It was hard to grasp. King stood gazing out over the Burren.

He turned abruptly and clapped his hands together. 'So now you know, Jamie. A hero with feet of clay. Howzat, as they say in cricket?'

'I don't know what to say, Father.'

'You don't have to say anything. But *I* want to say something. Jamie, in a way you're that child I never had. And it has meant so much to me that you've let me be a father to you. I've so wanted to help you through all that misery. I've regretted those times being away when I couldn't help. And I've rejoiced to see you come through it all in the end. Come through it so splendidly.'

Another sigh. 'Jamie, that's why I want you to come through this last awfulness. This hatred. Because it's the worst thing in all of life. Literally.

'I saw what it did in Germany. Remember the Hell that used to bother you so much? Well, hatred *is* that Hell. That I promise you. By the way, what I just told you must never go beyond these walls. Remember, you're the only one in the world that knows.'

'You said you had two things to tell me.'

'Yes. The second thing is – you must promise me to keep it to yourself – Jamie, a while back they gave me six months to live. That was four months ago.'

***

IT was as if Jamie's own death sentence had been pronounced. He walked in a daze. And every now and then it came back with a lurch – King was going to die. *Going to die.* Going to die soon. And Jamie couldn't tell anyone – King had sworn him to silence.

Jamie broke his promise and told Cairns. About King going to die – not the other thing. He just had to tell someone. Cairns would never tell. That's the kind of fellow he was. Then Jamie admitted to King that he had told Cairns, and King hadn't minded that much. 'We can trust Brother Cairns,' was all he said.

'*Now* do you know why I want you to let go of that hatred?' King said to him a day or two later. 'I don't want to die leaving you like that. Leaving you with a poison inside you that will destroy you. Do you understand now, Jamie?'

'But what can I do, Father? I hate him. I can't help hating him.'

'Pray, Jamie. Remember I showed you how to pray? Well, pray like that. Remind yourself what Jesus promised – *ask and you shall receive?* Well, ask him to take away your hatred. He'd have to, wouldn't he?

'But you must really *want* it to happen. Ask, and ask and ask. Beg. He'll hear you. And He'll keep that promise. But the other thing you must do is pray for the man you hate. Pray that his misery be taken away. Pray for his happiness. Pray for

281

his conversion, for I think he needs it. Pray for him to find the light. As *you* must find it.'

***

JAMIE tried. He prayed as best he knew. His mind swung from the lurching horror of King's impending death – a father's death – and begging in prayer for it not to happen, but knowing that it would – his mind swung from that to thoughts of Smegs and trying to pray for the bastard even though it choked him. For the bastard's conversion. That things would be OK for the bastard. But you can't go on calling him a bastard if you want things to be OK for him. It was all a bit complicated.

In the end what happened was a completely new thought altogether. It came to Jamie during one of those FCA route marches, the last one, just before the end of term. It's amazing how thoughts can run so free when you're doing something physical. Like the way thoughts come to you when you're lazily doing the crawl up and down the pool.

Anyhow the fellows were tramping down one of those little Burren roads, rifles at the shoulder. The initial stiffness had gone and the rhythm of the march had become relaxing. The fellows were whistling *Colonel Bogey*. And Jamie was thinking about King going to die. Why him? Who could ever take his place?

Then the thought struck. *You* could. You could take his place. You could become a priest like him. Join the order – the congregation, whatever it's called. Come back to the college some day as a priest. No you couldn't. You could never be like him. No, but you could *try*. And leave the rest to God. Sure it'd take years. Still, if God wanted it he'd help you grow into somebody like King. Well, maybe not all the way. But – well, must ask King what he thinks about the idea.

***

BY the time Jamie got to King's room that evening he was all worked up about the wonderful notion of becoming a priest. And felt quite miffed when he discovered King wasn't at all keen on the idea. Jamie had thought he'd be delighted.

'You actually want to come back to Woodcock as a priest, Jamie?' King was astounded at the idea. 'After all it has done to you?'

'I saw what *you* could do here. Couldn't I do that too – I mean if I prayed enough?'

'Jamie, there are some things I would normally never say to anyone. Certainly not to a student here. But I'm going to tell *you*, because of this notion that's got into you. Woodcock is finished. It needs to be levelled to the ground and salt strewn on the ruins. So that nothing will ever grow here again.'

He gave a chuckle. 'That's what Scipio did to Carthage, by the way, or wanted to, anyhow, and I don't quite mean it. What I *do* mean is this. By the way, it's not just this college – it's our whole religious order that's gone wrong. Listen. At some point back along, a decision was made to educate the children of the rich. And a laudable decision it was. Somebody has to do it, and on the missions the idea was to educate the future leaders so they'd bring the rest along with them.'

'So what went wrong, then?'

'Here's what went wrong, Jamie. At some point it all went into reverse. Instead of our teaching compassion and humility,

283

we took on the ethos of the rich, which is competition and pride. And contempt. We became like them. It's as simple as that.'

'But *you're* not like that.'

'I've been close enough at times, Jamie. We all have. It's an insidious thing, the ethos of the rich. It gets into your bones before you know. The sense of elitism, that we're somehow special. Even snobbery: haven't you learnt, here, without anyone ever needing to say it, to look down on everyone else?'

'I think I learned it before I ever came here, Father.'

'No doubt you did, Jamie. And you were sent here to reinforce it. And look at the consequences here. Remember what Jesus said, *By their fruits ye shall know them*? Jamie, what are the fruits here of win-at-all-costs?'

'Bullying?'

'Unto death, Jamie. *Unto death.* Remember young Bates? And a revvo who could have died? But those are only the tips of the iceberg – it's what's done to the souls of the lads here that's the real evil. Nothing matters but winning. And contempt for others. Brutality – from the priests to the boys. From the boys to each other. Trample on everyone. Get it all for yourself. Sometimes I think our school motto should be *Snobbery with Violence.*

'As you know, the motto here is *Conquer for Christ*, but Christ is long gone and all that's left is conquer. And despise. And hate. You've been a pretty good hater yourself, Jamie.'

'I have, haven't I?'

'Jamie. There's no place for you here. There's no place for anyone here any more. Do you know that institutions die, just like people? Look at the priests here – sure *they* know it. Imagine, they joined to give their life to the missions, and instead found themselves stuck teaching the spoiled rich brats of Ireland. That's why they've no interest, why all they care about is golf. Why do you think we haven't replaced the Provost? You know he's an alcoholic, don't you? They've simply no one to send in his place. Religious orders are human institutions, and this one's sick unto death.' A wry smile. 'A bit like myself.'

'Don't say that please, Father.'

'Facts, Jamie. We have to face facts.'

'Aren't there other orders I could join? Like the Dominicans? Or the Blackrock crowd? Or Glenstal? They'd be nothing like here, would they?'

'Now you're making a bit more sense, Jamie. None of them seem to have lost it like we have. I'm not sure why – maybe they say their prayers better. But Jamie, *not yet*. How old are you, by the way?'

'I'll be seventeen in April.'

'You're miles too young, Jamie. Listen, we'll talk more about it tomorrow. I'm a bit tired now. You wouldn't mind?'

The next morning some of the fellows saw a white ambulance going down the avenue, and Jamie knew it had to be King in it. There hadn't even been a chance to say goodbye. He got a sudden urge to cry, but you don't do that at seventeen. Besides, if the fellows saw you...

Anyhow five days later Jamie headed home for the Easter break.

April 1951

A S usual there was no one at home when Jamie arrived for the last break of his schooldays. He still missed Sheila bustling from the kitchen to give him her big welcoming hug. Presumably Aunt May was out at her detested dentist's receptionist job. King had been wrong on that one: she hadn't ever grown to like the work.

A white envelope lay on the mat in the hall. The writing familiar. King's hand:

> Sorry for doing a runner like that,' the letter said [*Touch of the old humour*]. Anyhow just to let you know I've rallied quite a bit. These new drugs can work wonders. Looks like I may get a bit more time.
>
> I'm sorry we didn't finish what we were talking about the other evening. About you being seventeen and all that. I'll have a bit more to say about it when I get back next term. For the moment I'm here in Dublin, getting some more treatment at St Luke's.
>
> Meanwhile just keep in mind what I said: that you are miles too young for any such decision about your life. Remember the priesthood is not like being a doctor or a solicitor. There is one colossal difference, and that is celibacy. It is not something

287

to be taken lightly. Far from it. Certainly not at the age of seventeen. Just keep that in mind until we can meet. Meanwhile pray for this poor old sinner. May God bless you and keep you, my dear Jamie. Son!

Yours affectionately (I hope I'm entitled to say that!)

Ralph King

Jamie slid the letter inside his jacket. He hung his blazer on the newel post at the end of the banisters, lifted his racket, took it out of its press, opened the case to take out his tennis shoes, and headed down to the tennis club.

***

THERE were only a few playing at the club when Jamie got there. Ann Morgan and Dinny McCracken were on the centre court. They looked great in the whites. They beckoned him over when they saw him.

Ann gave him a kiss on the cheek. God, it felt good. 'C'mon y'boyo,' Ann said. 'Let's see what you've learnt at that fancy school of yours. You can take on the pair of us!'

The game was even enough at the start, and Jamie was well able for them. Except for one thing – Ann and that wee white skirt. He wasn't quite able for that. He could hardly take his eyes off her. And when she went up for those serves – Oh, forget it.

Maybe it was that Jamie hadn't seen a woman in months, in that crazy all-male establishment, or maybe it was that Ann had suddenly blossomed into some gorgeous glimmering girl – anyhow, by the third set Jamie had lost it. Lost the match and lost his heart too.

And then, as the three of them walked into the pavilion came the lurching realization that Ann and Dinny were an item. Which should have been clear from the start. Bloody Hell. But sure what could you expect? A plague on that bloody school that locks us away like that.

***

'JEALOUS, again, are we, Jamie?' King said from his hospital bed. 'You know it's your predominant passion, don't you?'

Jamie had taken a day trip on the train to Dublin to visit King in the hospital, and was telling him about how he felt about Ann and Dinny. 'What d'you mean, predominant – whatever?'

'It's in the catechism – remember? We each have our own particular weakness, our predominant shortcoming, if you will. Yours is jealousy – I've seen enough of you to know that. Don't worry: you could have worse.' He smiled wanly. 'You'd never guess what mine is – *my* predominant passion. And I'm not telling you!' He paused. 'Come to think of it, Jamie, you've got *two* predominant passions, which is quite an achievement.'

'So what's my other one?'

'*Hating*, Jamie. You've been pretty good at that, haven't you? Or should I say pretty bad?'

'Och, give us a break now, Father, I've really been working on that. I'm *tryin'*.'

'I do believe you are, Jamie.'

'D'you know I've actually been trying to pray for Smegs?'

'Best news I've heard in a while.' King chuckled. 'Do the prayers stick in your craw?'

'Will you give over, Father!'

Both men laughed, until King began coughing.

'All right, then,' King said, when the coughing fit was over. 'Let's get back to the jealousy. Isn't that what you felt towards those two young tennis players? I think it's a classic plot – straight out of a romantic novel. You pining away like that.'

'You're not taking me seriously, Father. I just lost my heart.' Jamie was beginning to see the funny side too.

'There'll be lots more of that, Jamie. Before you're much older. Hearts are made to be broken. Or didn't you know that?'

King seemed to be in some pain as he eased himself up in the bed. He was thinner and his skin had that yellowish colour. But the old smile was still there.

'Seriously, though, Jamie, there's a bit of a lesson there for you. One glimpse of a girl and you're smitten. And yet you're talking about becoming a priest and giving up girls altogether. Forever. Something strike you as not quite right there?'

'There's lots of others have done it.'

'There's lots have *tried*, Jamie. They haven't all succeeded. And it can get pretty messy when they fail.'

'Isn't God supposed to give you the strength? Like, to stick with it?'

'Let me explain something, Jamie. Some of the best men I have ever known are priests: they are men who are genuinely true to their promise of celibacy. A celibacy they've freely chosen. They have the most extraordinary love – they've taken that love that normally goes to a woman, and transformed it into love of all the people around them. Particularly for those who are suffering. Men like that can work wonders, and they're extraordinary people to meet. But it's a very special gift from

290

God – a very rare one – and the gift can only be retained through years of prayer and struggle and generosity.'

A bit like yourself, Jamie was thinking, but didn't say it.

'My German friend Father Franz was a man like that. He loved women and by golly they loved him. But he lived his celibacy to the full, and devoted his life to people who suffer. Indeed he cared so much for the people suffering in the war that he refused to serve in Hitler's army. You know, they did everything to get him to take the military oath, even offering him a place in the *Sanitätskorps* – the Medical Corps – so he wouldn't have to carry a gun. But he still said no. It was an unjust war, he said, and he simply wouldn't serve in it. So in the end he was beheaded. I keep that man in mind whenever I feel I'm losing heart.'

'*You* don't ever lose heart. Not you. You couldn't.'

'We're all cut from the same cloth, Jamie. Of course I can lose heart. Especially here in hospital. But I just keep trying. And keeping Father Franz in mind usually gives me the courage to go on.'

'Gee, Father, I never knew.'

'There's a lot you don't know yet, little brother. But you'll learn. But do remember that not everyone can be like Father Franz. Not everyone *has* that gift of celibacy, but the problem is, it's slapped on to the priesthood as a package deal. You want to be a priest – then, mister, you take on the celibacy too. And young fellows like yourself take it on, full of idealism and goodness. And wake up in their thirties to find they can't hack it. Can't hack the celibacy bit. Which was never right for them anyhow.'

'Was that what happened to Smegs?'

'God knows what happened there. Father Smith's a sad case, God knows. But look at some of the others back at the college. The grey, disappointed faces. The golf and the booze. The frustration – you can see it in some of the faces. Not all of them, of course, thank God. But some. Strictly speaking, Jamie, I shouldn't be telling you any of this. But you need to know it if you're thinking of becoming a priest. And no one else is going to tell you.'

A spasm of pain tightened the face momentarily. Then it passed.

'Remember what I just said about what a good priest can achieve? The good they can do is out of this world. Literally. Like Father Franz. But there are lots of others like him –the Cure of Ars, for example. Or Father Willie Doyle – a soldier on leave knelt down on a Dublin street and prayed when he heard that Father Willie had been blown to bits in the trenches. He'd been his chaplain. Men like that literally bring people to God. Bring God to people.

'But when a priest goes wrong, Jamie, the harm he can do is also out of this world. The consequences are immense. Literally, the evil is almost limitless. The terrible thing is that a bad priest – no, better say, a priest who does bad things – lessens people's belief in their religion, even their belief in God. It shouldn't be so – people should say it's just a frail human being gone wrong. But they don't. I think people often use such scandals as an excuse to give up their religion or their belief in God. They think they'll have more freedom that way – that life will be easier without religion or God. They couldn't be more wrong.'

'And are you saying that's what would happen to me?'

'You mean, fail as a priest? Indeed no, Jamie. You could some day be a wonderful priest, even a holy priest, if God is really calling you and has given you the gift of celibacy, and if you co-operate with his grace. And if you take up a life of genuine prayer.'

***

Both men were silent for a moment, as Jamie contemplated what King had said.

'So, Father, how do I know if God is calling me?'

'You don't, Jamie. Not yet, anyway. And not for a long time yet. Do you realise that most of those frustrated men joined at the age you are now? Seventeen or eighteen? When they hadn't a notion what they were giving up? When they hadn't a notion what celibacy really means? Jamie, it means never having a family. Never having a little daughter to bounce on your knee. Never having someone waiting for you to come home at night – someone to confide in, to tell your fears to.' King paused for breath. He spoke more quietly now. 'Never having *sex*, Jamie, which is the strongest drive inside you, after hunger and the need to breathe. You eat and breathe to stay alive – well, sex is for the human race to stay alive. Without it we'd die out. Become extinct like the dinosaurs. That's why it's such a powerful drive. *You* know that, Jamie – God knows it's led you a merry dance in the past. And you're going to walk away from all that – *at seventeen?*'

The talking seemed to have tired King. He leaned back on the pillow and closed his eyes. Jamie stayed silent and thought of Ann Morgan going up for the serve.

'Jamie.' The voice was weaker now. 'Jamie, the psychologists have a word for it – they call it *early foreclosure.* It's when the life choices of a young person are closed too soon. It can stunt your development terribly, and I don't want that to happen to you.'

'So what do I do, then?'

'You simply don't make any decision yet, Jamie. Why not university for a few years? The money's there now. Take arts – it's broad, and will broaden you immensely. Meet girls – lots of them. Have fun. Then work for a few years – you'd make a pretty good journalist, given the way you can write. *Then* decide. That's what *I* did – I was a psychologist for years before I decided to become a priest.'

'I'll think about it.' Jamie stood up. 'Thanks, Father. I really will think about it.' He leaned down to take the man's hand and say goodbye.

King put both his hands on Jamie's head and prayed a silent blessing.

May 1951

JAMIE managed to see King a few more times during his final term at Cock. They had moved him back to Barrington's Hospital in Limerick, where he had a room to himself overlooking the river. Jamie would cycle in to Corofin, usually on a Saturday when there were no classes, and there get the morning bus to Limerick, coming back in the evening on the late bus. He didn't even bother asking permission, and nobody bothered to stop him.

That's the way things were at Cock then. You could pretty well do as you wanted. Sometimes Jamie would even stay overnight with Cairns's people on the Ennis Road, and cycle back on the Sunday.

In later years Jamie would remember those weeks as a time of blue skies; of the smell of new-mown grass; of cricket under a warm sun; of concentrated study for the impending Leaving Cert – study that was surprisingly exhilarating – and the long evening cycles back from Corofin. It was a time of youth and of promise – paradoxically so, for it was also a time of watching someone passing towards death.

King was that bit thinner each time Jamie saw him. And that bit yellower. And that bit weaker. But always the smile of greeting, and always a few further smiles at something that might tickle the man's humour – often indeed at Jamie's expense. But always kindly.

There came the moment when Jamie realised he was looking at a man who could never recover. There was really nothing left *to* recover: the shrunken arms like those men in Belsen; eyes withdrawing into their sockets (even though they still sometimes sparkled with humour); the wisps of damp hair; the chest foraging for air. Although Jamie had long known that King was dying, the sudden realization came with a lurch that death was here in the room, waiting.

And when the flesh shrank tight around the skull, and the lips began to draw back from the teeth, he had a second sudden realization – that that's what had happened to his mother's face all those long years ago. And then he found himself thinking, he had lost a mother and found a father. For this little while, anyhow.

What surprised Jamie was how few of the priests from the college ever seemed to visit King. He asked him about it.

'Consequence of celibacy, Jamie. *Monks live unloved and die unwept,* as Voltaire once said. Do you know, one of the rarest things is to see a priest weeping at another priest's funeral. I saw it once, just the once. That was for a very special priest indeed.'

'I'll weep at your funeral,' Jamie said.

A smile. 'Thanks, Jamie. I'll be looking forward to that.'

'I mean it, Father. Please don't make fun of me.'

'I know you mean it, Jamie. And I know it will be a son weeping for a father.' He took Jamie's hand in his. 'But it's another lesson to you if you're thinking of becoming a priest. You can't really blame the men back at the college: they live separate, individual lives, even though they're supposed to be a community. Jamie, one of the most terrible things about being a priest is the loneliness. It's wives and children that weep for a man. It's *families* that love and care. But there won't *be* any family, Jamie. Not if you're genuinely celibate.'

'But what about the people you've dedicated your lives to? Shouldn't they come around?'

'Well, *you* come, don't you? But yes, you're right in that. The people I worked for in Africa would certainly not have let me die alone. They'd have rallied around, to be sure. But, well, they're there and I'm here. And that's it. Actually that's why so many of our men have preferred to live out their lives on the missions, and die there. There's really nothing to come back to, here.' A pause. 'But you make up for it, Jamie. You make up for it more than you can know. Your visits mean more than I can ever tell you.'

Jamie saw a tear, and felt one of his own.

***

SOMETIMES the two men prayed together. It began one day when Jamie came in to find King lying back with a rosary beads in his hand.

'Would you like to join me?' he asked.

Jamie felt slightly embarrassed at praying a rosary with another man, but he nodded. 'I've no beads,' he added.

'You'll do fine without them. Just a decade, now – I'm a bit tired. We'll meditate on the Agony in the Garden. *Our Father, who art in heaven...*

There were other times when they prayed silently together. Jamie would hold King's hand as he lay there, and they would both try to feel the presence of God in the room with them. And go quiet together, so that maybe God might have something to say to them. The way King had taught him to do.

That's what they were doing one Saturday afternoon, when a nurse came in to draw the curtains, so as to keep the June sunlight out of King's eyes. She lifted the watch pinned to her blouse, took his pulse, put a hand on his forehead, and went quietly away, leaving Jamie still with King's hand in his.

Twenty minutes later she came back in, felt the forehead and took his pulse again. 'He's gone,' she said.

'*Gone?* He couldn't be. When did he go?'

'He's gone these ten minutes.' The nurse reached over and gently closed the eyes. 'May God grant him rest,' she said.

Jamie just couldn't speak.

'Would you look at that face,' the nurse said. 'Sure isn't it the face of a man gone straight to heaven?'

Epilogue

JAMIE found himself trying to weep, all the way back in the bus to Corofin. But no tears would come. *Monks live unloved and die unwept* – no, that wasn't it – the tears were there all right: they just wouldn't come out, that's all.

And there'd be hardly anyone to tell at the college, as the fellows were all gone home after the Leaving Cert, except the few who had to stay on till Monday, for the exams in Art and Mechanical Drawing. Well, at least Cairns would be there.

It was when he climbed on his bike and cycled down the road from Corofin, that the tears came. They came with a roar and a torrent. He cried and he cried as he cycled that narrow road between the little stone walls. He cried shamelessly, his cries echoing over the limestone acres of the Burren. He cried until his ribs ached.

He was still weeping as a fire engine came towards him, closely followed by another. They were cruising quietly, and neither had their bells ringing. Obviously on their way back to Ennis after some call out.

Jamie was still weeping as he reached the great stone gateway to Woodcock College and, as he did so, another fire engine came out from the gateway.

That was the end of the weeping. It was now a gasping, as Jamie raced his bike along the avenue that curved through the trees. His lungs were hardly able for it, after the violent weeping.

A few wisps of smoke or steam still rose from the ruins. The spire still rose above the trees, but it was all that was left. Even the Manor House was gutted, as were the dormitory and classroom wings. Even the chapel. A fire engine and a couple of Garda cars stood nearby.

'It was the Hutch did it.' Cairns's voice, as he came up beside him.

'Hutchinson? God almighty.'

"Came when we were all asleep. Had a Volvo packed with petrol cans. Got in through a classroom window, Gardai say, and poured petrol along the corridors. Then he got back in the car and rammed it through the Manor House front door. He exploded it inside. Him in it.'

'Anyone else dead?'

'No. Fire-escapes, thank God. And there were only a few of us left, for Monday's exam. And thank God that fucker Fitz wasn't here to lock the doors.'

'The Hutch. I can't believe it. Revenge, d'you think? For expelling him? How'd they know it was him, anyway?'

'Family saw the car gone and called the Gardai. Of course it was all over by then.'

'It's time, then.'

'Time? Time for what?'

'To strew salt on the ruins.'

THE END

More books you may enjoy from RED 🦌 STAG (a Mentor imprint)

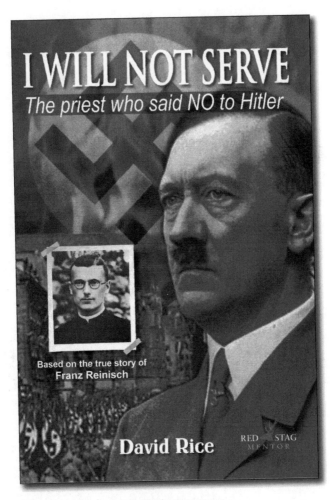

I WILL NOT SERVE

Over 17,000 Roman Catholic priests were called up to serve in Hitler's armed forces during World War 2. One refused.

This is the fascinating true story of Franz Reinisch who, in a remarkably brave and principled act of conscience, refused to swear allegiance to Adolf Hitler and was put to death by guillotine as a result. His refusal to serve was based on what he witnessed of the persecution of the Jewish people.

The story begins with Reinisch's refusal to take the oath in 1942 before tracing his origins in Austria: his troublesome youth, his romantic involvements, his decision to become a priest and his maturing into a spiritual leader whose decision of conscience led to his harrowing ordeal and ultimate demise.

Based on historical fact and painstakingly researched, *I Will Not Serve* is beautifully written in a vivid and evocative fictional format – an inspiring story from a dark era.

Franz Reinisch has been in the process of beatification since 2013.

From leading bookshops or RED STAG (Mentor Books) www.redstag.ie

RED 🦌 STAG (Mentor Books) ▪ 43 Furze Road ▪ Sandyford Industrial Estate ▪ Dublin 18
Tel: (01) 295 2112/3 ▪ Fax: (01) 295 2114 ▪ Email: admin@mentorbooks.ie

More books you may enjoy from RED 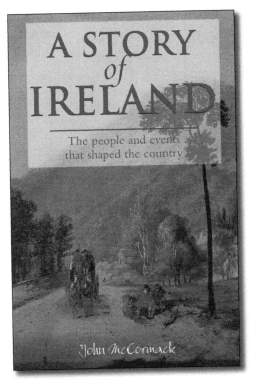 STAG (a Mentor imprint)

A STORY OF IRELAND

An historical journey that brings to life the
Ireland of Strongbow and Sarsfield, Tone and
Emmet, Pearse and Collins and a host of others
in an engaging and entertaining read. Beautifully
illustrated with original drawings and filled with
anecdotes and delightful nuggets of information,
A Story of Ireland is an account of the history
of Ireland from earliest times to the present day.

A STORY OF DUBLIN

An historical journey from the revels of
Donnybrook Fair to the revelations of tribunals,
via the Black Death and the Glimmer Man. The
Dublin of Brian Boru, Lord Edward Fitzgerald,
Jonathan Swift, Daniel O'Connell, Pádraig Pearse,
Eamon de Valera and countless others is recalled
in this engaging book.

From leading bookshops or RED STAG (Mentor Books) www.redstag.ie
RED STAG (Mentor Books) ▪ 43 Furze Road ▪ Sandyford Industrial Estate ▪ Dublin 18
Tel: (01) 295 2112/3 ▪ Fax: (01) 295 2114 ▪ Email: admin@mentorbooks.ie

More books you may enjoy from RED  STAG (a Mentor imprint)